Turn these pages and look back to the Wonder Years—a time when science fiction was the new kid in town.

. . . Marvel at the imagination and foresight of the men and women who pioneered the genre.

. . . View space travel and nuclear fission at a time when neither had occurred.

. . . Travel in time with writers predicting the events of today and the centuries beyond.

Above all, enjoy these stories for their newness in another era—a time when science fiction was first hitting the magazine stands in the pages of *Amazing® Stories*, the world's first magazine devoted to science fiction.

AMAZING™

SCIENCE FICTION ANTHOLOGY

THE WONDER YEARS

1926-1935

EDITED BY
MARTIN H. GREENBERG

ILLUSTRATIONS BY
GEORGE BARR
HANK JANKUS
PAUL JAQUAYS

TSR™

TSR, Inc.

ACKNOWLEDGEMENTS

"Introduction" - Copyright 1987 by Jack Williamson.

"The Metal Man" - Copyright 1928 by Experimenter Publishing Company; renewed ©1956, 1984 by Jack Williamson. Reprinted by permission of the author.

"The Jameson Satellite" - Copyright 1931 by Teck Publishing Corporation. Reprinted by permission of Mrs. Neil R. Jones.

"The Man Who saw the Future" - Copyright 1930 by Radio-Science Publications; renewed ©1958 by Edmond Hamilton. Reprinted by permission of the agents for the author's Estate, the Scott Meredith Literary Agency, Inc., 845 Third Ave., New York, NY 10022.

"The Machine Man of Ardathia" - Copyright 1927 by Experimenter Publishing Company. Reprinted by arrangement with Agent Forrest J Ackerman, 2495 Glendower Avenue, Hollywood, CA 90027.

"The Tissue-Culture King" - Copyright 1927 by Experimenter Publishing Company. Reprinted by permission of A.D. Peters, Ltd., London.

"The Voice from the Ether" - Copyright 1931 by Teck publications; copyright renewed © 1959; reprinted by permission of the author and the author's agent, James Allen.

"The Coming of the Ice" - Copyright 1926 by Experimenter Publishing Company. Reprinted by arrangement with Agent Forrest J Ackerman, 2495 Glendower Avenue, Hollywood, CA 90027.

"The Miracle of the Lily" - Copyright 1928 by Experimenter Publishing Company. Reprinted by arrangement with Agent Forrest J Ackerman, 2495 Glendower Avenue, Hollywood, CA 90027.

"The Man with the Strange Head" - Copyright 1926 by Experimenter Publishing Company. Reprinted by arrangement with Agent Forest J Ackerman, 2495 Glendower Avenue, Hollywood, CA 90027.

"Omega" - Copyright 1932 by Teck Publishing Corporation. Reprinted by arrangement with Agent Forrest J Ackerman, 2495 Glendower Avenue, Hollywood, CA 90027.

"The Plutonian Drug" - Copyright 1934 by Teck Publishing Corporation. Reprinted by permission of the agents for the author's Estate, the Scott Meredith Literary Agency, Inc., 845 Third Ave., New York, NY 10022.

"The Last Evolution" - Copyright 1932 by Teck Publishing Corporation; renewed ©1960 by John W. Campbell, Jr. Reprinted by permission of the agents for the author's Estate, the Scott Meredith Literary Agency, Inc., 845 Third Ave., New York, NY 10022.

"The Colour out of Space" - Copyright 1927 by Experimenter Publishing Company. Reprinted by permission of the agents for the author's Estate, the Scott Meredith Literary Agency, Inc., 845 Third Ave., New York, NY 10022.

Distributed to the book trade in the United States by Random House, Inc., and in Canada by Random House of Canada, Ltd. Distributed in the United Kingdom by TSR UK, Ltd. Distributed to the toy and hobby trade by regional distributors.

9 8 7 6 5 4 3 2 1

First printing: January 1987
Printed in the United States of America
Library of Congress Catalog Card Number: 86-51271
ISBN: 0-88038-439-5

TSR, Inc.
P.O. Box 756
Lake Geneva, WI
53147

TSR UK, Ltd.
The Mill, Rathmore Road
Cambridge CB1 4AD
United Kingdom

CONTENTS

INTRODUCTION

by Jack Williamson

For me, the years of wonder began in 1926, when Hugo Gernsback launched *Amazing Stories*. The first science fiction magazine, though he called it "scientifiction" until he invented the new name in 1929. I don't think anybody today can entirely understand what it meant to me and many like me then.

"The sense of wonder!"

That phrase is famous now. We had never heard the words, but we found sheer wonder in *Amazing Stories*, a rich new revelation of exciting things to come, a dazzling vision of new ideas and discoveries and inventions that could push our future frontiers wider, make all our lives richer.

The tattered and time-yellowed copies of those early issues recall that old excitement when I look at them now. They were big, "bed-sheet sized," printed on thick gray paper, with covers and inside pictures by Frank R. Paul. An architect by training, Paul drew human figures that looked like wooden dummies, but that didn't matter.

He showed us other worlds. The cities of the future, mysterious new machines, spaceships, alien monsters, the landscapes of Mars. All real to us then, even more thrilling than the new cities and creatures and ships of space in the stories themselves. I wrote a letter to Gernsback, begging for colored pictures inside.

That was too expensive; Gernsback watched his pennies. A native of Luxembourg and a passionate gadgeteer, he had arrived in America in 1904 with only a few dollars but a head full of new ideas. He invented the first home radio set and published catalogs that evolved into electronic hobby magazines. He wrote futuristic fiction of his own for them, and finally began *Amazing Stories* with the issue of May, 1926.

You can't imagine what the magazine meant to me. Still a

the world's best specialists, and that he was pouring out his millions in the establishment of scholarships and endowments as if he expected to die soon.

One cold, stormy day, when the sea was running high on the unprotected coast which the cottage overlooks, I saw a sail out to the north. It rapidly drew nearer until I could tell that it was a small sailing schooner with auxiliary power. She was running with the wind, but a half mile offshore she came up into it and the sails were lowered. Soon a boat had put off in the direction of the shore. The sea was not so rough as to make the landing hazardous, but the proceeding was rather unusual, and, as I had nothing better to do, I went out in the yard before my modest house, which stands perhaps two hundred yards above the beach, in order to have a better view.

When the boat touched, four men sprang out and rushed it up higher on the sand. As a fifth tall man arose in the stern, the four picked up a great chest and started up in my direction. The fifth person followed leisurely. Silently, and without invitation, the men brought the chest up the beach, and into my yard, and set it down in front of the door.

The fifth man, whom I now knew to be a hard-faced Yankee skipper, walked up to me and said gruffly,

"I am Captain McAndrews."

"I'm glad to meet you, Captain," I said, wondering. "There must be some mistake. I was not expecting—"

"Not at all," he said abruptly. "The man in that chest was transferred to my ship from the liner *Plutonia* three days ago. He had paid me for my services, and I believe his instructions have been carried out. Good day, sir."

He turned on his heel and started away.

"A man in the chest!" I exclaimed.

He walked on unheeding, and the seamen followed. I stood and watched them as they walked down to the boat, and rowed back to the schooner. I gazed at its sails until they were lost against the dull blue of the clouds. Frankly, I feared to open the chest.

At last I nerved myself to do it. It was unlocked. I threw back the lid. With a shock of uncontrollable horror that left me half sick for hours, I saw in it, stark naked, with the strange crimson mark standing lividly out from the pale green of the breast, the Metal Man, just as you may see him in the Museum.

Of course, I knew at once that it was Kelvin. For a long time I bent, trembling and staring at him. Then I saw an old canteen, purple-stained, lying by the head of the figure, and under it, a sheaf of manuscript. I got the latter out, walked with shaken steps to the easy chair in the house, and read the story that follows:

"Dear Russell,

"You are my best—my only—intimate friend. I have arranged to have my body and this story brought to you. I just drank the last of the wonderful purple liquid that has kept me alive since I came back, and I have scant time to finish this necessarily brief account of my adventure. But my affairs are in order and I die in peace. I had myself transferred to the schooner today, in order to reach you as soon as could be and to avoid possible complications. I trust Captain McAndrews. When I left France, I hoped to see you before the end. But Fate ruled otherwise.

"You know that the goal of my expedition was the headwaters of El Rio de la Sangre, 'The River of Blood.' It is a small stream whose strangely red waters flow into the Pacific. On my trip last year I had discovered that its waters were powerfully radioactive. Water has the power of absorbing radium emanations and emitting them in turn, and I hoped to find radium-bearing minerals in the bed of the upper river. Twenty-five miles above the mouth, the river emerges from the Cordilleras. There ber thinking that in such enormous quantities as undoubtedly the crater contained it, radium might possess qualities unnoticed in small amounts, or, again, that there might be present radioactive minerals at present unknown. It occurred to me also that perhaps some other scientists had already discovered the deposits and that what I had witnessed had been the trial of an airship in which radium was utilized as a propellent. I was considerably shaken, but not much alarmed. What happened later would have seemed incredible to me then.

"And then I noticed that a pale bluish luminosity was gathering about the cowl of the cockpit, and in a moment I saw that the whole machine, and even my own person, was covered with it. It was something like St. Elmo's Fire, except that it covered all surfaces indiscriminately, instead of being restricted to sharp points. All at once I connected the phenomenon with the thing I had seen. I felt no physical discomfort, and the motor continued to run, but as the blue radiance continued to increase, I observed that my body felt heavier, and that the machine was being drawn downward! My mind was flooded with wonder and terror. I fought to retain sufficient self-possession to fly the ship. My arms were soon so heavy that I could hold them upon the controls only with difficulty, and I felt a slight dizziness, due, no doubt, to the blood's being drawn from my head. When I recovered, I was already almost upon the green. Somehow, my gravitation had been increased and I was being drawn into the pit! It was possible to keep the plane under control only by diving and keeping it at high speed.

"I plunged into the green pool. The gas was not suffocating, as I had anticipated. In fact, I noticed no change in the atmosphere, save that my vision was limited to a few yards around. The wings of the plane were still distinctly discernible. Suddenly a smooth, sandy plain was murkily revealed below, and I was able to level the ship off enough for a safe landing. As I came to a stop I saw that the sand was slightly luminous, as the green mist seemed to be, and red. For a time I was confined to the ship by my own weight, but I noticed that the blue was slowly dissipating, and with it, its effect.

"As soon as I was able, I clambered over the side of the cockpit, carrying my canteen and automatic, which were themselves immensely heavy. I was unable to stand erect, but I crawled off over the coarse, shining, red sand, stopping at frequent intervals to lie flat and rest. I was in deathly fear of the force that had brought me down. I was sure it had been directed by intelligence. The floor was so smooth and level that I supposed it to be the bottom of an ancient lake.

"Sometimes I looked fearfully back, and when I was a hundred yards away I saw a score of lights floating through the green toward the airplane. In the luminous murk each bright point was surrounded by a disc of paler blue. I made no movement, but lay and watch them. They floated to the plane and wheeled about it with a slow, heavy motion. Closer and lower they came until they reached the ground about it. The mist was so thick as to obscure the details of the scene.

"When I went to resume my flight, I found my excess of gravity almost entirely gone, though I went on hands and knees for another hundred yards to escape possible observation. When I got to my feet, the plane was lost to view. I walked on for perhaps a quarter of a mile and suddenly realized that my sense of direction was altogether gone. I was completely lost in a strange world, inhabited by beings whose nature and disposition I could not even guess! And then I realized that it was a height of folly to walk about when any step might precipitate me into a danger of which I could know nothing. I had a peculiarly unpleasant feeling of helpless fear.

"The luminous red sand and the shining green of the

air lay about in all directions, unbroken by a single solid object. There was no life, no sound, no motion. The air hung heavy and stagnant. The flat sand was like the surface of a dead and desolate sea. The mist seemed to come closer; the strange evil in it seemed to grow more alert.

"Suddenly a darting light passed meteor-like through the green above and in my alarm I ran a few blundering steps. My foot struck a light object that rang like metal. The sharpness of the concussion filled me with fear, but in an instant the light was gone. I bent down to see what I had kicked.

"It was a metal bird—an eagle formed of metal—with the wings outspread, the talons gripping, the fierce beak set open. The color was white, tinged with green. It weighed no more than the living bird. At first I thought it was a cast model, and then I saw that each feather was complete and flexible. Somehow, a real eagle had been turned to metal! It seemed incredible, yet here was the concrete proof. I wondered if the radium deposits, which I had already used to explain so much, might account for this too. I knew that science held transmutation of elements to be possible—had even accomplished it in a limited way, and that radium itself was the product of the disintegration of ionium; and ionium that of uranium.

"I was struck with fright for my own safety. Might I be changed to metal? I looked to see if there were other metal things about. And I found them in abundance. Half-buried in the glowing sands were metal birds of every kind—birds that had flown over the surrounding cliffs. And, at the climax of my search, I found a pterosaur—a flying reptile that had invaded the pit in ages past—changed to ageless metal. Its wingspread was fully fifteen feet—it would be a treasure in any museum.

"I made a fearful examination of myself, and to my unutterable horror, I perceived that the tips of my fingernails, and the fine hairs upon my hands, *were already changed to light green metal!* The shock unnerved me completely. You cannot conceive my horror. I screamed aloud in agony of soul, careless of the terrible foes that the sound might attract. I ran off wildly. I was blind, unreasoning. I felt no fatigue as I ran, only stark terror.

"Bright, swift-moving lights passed above in the green, but I heeded them not. Suddenly I came upon the great sphere that I had seen above. It rested motionless in a cradle of black metal. The yellow fire was gone from the spikes, but the red surface shone with a metallic luster. Lights floated about it. They made little bright spots in the green, like lanterns swinging in a fog. I turned and ran again, desperately. I took no note of direction, nor of the passage of time.

"Then I came upon a bank of violet vegetation. Waist-deep it was, grass-like, with thick narrow leaves, dotted with clusters of small pink blooms, and little purple berries. And a score of yards beyond I saw a sluggish red steam—El Rio de la Sangre. Here was cover at last. I threw myself down in the violet growth and lay sobbing with fatigue and terror. For a long time I was unable to stir or think. When I looked again at my fingernails, the tips of metal had doubled in width.

"I tried to control my agitation, and to think. Possibly the lights, whatever they were, would sleep by day. If I could find the plane, or scale the walls, I might escape the fearful action of the radioactive minerals before it was too late. I realized that I was hungry. I plucked off a few of the purple berries and tasted them. They had a salty, metallic taste, and I thought they would be valueless for food. But in pulling them I had inadvertently squeezed the juice from one upon my fingers, and when I wiped it off I saw, to my amazement and my inexpressible joy, that the rim of metal was gone from the fingernails it had touched. I had discovered a means of safety! I suppose that the plants were able to exist there only because they had been so developed that they produced compounds counteracting the metal-forming emanations. Probably their evolution began when the action was far weaker than now, and only those able to withstand the more intense radiation had survived. I lost no time in eating a cluster of the berries, and then I poured the water from my canteen and filled it with their juice. I have analyzed the fluid and it corresponds in some ways with the standard formulas for the neutralization of radium burns and doubtless it saved me from the terrible burns caused by the action of ordinary radium.

"I lay there until dawn, dozing a little at times, only to start into wakefulness without cause. It seemed that some daylight filtered through the green, for at dawn it grew paler, and even the red sand appeared less luminous. After eating a few more of the berries, I ascertained the direction in which the stagnant red water was moving, and set off downstream, toward the west. In order to get an idea of where I was going, I counted my paces. I had walked about two and a half miles, along by the violet plants, when I came to an abrupt cliff. It towered up until it was lost in the green gloom. It seemed to be mostly of black pitchblende. The barrier seemed absolutely unscalable. The red river plunged out of sight by the cliff in a racing whirlpool.

"I walked off north around the rim. I had no very definite plan, except to try to find a way out over the cliff. If I failed in that, it would be time to hunt the plane. I had a mortal fear of going near it, or of encountering the strange lights I had seen floating about it. As I went I saw none of them. I supposed they slept when it was day.

"I went on until it must have been noon, though my watch had stopped. Occasionally I passed metal trees that had fallen from above, and once, the metallic body of a bear that had slipped off a path above, some time in past ages. And there were metal birds without number. They must have been accumulating through geological ages. All along up to this, the cliff had risen perpendicularly to the limit of my vision, but now I saw a wide ledge, with a sloping wall beyond it, dimly visible above. But the sheet wall rose a full hundred feet to the shelf, and I cursed at my inability to surmount it. For a time I stood there, devising impractical means for climbing it, driven almost to tears by my impotence. I was ravenously hungry, and thirsty as well.

"At last I went on.

"In an hour I came upon it. A slender cylinder of black metal, that towered a hundred feet into the greenish mist, and carried at the top a great mushroom-shaped orange flame. It was a strange thing. The first was as big as a balloon, bright and steady. It looked much like a great jet of combustible gas, burning as it streamed from the cylinder. I stood petrified in amazement, wondering vaguely at the what and why of the thing.

"And then I saw more of them back of it, dimly—scores of them—a whole forest of flames.

"I crouched back against the cliff, while I considered. Here, I supposed, was the city of the lights. They were sleeping now, but still I had not the courage to enter. According to my calculations I had gone about fifteen miles. Then I must be, I thought, almost diametrically opposite the place where the crimson river flowed under the wall, with half of the rim unexplored. If I wished to continue my journey, I must go around the city, if I may call it that.

"So I left the wall. Soon it was lost to view. I tried to keep in view of the orange flames, but abruptly they were gone in the mist. I walked more to the left, but I came upon nothing but the wastes of red sand, with the green murk above. On and on I wandered. Then the sand

and the air grew slowly brighter and I knew that night had fallen. The lights were soon passing to and fro. I had seen lights the night before, but they traveled high and fast. These, on the other hand, sailed low, and I felt that they were searching.

"I knew that they were hunting for me. I lay down in a little hollow in the sand. Vague, mist-veiled points of light came near and passed. And then one stopped directly overhead. It descended and the circle of radiance grew about it. I knew that it was useless to run, and I could not have done so, for my terror. Down and down it came.

"And then I saw its form. The thing was of a glittering, blazing crystal. A great six-sided, upright prism of red, a dozen feet in length it was, with a six-pointed structure like a snowflake about the center, deep blue, with pointed blue flanges running from the points of the star to angles of the prism! Soft scarlet fire flowed from the points. And on each face of the prism, above and below the star, was a purple cone that must have been an eye. Strange pulsating lights flickered in the crystal. It was alive with light.

"It fell straight toward me!

"It was a terribly, utterly alien form of life. It was not human, not animal—not even life as we know it at all. And yet it had intelligence. But it was strange and foreign and devoid of feeling. It is curious to say that even then, as I lay beneath it, the thought came to me, that the thing and its fellows must have crystallized when the waters of the ancient sea dried out of the crater. Crystallizing salts take intricate forms.

"I drew my automatic and fired three times, but the bullets ricocheted harmlessly off the polished facets.

"It dropped until the gleaming lower point of the prism was not a yard above me. Then the scarlet fire reached out caressingly—flowed over my body. My weight grew less. I was lifted, held against the point. You may see its mark upon my chest. The thing floated into the air, carrying me. Soon others were drifting about. I was overcome with nausea. The scene grew black and I knew no more.

"I awoke floating free in a brilliant orange light. I touched no solid object. I writhed, kicked about—at nothingness. I could not move or turn over, because I could get a hold on nothing. My memory of the last two days seemed a nightmare. My clothing was still upon me. My canteen still hung, or rather floated, by my shoulder. And my automatic was in my pocket. I had the sensation that a great space of time had passed. There was a curious stiffness in my side. I examined it and found a red scar. I believe those crystal things had cut into me. And I found, with a horror you cannot understand, the mark upon my chest. Presently it dawned on me that I was floating, devoid of gravity and free as an object in space, in the orange flame at the top of one of the black cylinders. The crystals knew the secret of gravity. It was vital to them. And peering about, I discerned, with infinite repulsion, a great flashing body, a few yards away. But its inner lights were dead, so I knew that it was day, and that the strange beings were sleeping.

"If I was ever to escape, this was the opportunity. I kicked, clawed desperately at the air, all in vain. I did not move an inch. If they had chained me, I could not have been more secure. I drew my automatic, resolved on a desperate measure. They would not find me again, alive. And as I had it in my hand, an idea came into my mind. I pointed the gun to the side, and fired six rapid shots. And the recoil of each explosion sent me drifting faster, rocket-wise, toward the edge.

"I shot out into the green. Had my gravity been suddenly restored, I might have been killed by the fall, but I descended slowly, and felt a curious lightness for several minutes. And to my surprise, when I struck the ground, the airplane was right before me! They had drawn it up by the base of the tower. It seemed to be intact. I started the engine with nervous haste, and sprang into the cockpit. As I started, another black tower loomed up abruptly before me, but I veered around it, and took off in safety.

"In a few moments I was above the green. I half expected the gravitational wave to be turned on me again, but higher and higher I rose unhindered until the accursed black walls were about me no longer. The sun blazed high in the heavens. Soon I had landed again at Vaca Morena.

"I had had enough of radium hunting. On the beach, where I landed, I sold the plane to a rancher at his own price, and told him to reserve a place for me on the next steamer, which was due in three days. Then I went to the town's single inn, ate, and went to bed. At noon the next day, when I got up, I found that my shoes and the pockets of my clothes contained a good bit of red sand from the crater that had been collected as I crawled about in flight from the crystal lights. I saved some of it for curiosity alone, but when I analyzed it I found it a radium compound so rich that the little handful was worth millions of dollars.

"But the fortune was of little value, for, despite frequent doses of the fluid from my canteen, and the best medical aid, I have suffered continually, and now that my canteen is empty, I am doomed.

"Your friend, Thomas Kelvin"

Thus the manuscript ends. If the reader doubts the truth of the letter, he may see the Metal Man in the Tyburn Museum.

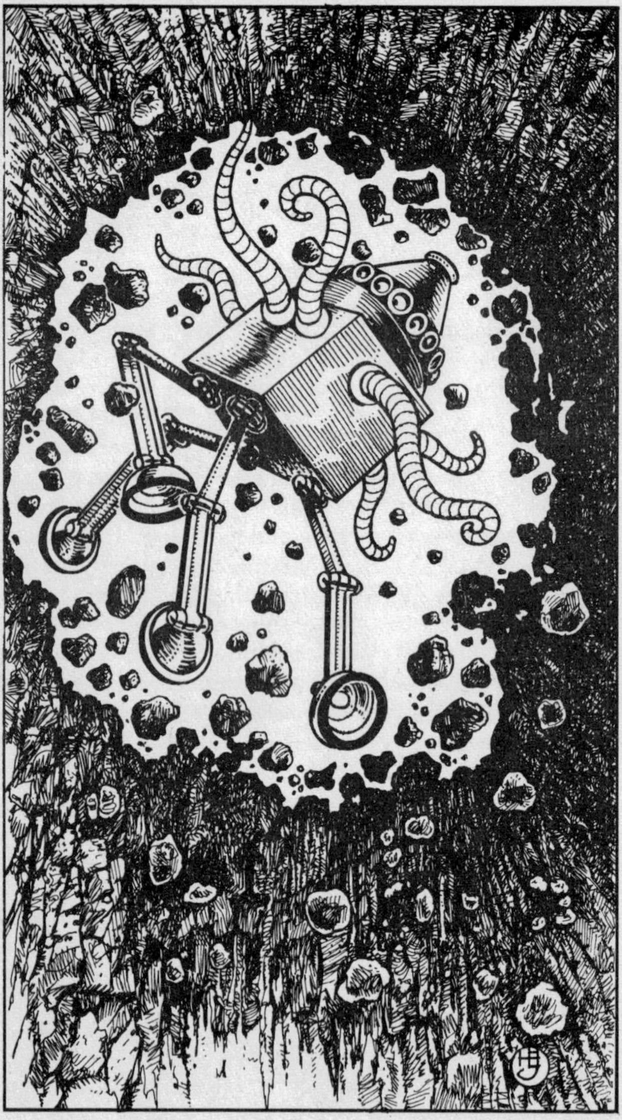

THE JAMESON SATELLITE

by Neil R. Jones

PROLOGUE

The Rocket Satellite

In the depths of space, some twenty thousand miles from the earth, the body of Professor Jameson within its rocket container cruised upon an endless journey, circling the gigantic sphere. The rocket was a satellite of the huge, revolving world around which it held its orbit. In the year 1958, Professor Jameson had sought a plan whereby he might preserve his body indefinitely after his death. He had worked long and hard upon the subject.

Since the time of the Pharaohs, the human race had looked for a means by which the dead might be preserved against the ravages of time. Great had been the art of the Egyptians in the embalming of their deceased, a practice which was later lost to humanity of the ensuing mechanical age, never to be rediscovered. But even the embalming of the Egyptians—so Professor Jameson had argued—would be futile in the face of millions of years, the dissolution of the corpses being just as eventual as immediate cremation following death.

The professor had looked for a means by which the body could be preserved perfectly forever. But eventually he had come to the conclusion that nothing on earth is unchangeable beyond a certain limit of time. Just as long as he sought an earthly means of preservation, he was doomed to disappointment. All earthly elements are composed of atoms which are forever breaking down and building up, but never destroying themselves. A match may be burned but the atoms are still unchanged, having resolved themselves into smoke, carbon dioxide, ashes, and certain basic elements. It was clear to the professor that he could never accomplish his purpose if he were to employ one system of atomic structure, such as embalming fluid or other concoction, to preserve another system of atomic structure, such as the human body, when all atomic structure is subject to universal change, no matter how slow.

He had then soliloquized upon the possibility of preserving the human body in its state of death until the end of all earthly time—to that day when the earth would return to the sun from which it had sprung. Quite suddenly one day he had conceived the answer to the puzzling problem which obsessed his mind, leaving him awed with its wild, uncanny potentialities.

He would have his body shot into space enclosed in a rocket to become a satellite of the earth as long as the earth continued to exist. He reasoned logically. Any material substance, whether of organic or inorganic origin, cast into the depths of space would exist indefinitely. He had visualized his dead body enclosed in a rocket flying off into the illimitable maw of space. He would remain in perfect preservation, while on earth millions of generations of mankind would live and die, their bodies to molder into the dust of the forgotten past. He would exist in this unchanged manner until the day when mankind, beneath a cooling sun, should fade out forever in the chill, thin atmosphere of a dying world. And still his body would remain intact and as perfect in its rocket container as on that day of the far-gone past when it had left earth to be hurled out on its career. What a magnificent idea!

At first he had been assailed with doubts. Suppose his funeral rocket landed upon some other planet or, drawn by the pull of the great sun, were thrown into the flaming folds of the incandescent sphere? Then the rocket might continue on out of the solar system, plunging through the endless seas of space for millions of years, to finally reenter the solar system of some far-off star, as meteors often enter ours. Suppose his rocket crashed upon a planet, or the star itself, or became a captive satellite of some celestial body?

It had been at this juncture that the idea of his rocket becoming the satellite of the earth had presented itself, and he had immediately incorporated it into his scheme. The professor had figured out the amount of radium necessary to carry the rocket far enough away from the earth so that it would not turn around and crash, and still be not so far away but what the earth's gravitational attraction would keep it from leaving the vicinity of the earth and the solar system. Like the moon, it would forever revolve around the earth.

He had chosen an orbit sixty-five thousand miles from the earth for his rocket to follow. The only fears he had entertained concerned the huge meteors which careened through space at tremendous rates of speed. He had overcome this obstacle, however, and eliminated the possibilites of a collision with these stellar juggernauts. In the rocket were installed radium repulsion rays which swerved all approaching meteors from the path of the rocket as they entered the vicinity of the space wanderer.

The aged professor had prepared for every emergency, and had set down to rest from his labors, reveling in the stupendous, unparalleled results he would obtain. Never would his body undergo decay; and never would his bones bleach to return to the dust of the earth from which all men originally came and to which they must return. His body would remain millions of years in a perfectly preserved state, untouched by the hoary palm of such time as only geologists and astronomers can conceive.

His efforts would surpass even the wildest dreams of H. Rider Haggard, who depicted the wondrous, embalming practices of the ancient nation of Kor in his immortal novel, *She*, wherein Holly, under the escort of the incomparable Ayesha, looked upon the magnificent, lifelike masterpieces of embalming by the long-gone people of Kor.

With the able assistance of a nephew, who carried out his instructions and wishes following his death, Professor Jameson was sent upon his pilgrimage into space within the rocket he himself had built. The nephew and heir kept the secret forever locked in his heart.

Generation after generation had passed upon its way. Gradually humanity had come to die out, finally disappearing from the earth altogether. Mankind was later replaced by various other forms of life which dominated the globe for their allotted spaces of time before they too became extinct. The years piled up on one another, running into millions and still the Jameson satellite kept its lonely vigil around the earth, gradually closing the distance between satellite and planet, yielding reluctantly to the latter's powerful attraction.

Forty million years later, its orbit ranged some twenty thousand miles from the earth while the dead world edged ever nearer the cooling sun whose dull, red ball covered a large expanse of the sky. Surrounding the flaming sphere, many of the stars could be perceived through the earth's thin, rarified atmosphere. As the earth cut in slowly and gradually toward the solar luminary, so was the moon revolving ever nearer the earth, appearing like a great gem glowing in the twilight sky.

The rocket containing the remains of Professor Jameson continued its endless travel around the great ball of the earth whose rotation had now ceased entirely—one side forever facing the dying sun. There it pursued its lonely way, a cosmic coffin, accompanied by its funeral cortege of scintillating stars amid the deep silence of eternal space which enshrouded it. Solitary it remained except for the occasional passing of a meteor flitting by at a remarkable speed on its aimless journey through the vacuum between the far-flung worlds.

Would the satellite follow its orbit to the world's end, or would its supply of radium soon exhaust itself after so many eons of time, converting the rocket into the prey of the first large meteor which chanced that way? Would it some day return to the earth as its nearer approach portended, and increase its acceleration in a long arc to crash upon the surface of the dead planet? And when the rocket terminated its career, would the body of Professor Jameson be found perfectly preserved or merely a crumbled mound of dust?

CHAPTER I

40,000,000 Years After

Entering within the boundaries of the solar system, a long, dark, pointed craft sped across the realms of space towards the tiny point of light which marked the dull red ball of the dying sun which would some day lie cold and dark forever. Like a huge meteor it flashed into the solar system from another chain of planets far out in the illimitable Universe of stars and worlds, heading towards the great red sun at an inconceivable speed.

Within the interior of the space traveler, queer creatures of metal labored at the controls of the space flyer which juggernauted on its way towards the far-off luminary. Rapidly it crossed the orbits of Neptune and Uranus and headed sunward. The bodies of these queer creatures were square blocks of metal closely resembling steel, while for appendages, the metal cube was upheld by four jointed legs capable of movement. A set of six tentacles, all metal, like the rest of the body, curved outward from the upper half of the cubic body. Surmounting it was a queer-shaped head rising to a peak in the center and equipped with a circle of eyes all the way around the head. The creatures, with their mechanical eyes equipped with metal shutters, could see in all directions. A single eye pointed directly upward, being situated in the space of the peaked head, resting in a slight depression of the cranium.

These were the Zoromes of the planet Zor which rotated on its way around a star millions of light years distant from our solar system. The Zoromes, several hundred thousand years before, had reached a stage in science, where they searched for immortality and eternal relief from bodily ills and various deficiencies of flesh and blood anatomy. They had sought freedom from death, and had found it, but at the same time they had destroyed the propensities of birth. And for several hundred thousand years there had been no births and few deaths in the history of the Zoromes.

This strange race of people had built their own mechanical bodies, and by operation upon one another had removed their brains to the metal heads from which they directed the functions and movements of their inorganic anatomies. There had been no deaths due to worn-out bodies. When one part of the mechanical men wore out, it was replaced by a new part, and so the Zoromes continued living their immortal lives which saw few casualties. It was true that, since the innovation of the machines, there had been a few accidents which had seen the destruction of the metal heads with their brains. These were irreparable. Such cases had been few, however, and the population of Zor decreased but little. The machine men of Zor had no use for atmosphere, and had it not been for the terrible coldness of space, could have just as well existed in the ether void as upon some planet. Their metal bodies, especially their metal-encased brains, did require a certain amount of heat even though they were able to exist comfortably in temperatures which would instantly have frozen to death a flesh-and-blood creature.

The most popular pastime among the machine men of Zor was the exploration of the Universe. This afforded them a never ending source of interest in the discovery of the variegated inhabitants and conditions of the various planets on which they came to rest. Hundreds of spaceships were sent out in all directions, many of them being upon their expeditions for hundreds of years before they returned once again to the home planet of far-off Zor.

This particular spacecraft of the Zoromes had entered the solar system whose planets were gradually circling in closer to the dull red ball of the declining sun. Several of the machine men of the spacecraft's crew, which numbered some fifty individuals, were examining the various planets of this particular planetary system carefully through telescopes possessing immense power.

These machine men had no names and were indexed according to letters and numbers. They conversed by means of thought impulses, and were capable neither of making a sound vocally nor of hearing one uttered.

"Where shall we go?" queried one of the men at the controls questioning another who stood by his side examining a chart on the wall.

"They all appear to be dead worlds, 4R-3579," replied the one addressed, "but the second planet from the sun appears to have an atmosphere which might sustain a few living creatures, and the third planet may also prove interesting for it has a satellite. We shall examine the inner planets first of all, and explore the outer ones later if we decide it is worth the time."

"Too much trouble for nothing," ventured 9G-721. "This system of planets offers us little but what we have seen many times before in our travels. The sun is so cooled that it cannot sustain the more common life on its planets, the type of life forms we usually find in our travels. We should have visited a planetary system with a brighter sun."

"You speak of common life," remarked 25X-987. "What of the uncommon life? Have we not found life existent on cold, dead planets with no sunlight and atmosphere at all?"

"Yes, we have," admitted 9G-721, "but such occasions are exceedingly rare."

"The possibility exists, however, even in this case," reminded 4R-3579, "and what if we do spend a bit of unprofitable time in this one planetary system—haven't we all an endless lifetime before us? Eternity is ours."

"We shall visit the second planet first of all," directed 25X-987, who was in charge of this particular expedition of the Zoromes, "and on the way there we shall cruise along near the third planet to see what we can of the surface. We may be able to tell whether or not it holds anything of interest to us. If it does, after visiting the second planet, we shall then return to the third. The first world is not worth bothering with.

The spaceship from Zor raced on in a direction which would take it several thousand miles above the earth and then on to the planet which we know as Venus. As the spaceship rapidly neared the earth, it slackened its speed, so that the Zoromes might examine it closely with their glasses as the ship passed the third planet.

Suddenly, one of the machine men ran excitedly into

the room where 25X-987 stood watching the topography of the world beneath him.

"We have found something!" he exclaimed.

"What?"

"Another spaceship!"

"Where?"

"But a short distance ahead of us on our course. Come into the foreport of the ship and you can pick it up with the glass."

"Which is the way it's going?" asked 25X-987.

"It is behaving queerly," replied the machine man of Zor. "It appears to be in the act of encircling the planet."

"Do you suppose that there really is life on that dead world—intelligent beings like ourselves, and that this is one of their spacecraft?"

"Perhaps it is another exploration craft like our own from some other world," was the suggestion.

"But not of ours," said 25X-987.

Together, the two Zoromes now hastened into the observation room of the spaceship where more of the machine men were excitedly examining the mysterious spacecraft, their thought impulses flying thick and fast like bodiless bullets.

"It is very small!"

"Its speed is slow!"

"The craft can hold but few men," observed one.

"We do not yet know of what size the creatures are," reminded another. "Perhaps there are thousands of them in that spacecraft out there. They may be of such a small size that it will be necessary to look twice before finding one of them. Such beings are not unknown."

"We shall soon overtake it and see."

"I wonder if they have seen us?"

"Where do you suppose it came from?"

"From the world beneath us," was the suggestion.

"Perhaps."

CHAPTER II

The Mysterious Spacecraft

The machine men made way for their leader, 25X-987, who regarded the spacecraft ahead of them critically.

"Have you tried communicating with it yet?" he asked.

"There is no reply to any of our signals," came the answer.

"Come alongside of it then," ordered their commander. "It is small enough to be brought inside our carrying compartment, and we can see with our penetration rays just what manner of creatures it holds. They are intelligent, that is certain, for their spaceship does imply as much.

The space flyer of the Zoromes slowed up as it approached the mysterious wanderer of the cosmic void which hovered in the vicinity of the dying world.

"What a queer shape it has," remarked 25X-987. "It is even smaller than I had previously calculated."

A rare occurrence had taken place among the machine men of Zor. They were overcome by a great curiosity which they could not allow to remain unsatiated. Accustomed as they were to witnessing strange sights and still stranger creatures, meeting up with weird adventures in various corners of the Universe, they had now become hardened to the usual run of experiences which they were in the habit of encountering. It took a great deal to arouse their unperturbed attitudes. Something new, however, about this queer spacecraft had gripped their imaginations, and perhaps a subconscious influence asserted in their minds that here they have come across an adventure radically unusual.

"Come alongside it," repeated 25X-987 to the operator as he returned to the control room and gazed through the side of the spaceship in the direction of the smaller cosmic wanderer.

"I'm trying to," replied the machine man, "but it seems to jump away a bit every time I get within a certain distance of it. Our ship seems to jump backward a bit too."

"Are they trying to elude us?"

"I don't know. They should pick up more speed if that was their object."

"Perhaps they are now progressing at their maximum speed and cannot increase their acceleration any more."

"Look!" exclaimed the operator. "Did you see that? The thing has jumped away from us again!"

"Our ship moved also," said 25X-987. "I saw a flash of light shoot from the side of the other ship as it jumped."

Another machine man now entered and spoke to the commander of the Zorome expedition.

"They are using radium repellent rays to keep us from approaching," he informed.

"Counteract it," instructed 25X-987.

The man left, and now the machine man at the controls of the craft tried again to close with the mysterious wanderer of the space between planets. The effort was successful, and this time there was no glow of repulsion rays from the side of the long metal cylinder.

They now entered the compartment where various objects were transferred from out of the depths of space to the interplanetary craft. Then patiently they waited for the rest of the machine men to open the side of their spaceship and bring in the queer elongated cylinder.

"Put it under the penetration ray!" ordered 25X-987. "Then we shall see what it contains!"

The entire group of Zoromes were assembled about the long cylinder whose low nickel-plated sides shone brilliantly. With interest they regarded the fifteen-foot object which tapered a bit towards its base. The nose was pointed like a bullet. Eight cylindrical protuberances were affixed to the base while the four sides were equipped with fins such as are seen on aerial bombs to guide them in a direct, unswerving line through the atmosphere. At the base of the strange craft there projected a lever, while in one side was a door which apparently opened outward. One of the machine men reached forward to open it but was halted by the admonition of the commander.

"Do not open it yet!" he warned. "We are not aware of what it contains!"

Guided by the hand of one of the machine men, a series of lights shone down upon the cylinder. It became enveloped in a haze of light which rendered the metal sides of the mysterious spacecraft dim and indistinct while the interior of the cylinder was as clearly revealed as if there had been no covering. The machine men, expecting to see at least several, perhaps many, strange creatures moving about within the metal cylinder, stared aghast at the sight they beheld. There was but one creature, and he was lying perfectly still, either in a state of suspended animation or else of death. He was about twice the height of the mechanical men of Zor. For a long time they gazed at him in a silence of thought, and then their leader instructed them.

"Take him out of the container."

The penetration rays were turned off, and two of the machine men stepped eagerly forward and opened the door. One of them peered within at the recumbent body of the weird-looking individual with the four appendages. The creature lay up against a luxuriously upholstered interior, a strap affixed to his chin while four more straps held both the upper and lower appendages securely to the insides of the cylinder. The machine man released these, and with the help of his comrade removed the body of the creature from the cosmic coffin in which they had found it.

"He is dead!" pronounced one of the machine men after a long and careful examination of the corpse. "He has been like this for a long time."

"There are strange thought impressions left upon his mind," remarked another.

One of the machine men, whose metal body was a different shade than that of his companions, stepped forward. His cubic body bent over that of the strange, cold creature who was garbed in fantastic accoutrements. He examined the dead organism a moment and then he turned to his companions.

"Would you like to hear his story?" he asked.

"Yes!" came the concerted reply.

"You shall, then," was the ultimatum. "Bring him into my laboratory. I shall remove his brain and stimulate the cells into activity once more. We shall give him life again, transplanting his brain into the head of one of our machines."

With these words he directed two of the Zoromes to carry the corpse into the laboratory.

As the spaceship cruised about in the vicinity of this third planet which 25X-987 had decided to visit on finding the metal cylinder with its queer inhabitant, 8B-52, the experimenter, worked unceasingly in his laboratory to revive the long-dead brain cells to action once more. Finally, after consumating his desires and having his efforts crowned with success, he placed the brain within the head of a machine. The brain was brought to consciousness. The creature's body was discarded after the all-important brain had been removed.

CHAPTER III

Recalled to Life

As Professor Jameson came to, he became aware of a strange feeling. He was sick. The doctors had not expected him to live, they had frankly told him so—but he had cared little in view of the long, happy years stretched out behind him. Perhaps he was not to die yet. He wondered how long he had slept. How strange he felt—as if he had no body. Why couldn't he open his eyes? He tried very hard. A mist swam before him. His eyes had been open all the time but he had not seen before. That was queer, he ruminated. All was silent about his bedside. Had all the doctors and nurses left him to sleep—or to die?

Devil take the mist which now swam before him, obscuring everything in line of vision. He would call his nephew. Vainly he attempted to shout the word "Douglas," but to no avail. Where was his mouth? It seemed as if he had none. Was it all delirium? The strange silence—perhaps he had lost his sense of hearing along with his ability to speak— and he could see nothing distinctly. The mist had transferred itself into a confused jumble of indistinct objects, some of which moved about before him.

He was now conscious of some impulse in his mind which kept questioning him as to how he felt. He was conscious of other strange ideas which seemed to be impressed upon his brain, but this one thought concerning his indisposition clamored insistently over the lesser ideas. It even seemed just as if someone was addressing him, and impulsively he attempted to utter a sound and tell them how queer he felt. It seemed as if speech had been taken from him. He could not talk, no matter how hard he tried. It was no use. Strange to say, however, the impulse within his mind appeared to be satisfied with the effort, and it now put another question to him. Where was he from? What a strange question—when he was at home. He told them as much. Had he always lived there? Why, yes, of course.

The aged professor was now becoming more astute as to his condition. At first it was only a mild, passive wonderment at his helplessness and the strange thoughts which raced through his mind. Now he attempted to arouse himself from the lethargy.

Quite suddenly his sight cleared, and what a surprise! He could see all the way around him without moving his head! And he could look at the ceiling of his room! His room? Was it his room? No—It just couldn't be. Where was he? What were those queer machines before him? They moved on four legs. Six tentacles curled outward from their cubical bodies. One of the machines stood close before him. A tentacle shot out from the object and rubbed his head. How strange it felt upon his brow. Instinctively he obeyed the impulse to shove the contraption of metal from him, with his hands.

His arms did not rise, instead six tentacles projected upward to force back the machine. Professor Jameson gasped mentally in surprise as he gazed at the result of his urge to push the strange, unearthly looking machine-caricature from him. With trepidation he looked down at his own body to see where the tentacles had come from, and his surprise turned to sheer fright and amazement. His body was like the moving machine which stood before him! Where was he? What ever had happened to him so suddenly? Only a few moments ago he had been in his bed, with the doctors and his nephew bending over him, expecting him to die. The last words he had remembered hearing was the cryptic announcement of one of the doctors.

"He is going now."

But he hadn't died after all, apparently. A horrible thought struck him! Was this the life after death? Or was it an illusion of the mind? He became aware that the machine in front of him was attempting to communicate something to him. How could it, thought the professor, when he had no mouth. The desire to communicate an idea became more insistent. The suggestion of the machine man's question was in his mind. Telepathy, thought he.

The creature was asking about the place whence he had come. He didn't know; his mind was in such a turmoil of thoughts and conflicting ideas. He allowed himself to be led to a window where the machine with waving tentacle pointed towards an object outside. It was a queer sensation to be walking on the four metal legs. He looked from the window and he saw that which caused him to nearly drop over, so astounded was he.

The professor found himself gazing out from the boundless depths of space across the cosmic void to where a huge planet lay quiet. Now he was sure it was an illusion which made his mind and sight behave so queerly. He was troubled by a very strange dream. Carefully he examine the topography of the gigantic globe which rested off in the distance. At the same time he could see back of him the concourse of mechanical creatures crowding up behind him, and he was aware of a telepathic conversation which was being carried on behind him—or just before him. Which was it now? Eyes extended all the way around his head, while there existed no difference on any of the four sides of his cubed body. His mechanical legs were capable of moving in any of four given directions with perfect ease, he discovered.

The planet was not the earth—of that he was sure. None of the familiar continents lay before his eyes. And then he saw the great dull red ball of the dying sun. That was not the sun of the earth. It had been a great deal more brilliant.

"Did you come from that planet?" came the thought impulse from the mechanism by his side.

"No," he returned.

He then allowed the machine men—for he assumed that they were machine men, and he reasoned that, somehow or other they had by some marvelous transformation made him over just as they were—to lead him through the craft of which he now took notice for the first time. It was an interplanetary flyer, or spaceship, he firmly believed.

25X-987 now took him to the compartment which they had removed him to from the strange container they had found wandering in the vicinity of the nearby world. There they showed him the long cylinder.

"It's my rocket satellite!" exclaimed Professor Jameson to himself, though in reality every one of the machine men received his thoughts plainly. "What is it doing here?"

"We found your dead body within it," answered 25X-987. "Your brain was removed to the machine after having been stimulated into activity once more. Your carcass was thrown away."

Professor Jameson just stood dumbfounded by the words of the machine man.

"So I did die!" exclaimed the professor. "And my body was placed within the rocket to remain in everlasting preservation until the end of all earthly time! Success! I have now attained unrivaled success!"

He then turned to the machine man.

"How long have I been that way?" he asked excitedly.

"How should we know?" replied the Zorome. "We picked up your rocket only a short time ago, which, according to your computation, would be less than a day. This is our first visit to your planetary system and we chanced upon your rocket. So it is a satellite? We didn't watch it long enough to discover whether or not it was a satellite. At first we thought it to be another traveling spacecraft, but when it refused to answer our signals we investigated."

"And so that was the earth at which I looked," mused the professor. "No wonder I didn't recognize it. The topography has changed so much. How different the sun appears—it must have been over a million years ago when I died!"

"Many millions," corrected 25X-987. "Suns of such size as this one do not cool in so short a time as you suggest."

Professor Jameson, in spite of all his amazing computations before his death, was staggered by the reality.

"Who are you?" he suddenly asked.

"We are the Zoromes from Zor, a planet of a sun far across the Universe."

25X-987 then went on to tell Professor Jameson something about how the Zoromes had attained their high stage of development and had instantly put a stop to all birth, evolution and death of their people, by becoming machine men.

CHAPTER IV

The Dying World

"And now tell us of yourself," said 25X-987, "and about your world."

Professor Jameson, noted in college as a lecturer of no mean ability and perfectly capable of relating intelligently to them the story of the earth's history, evolution and march of events following the birth of civilization up until the time he died, began his story. The mental speech hampered him for a time, but he soon became accustomed to it so as to use it easily, and he found it preferable to vocal speech after a while. The Zoromes listened interestedly to the long account until Professor Jameson had finished.

"My nephew," concluded the professor, "evidently obeyed my instructions and placed my body in the rocket I had built, shooting it out into space where I became a satellite of the earth for these many millions of years."

"Do you really want to know how long you were dead before we found you?" asked 25X-987. "It would be interesting to find out."

"Yes, I should like very much to know," replied the professor.

"Our greatest mathematician, 459C-79, will tell it to you." The mathematician stepped forward. Upon one side of his cube were many buttons arranged in long columns and squares.

"What is your unit of measuring?" he asked.

"A mile."

"How many times more is a mile than is the length of your rocket satellite?"

"My rocket is fifteen feet long. A mile is five thousand two hundred and eighty feet."

The mathematician depressed a few buttons.

"How far, or how many miles from the sun was your planet at that time?"

"Ninety-three million miles," was the reply.

"And your world's satellite—which you call the moon—from your planet earth?"

"Two hundred and forty thousand miles."

"And your rocket?"

"I figured it to go about sixty-five thousand miles from the earth."

"It was only twenty thousand miles from the earth when we picked it up," said the mathematician, depressing a few more buttons. "The moon and the sun are also much nearer your planet now."

Professor Jameson gave way to a mental ejaculation of amazement.

"Do you know how long you have cruised around the planet in your own satellite?" said the mathematician. "Since you began that journey, the planet which you called the earth has revolved around the sun over forty million times."

"Forty—million—years!" exclaimed Professor Jameson haltingly. "Humanity must then have all perished from the earth long ago! I'm the last man on earth!"

"It's a dead world now," interjected 25X-987.

"Of course," elucidated the mathematician, "those last few million years are much shorter than the ones in which you lived. The earth's orbit is of less diameter and its speed of revolution is greatly increased, due to its proximity to the cooling sun. I should say that your year was some four times as long as the time it now takes your old planet to circumnavigate the sun.

"How many days were there in your year?"

"Three hundred and sixty-five."

"The planet has now ceased rotating entirely."

"Seems queer that your rocket satellite should avoid the meteors so long," observed 459C-79, the mathematician.

"Automatic radium repulsion rays," explained the professor.

"The very rays which kept us from approaching your rocket," stated 25X-987, "until we neutralized them."

"You died and were shot out into space long before any life occurred on Zor," soliloquized one of the machine men. "Our people had not yet even been born when yours had probably disappeared entirely from the face of the earth."

"Hearken to 72N-4783," said 25X-987, "he is our philosopher, and he just loves to dwell on the past life of Zor when we were flesh and blood creatures with the threat of death hanging over our heads. At that time, like the life you knew, we were born, we lived and died, all within a very short time comparatively."

"Of course, time has come to mean nothing to us, especially when we are out in space," observed 72N-4783. "We never keep track of it on our expeditions, though back in Zor such accounts are accurately kept. By the way, do you know how long we stood here while you recounted to us the history of your planet? Our machine bodies never get tired, you know."

"Well," ruminated Professor Jameson, giving a generous allowance of time. "I should say about half a day, although it seemed scarcely as long as that."

"We listened to you for four days," replied 72N-4783.

Professor Jameson was really aghast.

"Really, I hadn't meant to be such a bore," he apologized.

"That is nothing," replied the other. "Your story has been interesting, and if it had been twice as long it would not have mattered, nor would it have seemed any longer. Time is merely relative, and in space actual time does not exist at all, any more than your forty million years' cessation of life seemed more than a few minutes to you. We saw that it was so when your first thought impressions reached us following your revival."

"Let us continue on to your planet earth," then said 25X-987. "Perhaps we shall find more startling disclosures there."

As the spaceship of the Zoromes approached the sphere from which Professor Jameson had been hurled in his rocket forty million years before, the professor was wondering how the earth would appear, and what radical changes he would find. Already he knew that the geographical conditions of the various continents were changed. He had seen as much from the spaceship.

A short time later the earth was reached. The space travelers from Zor, as well as Professor Jameson, emerged from the cosmic flyer to walk upon the surface of the planet. The earth had ceased rotating, leaving one-half its surface toward the sun. This side of the earth was heated to a considerable degree, while its antipodes, turned always away from the solar luminary, was a cold, frigid, desolate waste. The space travelers from Zor did not dare to advance very far into either hemisphere, but landed on the narrow, thousand-mile strip of territory separating the earth's frozen half from its sun-baked antipodes.

As Professor Jameson emerged from the spaceship with 25X-987, he stared in awe at the great transformation four hundred thousand centuries had wrought. The earth's surface, its sky and the sun were all so changed and unearthly appearing. Off to the east the blood red ball of the slowly cooling sun rested upon the horizon, lighting up the eternal day. The earth's rotation had ceased entirely, and it hung motionless in the sky as it revolved around its solar parent, its orbit slowly but surely cutting in toward the great body of the sun. The two inner planets, Mercury and Venus, were now very close to the blood red orb whose scintillating, dazzling brilliance had been lost in its cooling process. Soon, the two nearer planets would succumb to the great pull of the solar luminary and return to the flaming folds, from which they had been hurled out as gaseous bodies in the dim, age-old past, when their careers had just begun.

The atmosphere was nearly gone, so rarified had it become, and through it Professor Jameson could view with amazing clarity without discomfort to his eyes the bloated body of the dying sun. It appeared many times the size he had seen it at the time of his death, on account of its relative nearness. The earth had advanced a great deal closer to the great star around which it swung.

The sky toward the west was pitch black except for the iridescent twinkle of the fiery stars which studded that section of the heavens. As he watched, a faint glow suffused the western sky, gradually growing brighter, the full moon majestically lifted itself above the horizon, casting its pale ethereal radiance upon the dying world beneath. It was increased to many times the size Professor Jameson had ever seen it during his natural lifetime.

The earth's greater attraction was drawing upon the moon just as the sun was pulling the earth ever nearer itself.

This cheerless landscape confronting the professor represented the state of existence to which the earth had come. It was a magnificent spread of loneliness which bore no witness to the fact that it had seen the teeming life in better ages long ago. The weird, yet beautiful scene, spread in a melancholy panorama before his eyes, drove his thoughts into gloomy abstraction with its dismal, depressing influence. Its funereal, oppressive aspect smote him suddenly with the chill of a terrible loneliness.

25X-987 aroused Professor Jameson from his lethargic reverie. "Let us walk around and see what we can find. I can understand how you feel in regard to the past. It is quite a shock—but it must happen to all worlds sooner or later—even to Zor. When that time comes, the Zoromes will find a new planet on which to live. If you travel with us, you will become accustomed to the sight of seeing, dead, lifeless worlds as well as new and beautiful ones pulsating with life and energy. Of course, this world being your own, holds a peculiar sentimental value to you, but it is really one planet among billions."

Professor Jameson was silent.

"I wonder whether or not there are any ruins here to be found?" queried 25X-987.

"I don't believe so," replied the professor. "I remember hearing an eminent scientist of my day state that, given fifty thousand years, every structure and other creation of man would be obliterated entirely from off the earth's surface."

"And he was right," endorsed the machine man from Zor. "Time is a great effacer."

For a long time the machine men wandered over the dreary surface of the earth, and then 25X-987 suggested a change of territory to explore. In the spaceship, they moved around the earth to the other side, still keeping to the belt of shadowland which completely encircled the globe like some gigantic ring. Where they now landed arose a series of cones with hollow peaks.

"Volcanoes!" exclaimed the professor.

"Extinct ones," added the machine man.

Leaving the spaceship, the fifty or more machine men, including Professor Jameson, were soon exploring the curiously shaped peaks. The professor, in his wanderings had strayed away from the rest, and now advanced into one of the cup-like depressions of the peak, out of sight of his companions, the Zoromes.

CHAPTER V

Eternity or Death

He was well in the center of the cavity when the soft ground beneath him gave way suddenly and he catapulted below into the darkness. Through the Stygian gloom he fell in what seemed to be an endless drop. He finally crashed upon something hard. The thin crust of the volcano's mouth had broken through, precipitating him into the deep, hollow interior.

It must have been a long way to fall—or so it had seemed. Why was he not knocked senseless or killed? Then he felt himself over with three tentacles. His metal legs were four broken, twisted masses of metal, while the lower half of his cubic body was jammed out of shape and split. He could not move, and half of his six tentacles were paralyzed.

How would he ever get out of there? he wondered. The machine men of Zor might never find him. What would happen to him, then? He would remain in this deathless, monotonous state forever in the black hole of the volcano's interior unable to move. What a horrible thought! He could not starve to death; eating was unknown among the Zoromes, the machines requiring no food. He could not even commit suicide. The only way for him to die would be to smash the strong metal head, and in his present immovable condition, this was impossible.

It suddenly occurred to him to radiate thoughts for help. Would the Zoromes receive his message? He wondered how far the telepathic messages would carry. He concentrated the powers of his mind upon the call for help, and repeatedly stated his position and plight. He then left his mind clear to receive the thought answers of the Zoromes. He received none. Again he tried. Still he received no welcoming answer. Professor Jameson became dejected.

It was hopeless. The telepathic messages had not reached the machine men of Zor. They were too far away, just as one person may be out of earshot of another's voice. He was doomed to a terrible fate of existence! It were better that his rocket had never been found. He wished that the Zoromes had destroyed him instead of bringing him back to life—back to this!

His thoughts were suddenly broken in upon.

"We're coming!"

"Don't give up hope!"

If the professor's machine body had been equipped with a heart, it would have sung for joy at these welcome thought impressions. A short time later there appeared in the ragged break of the volcano's mouth, where he had fallen through, the metal head of one of the machine men.

"We shall have you out of there soon," he said.

The professor never knew how they managed it for he lost consciousness under some strange ray of light they projected down upon him in his prison. When he came to consciousness once more, it was to find himself inside the spaceship.

"If you had fallen and had smashed your head, it would have been all over for you," were the first thoughts which greeted him. "As it is, however, we can fix you up first rate."

"Why didn't you answer the first time I called you?" asked the professor. "Didn't you hear me?"

"We heard you, and we answered, but you didn't hear us. You see, your brain is different than ours, and though you can send thought waves as far as we can you cannot receive them from such a great distance."

"I'm wrecked," said the professor, gazing at his twisted limbs, paralyzed tentacles and jammed body.

"We shall repair you," came the reply. "It is your good fortune that your head was not crushed."

"What are you going to do with me?" queried the professor. "Will you remove my brains to another machine?"

"No, it isn't necessary. We shall merely remove your head and place it upon another machine body."

The Zoromes immediately set to work upon the task, and soon had Professor Jameson's metal head removed from the machine which he had wrecked in his fall down the crater. All during the painless operation, the professor kept up a series of thought exchanges in conversation with the Zoromes, and it seemed but a short time before his head surmounted a new machine and he was ready for further exploration. In the course of his operation, the spaceship had moved to a new position, and now as they emerged 25X-987 kept company with Professor Jameson.

"I must keep an eye on you," he said. "You will be getting into more trouble before you get accustomed to the metal bodies."

But Professor Jameson was doing a great deal of thinking. Doubtlessly, these strange machine men who had picked up his rocket in the depths of space and had brought him back to life, were expecting him to travel with them and become adopted into the ranks of the Zoromes. Did he want to go with them? He couldn't decide. He had forgotten that the machine men could read his innermost thoughts.

"You wish to remain here alone upon earth?" asked 25X-987. "It is your privilege if you really want it so."

"I don't know," replied Professor Jameson truthfully.

He gazed at the dust around his feet. It had probably been the composition of men, and had changed from time to time into various other atomic structures—of other queer forms of life which had succeeded mankind. It was the law of the atom which never died. And now he had within his power perpetual existence. He could be immortal if he wished. It would be an immortality of never-ending adventures in the vast, endless Universe among the galaxy of stars and planets.

A great loneliness seized him. Would he be happy among these machine men of another far-off world—among these Zoromes? They were kindly and solicitous of his welfare. What better fate could he expect? Still, a longing for his own kind arose in him—the call of humanity. It was irresistible. What could he do? Was it not in vain? Humanity had long since disappeared from the earth—millions of years ago. He wondered what lay beyond the pales of earth—the real death, where the body decomposed and wasted away to return to the dust of the earth and assume new atomic structures.

He had begun to wonder whether or not he had been dead all these forty million years—suppose he had been merely in a state of suspended animation. He had remembered a scientist of his day, who had claimed that the body did not die at the moment at which respiration, heart beats and the blood circulation ceased, but it existed in the semblance of life for several days afterward, especially in the cells of the bones, which died last of all.

Perhaps when he had been sent out into space in his rocket right after his death, the action of the cosmic void was to halt his slow death of the cells in his body, and hold him in suspended animation during the ensuing millions of years. Suppose he should really die—destroying his own brain? What lay beyond real death? Would it be a better plane of existence than the Zoromes could offer him? Would he rediscover humanity, or had they long since arisen to higher planes of existence or reincarnation? Did time exist beyond the mysterious portals of death? If not, then it was possible for him to join the souls of the human race. Had he really been dead all this time? If so, he knew what to expect in case he really destroyed his own brain! Oblivion!

Again the intense feeling of loneliness surged over him and held him within its melancholy grasp. Desperately, he decided to find the nearest cliff and jump from it—headfirst! Humanity called; no man lived to companion him. His four metal limbs carried him swiftly to the summit of a nearby precipice. Why not gamble on the hereafter? 25X-987, understanding his trend of thought, did not attempt to restrain him. Instead, the machine man of Zor waited patiently.

As Professor Jameson stood there meditating upon the jump which would hurl him now into a new plane of existence—or into oblivion, the thought transference of 25X-987 reached him. It was laden with the wisdom born of many planets and thousands of centuries' experience.

"Why jump?" asked the machine man. "The dying world holds your imagination within a morbid clutch. It is all a matter of mental condition. Free your mind of this fascinating influence and come with us to visit other worlds, many of them are both beautiful and new. You will then feel a great difference.

"Will you come?"

The professor considered for a moment as he resisted the impulse to dive off the declivity to the enticing rocks far below. An inspiration seized him. Backing away from the edge of the cliff, he joined 25X-987, once more.

"I shall come," he stated.

He would become immortal after all and join the Zoromes in their never-ending adventures from world to world. They hastened to the spaceship to escape the depressing dreary influence of the dying world, which had nearly driven Professor Jameson to take the fatal leap to oblivion.

THE MAN WHO SAW THE FUTURE

By Edmond Hamilton

Jean de Marselait, Inquisitor Extraordinary of the King of France, raised his head from the parchments that littered the rude desk at which he sat. His glance shifted along the long, stone-walled, torch-lit room to the file of mail-clad soldiers who stood like steel statues by its door. A word from him and two of them sprang forward.

"You may bring in the prisoner," he said.

The two disappeared through the door and in moments more came a clang of opening bolts and grating heavy hinges from somewhere in the building. Then the clang of the returning soldiers, and they entered the room with another man between them whose hands were fettered.

He was a straight figure, and was dressed in drab tunic and hose. His dark hair was long and straight, and his face held a dreaming strength, altogether different from the battered visages of the soldiers or the changeless mask of the Inquisitor. The latter regarded the prisoner for a moment, and then lifted one of the parchments from before him and read from it in a smooth, clear voice.

"Henri Lothiere, apothecary's assistant of Paris," he read, "is charged in this year of our Lord one thousand four hundred and forty-four with offending against God and the King by committing the crime of sorcery."

The prisoner spoke for the first time, his voice low but steady. "I am no sorcerer, sire."

Jean de Marselait read calmly on from the parchment. "It is stated by many witnesses that for long that part of

Paris, called Nanley by some, has been troubled by works of the devil. Ever and anon great claps of thunder have been heard issuing from an open field there without visible cause. They were evidently caused by a sorcerer of power since even exorcists could not halt them.

"It is attested by many that the accused, Henri Lothiere, did, in spite of the known diabolical nature of the thing, spend much time at the field in question. It is also attested that the said Henri Lothiere did state that in his opinion the thunderclaps were not of diabolical origin, and that if they were studied, their cause might be discovered.

"It being suspected from this that Henri Lothiere was himself the sorcerer causing the thunderclaps, he was watched and on the third day of June was seen to go in the early morning to the unholy spot with certain instruments. There he was observed going through strange and diabolical conjurations, when there came suddenly another thunderclap and the said Henri Lothiere did vanish entirely from view in that moment. This fact is attested beyond all doubt.

"The news spreading, many hundreds watched around the field during that day. Upon that night, before midnight, another thunderclap was heard and the said Henri Lothiere was seen by these hundreds to appear at the field's center as swiftly and as strangely as he had vanished. The fear-stricken hundreds around the field heard him tell them how, by diabolical power, he had gone for hundreds of years into the future, a thing surely possible only to the devil and his minions, and heard him tell other blasphemies before they seized him and brought him to the Inquisitor of the King, praying that he be burned and his work of sorcery thus halted.

"Therefore, Henri Lothiere, since you were seen to vanish and reappear as only the servants of the evil one might do, and were heard by many to utter the blasphemies mentioned, I must adjudge you a sorcerer with the penalty of death by fire. If anything there be that you can advance in palliation of your black offense, however, you may now do so before final sentence is passed upon you."

Jean de Marselait laid down the parchment, and raised his eyes to the prisoner. The latter looked round him quickly for a moment, a half-glimpsed panic for an instant in his eyes, then seemed to steady.

"Sire, I cannot change the sentence you will pass upon me," he said quietly, "yet do I wish well to relate once, what happened to me and what I saw. Is it permitted me to tell that from first to last?"

The Inquisitor's head bent, and Henri Lothiere spoke, his voice gaining in strength and fervor as he continued.

"Sire, I, Henri Lothiere, am no sorcerer but a simple apothecary's assistant. It was always my nature, from earliest youth, to desire to delve into matters unknown to men; the secrets of the earth and sea and sky, the knowledge hidden from us. I knew well that this was wicked, that the Church teaches all we need to know and that heaven frowns when we pry into its mysteries, but so strong was my desire to know, that many times I concerned myself with matters forbidden.

"I had sought to know the nature of the lightning, and the manner of flight of the birds, and the way in which fishes are able to live beneath the waters, and the mystery of the stars. So when these thunderclaps began to be heard in the part of Paris in which I lived, I did not fear them so much as my neighbors. I was eager to learn only what was causing them, for it seemed to me that their cause might be learned.

"So I began to go to that field from which they issued, to study them. I waited in it and twice I heard the great thunderclaps myself. I thought they came from near the field's center, and I studied that place. But I could see nothing there that was causing them. I dug in the ground, I looked up for hours into the sky, but there was nothing. And still, at intervals, the thunderclaps sounded.

"I still kept going to the field, though I knew that many of my neighbors whispered that I was engaged in sorcery. Upon that morning of the third day of June, it had occurred to me to take certain instruments, such as loadstones, to the field, to see whether anything might be learned with them. I went, a few superstitious ones following me at a distance. I reached the field's center, and started the examinations I had planned. Then came suddenly another thunderclap and with it I passed from the sight of those who had followed and were watching, vanished from view.

"Sire, I cannot well describe what happened in that moment. I heard the thunderclap come as though from all the air around me, stunning my ears with its terrible burst of sound. And at the same moment that I heard it, I was buffeted as though by awful winds and seemed falling downward through terrific depths. Then through the hellish uproar, I felt myself bumping upon a hard surface, and the sounds quickly ceased from about me.

"I had involuntarily closed my eyes at the great thunderclap, but now, slowly, I opened them. I looked around me, first in stupefaction, and then in growing amazement. For I was not in that familiar field at all, Sire, that I had been in a moment before. I was in a room, lying upon its floor, and it was such a room as I had never seen before.

"Its walls were smooth and white and gleaming. There were windows in the walls, and they were closed with sheets of glass so smooth and clear that one seemed looking through a clear opening rather than through glass. The floor was of stone, smooth and seamless as though carved from one great rock, yet seeming not, in some way, to be stone at all. There was a great circle of smooth metal inset in it, and it was on it that I was lying.

"All around the room were many great things the like of which I had never seen. Some seemed of black metal, seemed contrivances or machines of some sort. Black cords or wires connected them to each other and from part of them came a humming sound that did not stop. Others had glass tubes fixed on the front of them, and there were square black plates on which were many shining little handles and buttons.

"There was a sound of voices, and I turned to find that two men were bending over me. They were men like myself, yet they were at the same time like no men I had ever met! One was white-bearded and the other plump and bare of face. Neither of them wore cloak or tunic or hose. Instead they wore loose and straight-hanging garments of cloth.

"They were both greatly excited, it seemed, and were talking rapidly to each other as they bent over me. I caught a word or two of their speech in a moment, and found it was French they were talking. But it was not the French I knew, being so strange and with so many new words as to be almost a different language. I could understand the drift, though, of what they were saying.

" 'We have succeeded!' the plump one was shouting excitedly. 'We've brought someone through at last!'

" 'They will never believe it,' the other replied. 'They'll say it was faked.'

" 'Nonsense!' cried the first. 'We can do it again, Rastin; we can show them before their own eyes!'

"They bent toward me, seeing me staring at them.

" 'Where are you from?' shouted the plump-faced one. 'What time—what year—what century?'

" 'He doesn't understand, Thicourt,' muttered the white-bearded one. 'What year is this now, my friend?'

he asked me.

"I found voice to answer. 'Surely, sirs, whoever you be, you know that this is the year fourteen hundred and forty-four,' I said.

"That set them off again into a babble of excited talk, of which I could make out only a word here and there. They lifted me up, seeing how sick and weak I felt, and seated me in a strange, but very comfortable chair. I felt dazed. The two were still talking excitedly, but finally the white-bearded one, Rastin, turned to me. He spoke to me, very slowly, so that I understood him clearly, and he asked me my name. I told him.

" 'Henri Lothiere,' he repeated. 'Well, Henri you must try to understand. You are not now in the year 1444. You are five hundred years in the future, or what would seem to you the future. This is the year 1944.'

" 'And Rastin and I have jerked you out of your own time across five solid centuries,' said the other, grinning.

"I looked from one to the other. 'Messieurs,' I pleaded, and Rastin shook his head.

" 'He does not believe,' he said to the other. Then to me, 'Where were you just before you found yourself here, Henri?' he asked.

" 'In a field at the outskirts of Paris," I said.

" 'Well, look from that window and see if you still believe yourself in your fifteenth century Paris,' he told me.

"I went to the window. I looked out. Mother of God, what a sight before my eyes! The familiar gray little houses, the open fields before them, the saunterers in the dirt streets—all these were gone and it was a new and terrible city that lay about me! Its broad streets were of stone and great buildings of many levels rose on either side of them. Great numbers of people, dressed like the two beside me, moved in the streets and also strange vehicles or carriages, undrawn by horse or ox, that rushed to and fro at undreamed-of speed! I staggered back to the chair.

" 'You believe now, Henri?' asked the white-beard, Rastin, kindly enough, and I nodded weakly. My brain was whirling.

"He pointed to the circle of metal on the floor and the machines around the room. 'Those are what we used to jerk you from your own time to this one,' he said.

" 'But how, sirs?' I asked. 'For the love of God, how is it that you can take me from one time to another? Have ye become gods or devils?'

" 'Neither the one nor the other, Henri,' he answered. 'We are simply scientists, physicists—men who want to know as much as man can know and who spend our lives in seeking knowledge.'

"I felt my confidence returning. These were men such as I had dreamed might some day be. 'But what can you do with time?' I asked. 'Is not time a thing unalterable, unchanging?'

"Both shook their heads. 'No, Henri, it is not. But lately have our men of science found that out.'

"They went on to tell me of things that I could not understand. It seemed they were telling that their men of knowledge had found time to be a mere measurement, or dimension, just as length or breadth or thickness. They mentioned names with reverence that I had never heard—Einstein and De Sitter and Lorentz. I was in a maze at their words.

"They said that just as men use force to move or rotate matter from one point along the three known measurements to another, so might matter be rotated from one point in time, the fourth measurement, to another, if the right force were used. They said that their machines produced that force and applied it to the metal circle. They had set the force to rotate any matter on the circle from five hundred years before to this time of theirs.

"They had tried it many times, they said, but nothing had been on the spot at that time and they had rotated nothing but the air above it from the one time to the other, and the reverse. I told them of the thunderclaps that had been heard at the spot in the field and that had made me curious. They said that they had been caused by the changing of the air above that spot from the one time to the other in their trials. I could not understand these things.

"They said then that I had happened to be on the spot when they had again turned on their force and so had been rotated out of my own time into theirs. They said that they had always hoped to get someone living from a distant time in that way, since a living man from the past would be a proof to all the other men of knowledge of what they had been able to do.

"I could not comprehend, and they saw and told me not to fear. I was not fearful, but excited at the things that I saw around me. I asked of those things and Rastin and Thicourt laughed and explained some of them to me as best they could. Much they said that I did not understand but my eyes saw marvels in that room of which I had never dreamed.

"They showed me a thing like a small glass bottle with wires inside, and then told me to touch a button beneath it. I did so and the bottle shone with a brilliant light exceeding that of scores of candles. I shrank back, but they laughed, and when Rastin touched the button again, the light in the glass thing vanished. I saw that there were many of these things in the ceiling of the room and on the walls.

"They showed me also a rounded black object of metal with a wheel at the end. A belt ran around the wheel and around smaller wheels connected to many machines. They touched a lever on this object and a sound of humming came from it and the wheel turned very fast, turning all the machines with the belt. It turned far faster than any man could ever have turned it, yet when they touched the lever again, its turning ceased. They said that it was the power of the lightning in the skies that they used to make the light and to turn that wheel!

"My brain reeled at the wonders that they showed. One took an instrument from the table that he held to his face, saying that he would summon the other scientists or men of knowledge to see their experiment that night. He spoke into the instrument as though to different men, and let me hear voices from it answering him! They said that the men who answered were leagues separated from him!

"I could not believe—and yet somehow I did believe! I was half-dazed with wonder and yet excited too. The white-bearded man, Rastin, saw that, and encouraged me. They then brought a small box with an opening and placed a black disc on the box, and set it turning in some way. A woman's voice came from the opening of the box, singing. I shuddered when they told me that the woman was one who had died years before. Could the dead speak thus?

"How can I describe what I saw there? Another box or cabinet there was, with an opening also. I thought it was like that from which I had heard the dead woman singing, but they said it was different. They touched buttons on it and a voice came from it speaking in a tongue I knew not. They said that the man was speaking thousands of leagues from us, in a strange land across the uncrossed western ocean, yet he seemed to be speaking by my side!

"They saw how dazed I was by these things, and gave me wine. At that I took heart, for wine, at least, was as it had always been.

" 'You will want to see Paris—the Paris of our time,

Henri?' asked Rastin.

" 'But it is different—terrible—' I said.

" 'We'll take you,' Thicourt said, 'but first your clothes—'

"He got a long light coat that they had me put on, that covered my tunic and hose, and a hat of grotesque round shape that they put on my head. They led me then out of the building and into the street.

"I gazed astoundedly along that street. It had a raised walk at either side, on which many hundreds of people moved to and fro, all dressed in as strange a fashion. Many, like Rastin and Thicourt, seemed of gentle blood, yet, in spite of this, they did not wear a sword or even a dagger. There were no knights or squires, or priests or peasants. All seemed dressed much the same.

"Small lads ran to and fro selling what seemed sheets of very thin white parchment, many times folded and covered with lettering. Rastin said that these had written in them all things that had happened through all the world, even but hours before. I said that to write even one of these sheets would take a clerk many days, but they said that the writing was done in some way very quickly by machines.

"In the broad stone street between the two raised walks were rushing back and forth the strange vehicles I had seen from the window. There was no animal pulling or pushing any one of them, yet they never halted their swift rush, and carried many people at unthinkable speed. Sometimes those who walked stepped before the rushing vehicles, and then from them came terrible warning snarls or moans that made the walkers draw back.

"One of the vehicles stood at the walk's edge before us, and we entered it and sat side by side on a soft leather seat. Thicourt sat behind a wheel on a post, with levers beside him. He touched these and a humming sound came from somewhere in the vehicle and then it too began to rush forward. Faster and faster along the street it went, yet neither of them seemed afraid.

"Many thousands of these vehicles were moving swiftly through the streets about us. We passed on, between great buildings and along wider streets, my eyes and ears numbed by what I saw about me. Then the buildings grew smaller, after we had gone for miles through them, and we were passing through the city's outskirts. I could not believe, hardly, that it was Paris in which I was.

"We came to a great flat and open field outside the city and there Thicourt stopped and we got out of the vehicle. There were big buildings at the field's end, and I saw other vehicles rolling out of them across the field, ones different from any I had yet seen, with flat winglike projections on either side. They rolled out over the field very fast and then I cried out as I saw them rising from the ground into the air. Mother of God, they were flying! The men in them were flying!

"Rastin and Thicourt took me forward to the great buildings. They spoke to men there and one brought forward one of the winged cars. Rastin told me to get in, and though I was terribly afraid, there was too terrible a fascination that drew me in. Thicourt and Rastin entered after me, and we sat in seats with the other man. He had before him levers and buttons, while at the car's front was a great thing like a double-oar or paddle. A loud roaring came and that double-blade began to swirl so swiftly I could not see it. Then the car rolled swiftly forward, bumping on the ground, and then ceased to bump. I looked down, then shuddered. The ground was already far beneath! I too, was flying in the air!

"We swept upward at terrible speed, that increased steadily. The thunder of the car was terrific, and as the man at the levers changed their position, we curved around and over, downward and upward, as though birds. Rastin tried to explain to me how the car flew, but it was all too wonderful, and I could not understand. I only knew that a wild thrilling excitement held me, and that it were worth life and death to fly thus, if but for once, as I had always dreamed that men might some day do.

"Higher and higher we went. The earth lay far beneath and I saw now that Paris was indeed a mighty city, its vast mass of buildings stretching away almost to the horizons below us. A mighty city of the future that it had been given my eyes to look on!

"There were other winged cars darting to and fro in the air about us, and they said that many of these were starting or finishing journeys of hundreds of leagues in the air. Then I cried out as I saw a great shape coming near us in the air. It was many rods in length, tapering to a point at both ends, a vast ship sailing in the air! There were great cabins on its lower part and in them we glimpsed people gazing out, coming and going inside, dancing even! They told me that vast ships of the air like this sailed to and fro for thousands of leagues with hundreds inside them.

"The huge vessel of the air passed us and then our winged car began to descend. It circled smoothly down to the field like a swooping bird, and, when we landed there, Rastin and Thicourt led me back to the ground-vehicle. It was late afternoon by then, the sun sinking westward, and darkness had descended by the time we rolled back into the great city.

"But in that city was not darkness! Lights were everywhere in it, flashing brilliant lights that shone from its mighty buildings and that blinked and burned and ran like water in great symbols upon the buildings above the streets. Their glare was like that of day! We rode through these lanes of lights and stopped before a great building into which Rastin and Thicourt led me.

"It was vast inside and in it were many people in rows and rows of seats. I thought it a cathedral at first but saw soon that it was not. The wall at one end of it, toward which all in it were gazing, had on it pictures of people, great in size, and those pictures were moving as though themselves alive! And they were talking one to another too, as though with living voices! I trembled. What magic!

"With Rastin and Thicourt in seats beside me, I watched the pictures enthralled. It was like looking through a great window into strange worlds. I saw the sea, seemingly tossing and roaring there before me, and then saw on it a ship, a vast ship of size incredible, without sails or oars, holding thousands of people. I seemed on that ship as I watched, seemed moving forward with it. They told me it was sailing over the western ocean that never men had crossed. I feared!

"Then another scene, land appearing from the ship. A great statue, upholding a torch, and we on the ship seemed passing beneath it. They said that the ship was approaching a city, the city of New York, but mists hid all before us. Then suddenly the mists before the ship cleared and there before me seemed the city.

"Mother of God, what a city! Climbing range on range of great mountain-like buildings that aspired up as though to scale heaven itself! Far beneath narrow streets pierced through them and in the picture we seemed to land from the ship, to go through those streets of the city. It was an incredible city of madness! The streets and ways were mere chasms between the sky-toppling buildings! People—people—people—millions on millions of them rushed through the endless streets. Countless ground-vehicles rushed to and fro also, and other different ones that roared above the streets and still others below them!

"Winged flying-cars and great airships were sailing to and fro over the titanic city, and in the waters around it great ships of the sea and smaller ships were coming and going. They sailed beneath colossal bridges, such as man never dreamed of surely, that reached out from the mighty city on all sides. And with the coming of darkness, the city blazed with living light!

"The pictures changed, showed other mighty cities, though none so terrible as that one. It showed great mechanisms that appalled me. Giant metal things that scooped in an instant from the earth as much as a man might dig in days. Vast things that poured molten metal from them like water. Others that lifted loads that hundreds of men and oxen could not have stirred.

"They showed men of knowledge like Rastin and Thircourt beside me. Some were healers, working miraculous cures in a way that I could not understand. Others were gazing through giant tubes at the stars, and the picture showed what they saw, showed that all of the stars were great suns like our sun, and that our sun was greater than earth, that earth moved around it instead of the reverse! How could such things be, I wondered. Yet they said that it was so, that earth was round like an apple, and that with other earths like it, the planets, moved round the sun. I heard, but could scarce understand.

"At last Rastin and Thicourt led me out of that place of living pictures and to their ground-vehicle. We went again through the streets to their buildings, where first I had found myself. As we went I saw that none challenged my right to go, nor asked who was my lord. And Rastin said that none now had lords, but that all were lord, king and priest and noble, having no more power than any in the land. Each man was his own master! It was what I had hardly dared to hope for, in my own time, and this, I thought, was greatest of all the marvels they had shown me!

"We entered again their building but Rastin and Thicourt took me first to another room than the one in which I had found myself. They said that their men of knowledge were gathered there to hear of their feat, and to have it proved to them.

" 'You would not be afraid to return to your own time, Henri?' asked Rastin, and I shook my head.

" 'I want to return to it,' I told them. 'I want to tell my people there what I have seen—what the future is that they must strive for.'

" 'But if they should not believe you?' Thicourt asked.

" 'Still I must go—must tell them,' I said.

"Rastin grasped my hand. 'You are a man, Henri,' he said. Then throwing aside the cloak and hat I had worn outside, they went with me down to the big white-walled room where first I had found myself.

"It was lit brightly now by many of the shining glass things on ceiling and walls, and in it were many men. They all stared strangely at me and at my clothes, and talked excitedly so fast I could not understand. Rastin began to address them.

"He seemed explaining how he had brought me from my own time to his. He used many terms and words that I could not understand, incomprehensible references and phrases, and I could understand but little. I heard again the names of Einstein and De Sitter that I had heard before, repeated frequently by these men as they disputed with Rastin and Thicourt. They seemed disputing about me.

"One big man was saying, 'Impossible! I tell you, Rastin, you've faked this fellow!'

"Rastin smiled. 'You don't believe that Thicourt and I brought him here from his own time across five centuries?'

"A chorus of excited negatives answered him. He had me stand up and speak to them. They asked me many questions, part of which I could not understand. I told them of my life, and of the city of my own time, and of king and priest and noble, and of many simple things that they seemed quite ignorant of. Some appeared to believe me but others did not, and again their dispute broke out.

" 'There is a way to settle the argument, gentlemen,' said Rastin finally.

" 'How?' all cried.

" 'Thicourt and I brought Henri across five centuries by rotating the time-dimensions at this spot,' he said. 'Suppose we reverse that rotation and send him back before your eyes—would that be proof?'

"They all said that it would. Rastin turned to me. 'Stand on the metal circle, Henri,' he said. I did so.

"All were watching very closely. Thicourt did something quickly with the levers and buttons of the mechanisms in the room. They began to hum, and blue light came from the glass tubes on some. All were quiet, watching me as I stood there on the circle of metal. I met Rastin's eyes and something in me made me call goodbye to him. He waved his hand and smiled. Thicourt pressed more buttons and the hum of the mechanisms grew louder. Then he reached toward another lever. All in the room were tense and I was tense.

"Then I saw Thicourt's arm move as he turned one of the many levers.

"A terrific clap of thunder seemed to break around me, and as I closed my eyes before its shock, I felt myself whirling around and falling at the same time as though into a maelstrom, just as I had done before. The awful falling sensation ceased in a moment and the sound subsided. I opened my eyes. I was on the ground at the center of the familiar field from which I had vanished hours before, upon the morning of that day. It was night now, though, for that day I had spent five hundred years in the future.

"There were many people gathered around the field, fearful, and they screamed and some fled when I appeared in the thunderclap. I went toward those who remained. My mind was full of the things I had seen and I wanted to tell them of these things. I wanted to tell them how in the future would be the marvels that my eyes had beheld, and of the freedom that I had seen those people of the future have. I wanted to tell them how they must work ever toward that future time of wonder.

"But they did not listen. Before I had spoken minutes to them they cried out on me as a sorcerer and a blasphemer, and seized me and brought me here to the Inquisitor, to you, sire. And to you, sire, I have told the truth in all things. I know that in doing so I have set the seal on my own fate, and that only a sorcerer would ever tell such a tale, yet despite that I am glad. Glad that I have told one at least of this time of what I saw five centuries in the future. Glad that I saw! Glad that I saw the things that someday, sometime, must come to be—"

It was a week later that they burned Henri Lothiere. Jean de Marselait, lifting his gaze from his endless parchment accusations and examens on that afternoon, looked out through the window at the stone room's end and saw a thick curl of black smoke going up into the blue heavens from the distant square. There came dimly to his ears the thunderous shouting of the crowd there.

He rested for a moment thoughtful, his pen upon his chin. "Strange, that one," he mused. "A sorcerer, of course, but such a one as I had never heard before."

His eyes went out again to the thick black smoke, and a thought came to him. "I wonder," he half-whispered, "was there any truth in that wild tale of his? The future—

who can say—what men might do—?"

There was silence in the room as he brooded for a moment, and then he shook himself as one ridding himself of absurd speculations. "But tush—enough of these crazy fancies. They will have me for a sorcerer if I yield to these wild fancies and visions *of the future.*"

And bending again with his pen to the parchment before him, he went gravely on with his work.

O. Barr

THE MACHINE MAN OF ARDATHIA

By Francis Flagg

I do not know what to believe. Sometimes, I am positive I dreamed it all. But, then, there is the matter of the heavy rocking chair. That, indeniably, did disappear. Perhaps someone played a trick on me; but who would stoop to a deception so bizarre, merely for the purpose of befuddling the wits of an old man? Perhaps someone stole the rocking chair; but why should anyone want to steal it? It was, it is true, a sturdy piece of furniture, but hardly valuable enough to excite the cupidity of a thief. Besides, it was in its place when I sat down in the easy chair.

Of course, I may be lying. Peters, to whom I was misguided enough to tell everything on the night of its occurrence, wrote the story for his paper, and the editor says as much in his editorial when he remarks: "Mr Mathews seems to possess an imagination equal to that of an H. G. Wells." And, considering the nature of my story, I am quite ready to forgive him for doubting my veracity.

However, the few friends who know me better think that I had dined a little too wisely or too well, and was visited with a nightmare. Hodge suggested that the Jap who cleans my rooms had, for some reason, removed the rocking chair from its place, and that I merely took its presence for granted when I sat down in the other; but the Jap strenuously denies having done so.

I must explain that I have two rooms and a bath on the third floor of a modern apartment house fronting the Lake. Since my wife's death three years ago, I have lived thus, taking my breakfast and lunch at a restaurant, and my dinners, generally, at the club. I also have a room in a downtown office building where I spend a few hours every day working on my book, which is intended to be a critical analysis of the fallacies inherent in the Marxian theory of economics, embracing at the same time a thorough refutation of Lewis Morgan's *Ancient Society*. A rather ambitious undertaking, you will admit, and one not apt to engage the interest of a person given to inventing wild yarns for the purpose of amazing his friends.

No; I emphatically deny having invented the story. However, the future will speak for itself. I will merely proceed to put the details of my strange experience on paper—justice to myself demands that I should do so, so many garbled accounts have appeared in the press—and leave the reader to draw his own conclusions.

Contrary to my usual custom, I had dined that evening with Hodge at the Hotel Oaks. Let me emphatically state that, while it is well-known among his intimates that Hodge has a decided taste for liquor, I had absolutely nothing of an intoxicating nature to drink, and Hodge will verify this. About eight-thirty, I refused an invitation to attend the theatre with him, and went to my rooms. There I changed into my smoking-jacket and slippers, and lit a mild Havana.

The rocking chair was occupying its accustomed place near the center of the sitting-room floor. I remember that clearly because, as usual, I had either to push it aside or step around it, wondering for the thousandth time, as I did so, why that idiotic Jap persisted in placing it in such an inconvenient spot, and resolving, also for the thousandth time to speak to him about it. With a notebook and pencil placed on the stand beside me, and a copy of Frederick Engel's *Origin of the Family, Private Property, and The State*, I turned on the light in my green-shaded reading lamp, switched off all the others, and sank with a sigh of relief into the easy chair.

It was my intention to make a few notes from Engel's work relative to plural marriages, showing that he contradicted certain conclusions of Morgan's, but after a few minutes' work, I leaned back in my chair and closed my eyes. I did not doze; I am positive of that. My mind was actively engaged in trying to piece together a sentence that would clearly express my thoughts.

I can best describe what happened, then, by saying there was an explosion. It wasn't that, exactly; but, at the time, it seemed to me there must have been an explosion. A blinding flash of light registered with appalling vividness, through the closed lids, on the retinas of my eyes. My first thought was that someone had dynamited the building; my second, that the electric fuses had blown out. It was some time before I could see clearly. When I could:

"Good Lord!" I whispered weakly. "What's that?"

Occupying the space where the rocking chair had stood (though I did not notice its absence at the time) was a cylinder of what appeared to be glass, standing, I should judge, above five feet high. Encased in this cylinder was what seemed to be a caricature of a man—or a child. I say caricature because, while the cylinder was all of five feet in height, the being inside of it was hardly three; and you can imagine my amazement while I stared at this apparition. After a while, I got up and switched on all the lights, to better observe it.

You may wonder why I did not try to call someone in, but that never occurred to me. In spite of my age—I am sixty—my nerves are steady, and I am not easily frightened. I walked very carefully around the cylinder, and viewed the creature inside from all angles. It was sustained in the center, midway between top and bottom, by what appeared to be an intricate arrangement of glass and metal tubes. These tubes seemed to run at places into the body; and I noticed some dark fluid circulating through the glass tubes.

The head was very large and hairless; it had bulging brows, and no ears. The eyes were large and winkless, the nose well defined; but the lower part of the face and mouth ran into the small, round body with no sign of a chin. Its legs hung down, skinny, flabby; and the arms were more like short tentacles reaching down from where the head and body joined. The thing was, of course, naked.

I drew the easy chair up to the cylinder, and sat down facing it. Several times I stretched out my hand in an effort to touch its surface, but some force prevented my fingers from making contact, which was very curious. Also, I could detect no movement of the body or limbs of the weird thing inside the glass.

"What I would like to know," I muttered, "is what you are and where you came from; are you alive, and am I dreaming or am I awake?"

Suddenly the creature came to life. One of its tentacle-like hands, holding a metal tube, darted to its mouth. From the tube shot a white streak, which fastened itself to the cylinder.

"Ah!" came a clear, metallic voice. "English, Primitive; probably of the twentieth century." The words were uttered with an indescribable intonation, much as if a foreigner were speaking our language. Yet, more than that, as if he were speaking a language long dead. I don't know why that thought should have occurred to me, then. Perhaps . . .

"So you can talk!" I exclaimed.

The creature gave a metallic chuckle. "As you say, I can talk."

"Then tell me what you are."

"I am an Ardathian—a Machine Man of Ardathia.

And you . . . ? Tell me, is that really hair on your head?"

Yes," I replied.

"And those coverings you wear on your body, are they clothes?"

I answered in the affirmative.

"How odd! Then you really are a Primitive; a Prehistoric Man." The eyes behind the glass shield regarded me intently.

"I mean that you are one of that race of early men whose skeletons we have dug up, here and there, and reconstructed for our Schools of Biology. Marvelous how our scientists have copied you from some fragments of bone! The small head covered with hair, the beast-like jaw, the abnormally large body and legs, the artificial coverings made of cloth . . . even your language!"

For the first time, I began to suspect that I was the victim of a hoax. I got up again and walked carefully around the cylinder, but could detect no outside agency controlling the contraption. Besides, it was absurd to think that anyone would go to the trouble of constructing such a complicated apparatus as this appeared to be, merely for the sake of a practical joke. Nevertheless, I looked out on the landing. Seeing nobody, I came back and resumed my seat in front of the cylinder.

"Pardon me," I said, "but you referred to me as belonging to a period much more remote than yours."

"That is correct. If I am not mistaken in my calculations, you are thirty thousand years in the past. What date is this?"

"June 5th, 1939," I replied, feebly. The creature went through some contortions, sorted a few metal tubes with its hands, and then announced in its metallic voice:

"Computed in terms of your method of reckoning, I have traveled back through time exactly twenty-eight thousand years, nine months, three weeks, two days, seven hours and a certain number of minutes and seconds which it is useless for me to enumerate exactly."

It was at this point that I endeavored to make sure I was wide awake and in full possession of my faculties. I got up, selected a fresh cigar from the humidor, struck a light, and began puffing away. After a few puffs, I laid it beside the one I had been smoking earlier in the evening. I found it there, later. Incontestable proof . . .

I said that I am a man of steady nerves. Once more I sat down in front of the cylinder, determined this time to find out what I could about the incredible creature within.

"You say you have traveled back through time thousands of years. How is that possible?" I demanded.

"By verifying time as a fourth dimension, and perfecting devices for traveling in it."

"In what manner?"

"I do not know whether I can explain it exactly, in your language, and you are too primitive and unevolved to understand mine. However, I shall try. Know, then, that space is as much a relative thing as time. In itself, aside from its relation to matter, it has no existence. You can neither see nor touch it, yet you move freely in space. Is that clear?"

"It sounds like Einstein's theory."

"Einstein?"

"One of our great scientists and mathematicians," I explained.

"So you have scientists and mathematicians? Wonderful! That bears out what Hoomi says. I must remember to tell . . . However, to resume my explanation. Time is apprehended in the same manner as is space—that is, in its relation to matter. When you measure space, you do so by letting your measuring rod leap from point to point of matter; or, in the case of spanning the void, let us say, from the Earth to Venus, you start and end with matter, remarking that between lie so many miles of space.

"But it is clear that you see and touch no space, merely spanning the distance between two points of matter with the vision of the measuring rod. You do the same when you compute time with the sun, or by means of the clock which I see hanging on the wall there. Time, then, is no more of an abstraction than is space. If it is possible for man to move freely in space, it is possible for him to move freely in time, and we Ardathians are beginning to do so."

"But how?"

"I am afraid your limited intelligence could not grasp that. You must realize that compared with us, you are hardly as much as human. When I look at you, I perceive that your body is enormously larger than your head. This means you are dominated by animal passions, and that your mental capacity is not very high."

That this weirdly humorous thing inside a glass cylinder should come to such a conclusion regarding me, made me smile.

"If any of my fellow citizens should see you," I replied, "they would consider you—well, absurd."

"That is because they would judge me by the only standard they know—themselves. In Ardathia, you would be regarded as bestial; in fact, that is exactly how your reconstructed skeletons are regarded. Tell me, is it true that you nourish your bodies by taking food through your mouths into your stomachs?"

"Yes."

"And are still at that stage of bodily evolution when you eliminate the waste products through the alimentary canal?"

I lowered my head.

"How revolting."

The unwinking eyes regarded me intently. Then something happened which startled me greatly. The creature raised a glass tube to its face, and from the end of the tube leaped a purple ray which came through the glass casing and played over the room.

"There is no need to be alarmed," said the metallic voice. "I was merely viewing your habitat, and making some deductions. Correct me if I am wrong, please. You are an English-speaking man of the twentieth century. You and your kind live in cities and houses. You eat, digest, and reproduce your young, much as do the animals from which you have sprung. You use crude machines, and have an elementary understanding of physics and chemistry. Correct me if I am wrong, please."

"You are right, to a certain extent," I replied. "But I am not interested in having you tell me what I am; I know that. I wish to know what you are. You claim to have come from thirty thousand years in the future, but you advance no evidence to support the claim. How do I know you are not a trick, a fake, an hallucination of mine? You say you can move freely in time. Then how is it you have never come this way before? Tell me something about yourself; I am curious."

"Your questions are well put," replied the voice, "and I shall seek to answer them. It is true that we Machine Men of Ardathia are beginning to move in time as well as in space, but note that I say beginning. Our Time Machines are very crude, as yet, and I am the first Ardathian to penetrate the past beyond a period of six thousand years. You must realize that a time traveler runs certain hazards. At any place on the road, he may materialize inside of a solid of some sort. In that case, he is almost certain to be destroyed.

"Such was the constant danger until I perfected my enveloping ray. I cannot name or describe it in your tongue, but if you approach me too closely, you will feel its resistance. This ray has the effect of disintegrating and dispersing any body of matter inside which a time traveler may materialize. Perhaps you were aware of a great light when I appeared in your room? I probably took shape within a body of matter, and the ray destroyed it."

"The rocking chair!" I exclaimed. "It was standing on the spot you now occupy."

"Then it has been reduced to its original atoms. This is a wonderful moment for me! My ray has proved an unqualified success, for the second time. It not only removes any hindering matter from about the time traveler, but also creates a void within which he is perfectly safe from harm. But to resume . . .

"It is hard to believe that we Ardathians evolved from such creatures as you. Our written history does not go back to a time when men nourished themselves by taking food into their stomachs through their mouths, or reproducing their young in the animal-like fashion in which you do. The earliest men of whom we have any records were the Bi-Chanics. They lived about fifteen thousand years before our era, and were already well along the road of mechanical evolution when their civilization fell.

"The Bi-Chanics vaporized their food substances and breathed them through the nostril, excreting the waste products of the body through the pores of the skin. Their children were brought to the point of birth in ectogenetic incubators. There is enough authentic evidence to prove that Bi-Chanics had perfected the use of mechanical hearts, and were crudely able to make . . .

"I cannot find the words to explain what they made, but it does not matter. The point is that, while they had only partly subordinated machinery to their use, they are the earliest race of human beings of whom we possess any real knowledge, and it was their period of time that I was seeking when I inadvertently came too far and landed in yours.

The metallic voice ceased for a moment, and I took advantage of the pause to speak.

"I do not know a thing about the Bi-Chanics, or whatever it is you call them," I remarked, "but they were certainly not the first to make mechanical hearts. I remember reading about a Russian scientist who kept a dog alive four hours by means of a motor which pumped the blood through the dog's body."

"You mean the motor was used as a heart?"

"Exactly."

The Ardathian made a quick motion with one of its hands.

"I have made a note of your information; it is very interesting."

"Furthermore," I pursued, "I recall reading of how, some years ago, one of our surgeons was hatching out rabbits and guinea pigs in ecto-genetic incubators.

The Ardathian made another quick gesture with its hand. I could see that my remarks excited it.

"Perhaps," I said, not without a feeling of satisfaction (for the casual allusion to myself as hardly human had irked my pride), "perhaps you will find it as interesting to visit the people of five hundred years from now, let us say, as you would to visit the Bi-Chanics."

"I assure you," replied the metallic voice, "that if I succeed in returning to my native Ardathia, those periods will be thoroughly explored. I can only express surprise at your having advanced as far as you have, and wonder why it is you have made no practical use of your knowledge."

"Sometimes I wonder myself," I returned. "But I am very much interested in learning more about yourself and your times. If you would resume your story . . . ?"

"With pleasure," replied the Ardathian. "In Ardathia, we do not live in houses or in cities; neither do we nourish ourselves as do you, or as did the Bi-Chanics. The chemical fluid you see circulating through these tubes which run into and through my body, has taken the place of blood. The fluid is produced by the action of a light-ray on certain life-giving elements in the air. It is constantly being produced in those tubes under my feet, and driven through my body by a mechanism too intricate for me to describe.

"The same fluid circulates through my body only once, nourishing it and gathering all impurities as it goes. Having completed its revolution, it is dissipated by means of another ray which carries it back into the surrounding air. Have you noticed the transparent substance enclosing me?"

"The cylinder of glass, you mean?"

"Glass? What do you mean by glass?"

"Why, that there," I said, pointing to the window. The Ardathian directed a metal tube to the spot indicated. A purple streak flashed out, hovered a moment on a pane, and then withdrew.

"No," came the metallic voice; "not that. The cylinder, as you call it, is made of a transparent substance, very strong and practically unbreakable. Nothing can penetrate it but the rays which you see, and the two whose action I have just described, which are invisible.

"We Ardathians, you must understand, are not delivered of the flesh; nor are we introduced into incubators as ova taken from female bodies, as were the Bi-Chanics. Among the Ardathians, there are no males or females. The cell from which we are to develop is created synthetically. It is fertilized by means of a ray, and then put into a cylinder such as you observe surrounding me. As the embryo develops, the various tubes and mechanical devices are introduced into the body by our mechanics, and become an integral part of it.

"When the young Ardathian is born, he does not leave the case in which he has developed. That case—or cylinder, as you call it—protects him from the action of a hostile environment. If it were to break and expose him to the elements, he would perish miserably. Do you follow me?"

"Not quite," I confessed. "You say that you have evolved from men like us, and then go on to state that you are synthetically conceived and machine made. I do not see how this evolution was possible."

"And you may never understand! Nevertheless, I shall try to explain. Did you not tell me you had wise ones among you who experiment with mechanical hearts and ecto-genetic incubators? Tell me, have you not others engaged in tests tending to show that it is the action of the environment, and not the passing of time, which accounts for the ageing of organisms?"

"Well, I said, hesitatingly, "I have heard tell of chicken's hearts being kept alive in special containers which protect them from their normal environment."

"Ah!" exclaimed the metallic voice. "But Hoomi will be astounded when he learns that such experiments were carried on by prehistoric men fifteen thousand years before the Bi-Chanics! Listen closely, for what you have told me provides a starting-point from which you may be able to follow my explanation of man's evolution from your time to mine.

"Of the thousands of years separating your day from that of the Bi-Chanics, I have no authentic knowledge. My exact knowledge begins with the Bi-Chanics. They were the first to realize that man's bodily advancement lay in, and through, the machine. They perceived that man only became human when he fashioned tools; that the tools increased the length of the arms, the grip of his hands, the strength of his muscles. They observed that, with the aid of the machine, man could circle the Earth, speak to the planets, gaze intimately at the stars. We will increase our span of life on Earth, said the Bi-Chanics, by throwing the protection of the machine, the thing that the machine produces, around and into our bodies.

"This they did, to the best of their ability, and increased their longevity to an average of about two hundred years. Then came the Tri-Namics. More advanced than the Bi-Chanics, they reasoned that old age was caused, not by the passage of time, but by the action of the environment on the matter of which men were composed. It is this reasoning which causes the men of your time to experiment with chicken hearts. The Tri-Namics sought to perfect devices for safeguarding the flesh against the wear and tear of its environment. They made envelopes—cylinders—in which they attempted to bring embryos to birth, and to rear children; but they met with only partial success."

"You speak of the Bi-Chanics and of the Tri-Namics," I said, "as if they were two distinct races of people. Yet you imply that the latter evolved from the former. If the Bi-Chanics' civilization fell, did any period of time elapse between that fall and the rise of the Tri-Namics? And how did the latter inherit from their predecessors?"

"It is because of your language, which I find very crude and inadequate, that I have not already made that clear," answered the Ardathian. "The Tri-Namics were really a more progressive part of the Bi-Chanics. When I said the civilization of the latter fell, I did not mean what that implies in your language.

"You must realize that, fifteen thousand years in your future, the race of man was, scientifically speaking, making rapid strides. But it was not always possible for backward or conservative minds to adjust themselves to new discoveries. Minority groups, composed mostly of the young, forged ahead, proposed radical changes, entertained new ideas, and finally culminated in what I have alluded to as the Tri-Namics. Inevitably, in the course of time, the Bi-Chanics died off, and conservative methods with them. That is what I meant when I said their civilization fell.

"In the same fashion did we follow the Tri-Namics. When the latter succeeded in raising children inside the cylinder, they destroyed themselves. Soon, all children were born in this manner; and in time, the fate of the Bi-Chanics became that of the Tri-Namics leaving behind them the Machine Men of Ardathia, who differed radically from them in bodily structure, yet were nonetheless their direct descendants."

At last, I began to get an inkling of what the Ardathian meant when it alluded to itself as a Machine-Man. The appalling story of man's final evolution into a controlling center that directed a mechanical body, awoke something akin to fear in my heart. If it were true, what of the soul, the spirit . . . ? The metallic voice went on.

"You must not imagine that the early Ardathians possessed a cylinder as invulnerable as the one that protects me. The first envelopes of this nature were made of a pliable substance, which wore out within three centuries. But the substance composing the envelope has gradually been improved, perfected, until now it is immune for fifteen hundred years to anything save a powerful explosion or some other major catastrophe."

"Fifteen hundred years!" I exclaimed.

"Barring accident, that is the length of time an Ardathian lives. But to us, fifteen hundred years is no longer than a hundred would be to you. Remember, please, that time is relative; twelve hours of your time is a second of ours, and a year . . . But suffice to say that very few Ardathians live out their allotted span. Since we are constantly engaged in hazardous experiments and dangerous expeditions, accidents are many. Thousands of our brave explorers have plunged into the past and never returned. They probably materialized inside solids, and were annihilated; but I believe I have finally overcome this danger with my disintegrating ray."

"And how old are you?"

"As you count time, five hundred and seventy years. You must understand that there has been no change in my body since birth. If the cylinder were everlasting, or proof against accident, I should live forever. It is the wearing out, or breaking up, of the envelope, which exposes us to the dangerous forces of nature and causes death. Some of our scientists are trying to perfect means for building up the cylinder as fast as the wear and tear of environment breaks it down; others are seeking to rear embryos to birth with nothing but rays for covering—rays incapable of harming the organism, yet immune to dissipation by environment and incapable of destruction by explosion. So far, they have been unsuccessful; but I have every confidence in their ultimate triumph. Then we shall be as immortal as the planet on which we live."

I stared at the cylinder, at the creature inside the cylinder, at the ceiling, the four walls of the room, and then back again at the cylinder, I pinched the soft flesh of my thigh with my fingers. I was awake, all right; there could be no doubt about that.

"Are there any questions you would like to ask?" came the metallic voice.

"Yes," I said at last, half-fearfully. "What joy can there be in existence for you? You have no sex; you cannot mate. It seems to me—" I hesitated. "It seems to me that no hell could be worse than centuries of being caged alive inside that thing you call an envelope. Now, I have full command of my limbs and can go where I please. I can—"

I came to a breathless stop, awed by the lurid light which suddenly gleamed in the winkless eyes.

"Poor prehistoric mammal," came the answer, "how could you, groping in the dawn of human existence, comprehend what is beyond your lowly environment!

Compared to you, we are as gods. No longer are our loves and hates the reactions of viscera. Our thoughts, our thinking, our emotions, are conditioned, molded to the extent we control our immediate environment. There is no such thing as—

"But it is impossible to continue. Your mentality—it is not the word I like to use but, as I have repeatedly said, your language is woefully inadequate—has a restricted range of but a few thousand words: therefore, I cannot explain further. Only the same lack—in a different fashion, of course, and with objects instead of words—hinders the free movement of your limbs. You have command of them, you say. Poor primitive, do you realize how shackled you are with nothing but your hands and feet? You augment them, of course, with a few machines, but they are crude and cumbersome. It is you who are caged alive, and not I. I have broken through the walls of your cage, have shaken off the shackles—have gone free. Behold the command I have of my limbs!"

From an extended tube shot a streak of white, like a funnel, whose radius was great enough to encircle my seated body. I was conscious of being scooped up, and drawn forward, with inconceivable speed. For one breathless moment, I hung suspended against the cylinder itself, the winkless eyes not an inch from my own. In that moment, I had the sensation of being probed, handled. Several times I was revolved, as a man might twirl a stick. Then I was back in the easy chair again, white and shaken.

"It is true that I never leave the envelope in which I am encased," continued the metallic voice, "but I have at my command rays which can bring me anything I desire. In Ardathia are machines—it would be useless for me to describe them to you—with which I can walk, fly, move mountains, delve in the earth, investigate the stars, and loose forces of which you have no conception. These machines are mechanical parts of my body, extensions of my limbs, I take them off and put them on at will. With their help, I can view one continent while busily employed in another, I can make time machines, harness rays, and plunge thirty thousand years into the past. Let me again illustrate."

The tentacle-like hand of the Ardathian waved a tube. The five-foot cylinder glowed with an intense light, spun like a top, and so spinning dissolved into space. Even as I gaped, like one petrified, the cylinder reappeared with the same rapidity. The metallic voice announced:

"I have just been five years into your future."

"My future!" I exclaimed. "How can that be when I have not lived it yet?"

"But of course you have lived it!"

I stared, bewildered.

"Could I visit my past if you had not lived your future?" the creature persisted.

"I do not understand," I said feebly. "It doesn't seem possible that while I am here, actually in this room, you should be able to travel ahead in time and find out what I shall be doing in a future I haven't reached yet."

"That is because you are unable to grasp intelligently what time is. Think of it as a dimension—a fourth dimension—which stretches like a road ahead and behind you."

"But even then," I protested, "I could only be at one place at a given time, on that road, and not where I am and somewhere else in the same second."

"You are never anywhere at any time," replied the metallic voice, "save always in the past and future. But it is useless trying to acquaint you with a simple truth, thirty thousand years ahead of your ability to understand it. As I said, I traveled five years into your future. Men were wrecking this building."

"Tearing down this place? Nonsense! It was only erected two years ago."

"Nevertheless, they were tearing it down. I sent forth my visual-ray to locate you. You were in a great room with numerous other men. They were all doing a variety of odd things. There was—"

At that moment came a heavy knock on the door of my room.

"What's the matter, Matthews?" called a loud voice. "What are you talking about, all this time? Are you sick?"

I uttered an exclamation of annoyance, because I recognized the voice of John Peters, a newspaperman who occupied the apartment next to mine. My first impulse was to tell him I was busy, but the next moment I had a better idea. Here was someone to whom I could show the cylinder, and the creature inside it; someone to bear witness to having seen it, besides myself! I hurried to the door and threw it open.

"Quick!" I said, grasping Peters by the arm and hauling him into the room. "What do you think of that?"

"Think of what?" he demanded.

"Why of that, there," I pointed with my finger, and then stopped short with my mouth wide open; for on the spot where, a few seconds before, the cylinder had stood, there was nothing. The envelope and the Ardathian had disappeared.

* * *

AUTHOR'S NOTE

The material for this manuscript came into my hands in an odd fashion. About a year after the Press had ceased to print garbled versions of Matthews' experience, I made the acquaintance of his friend, Hodge, with whom he had dined on that evening. I asked him about Matthews. He said:

"Did you know they've put him in an asylum? You didn't? Well, they have. He's crazy enough now, poor devil; though he was always a little queer, I thought. I went to visit him the other day, and it gave me quite a shock to see him in a ward with a lot of other men, all doing something queer.

"By the way, Peters told me the other day that the apartment house where Matthews lived is to be torn down. They are going to demolish several houses along the Lake Shore, to widen the boulevard; but he says they won't wreck them for three or four years yet. Funny, eh? Would you like to see what Matthews wrote about the affair himself?"

J. Barr

THE TISSUE-CULTURE KING

By Julian Huxley

We had been for three days engaged in crossing a swamp. At last we were out on dry ground, winding up a gentle slope. Near the top the brush grew thicker. The look of a rampart grew as we approached; it had the air of having been deliberately planted by men. We did not wish to have to hack our way through the spiky barricade, so turned to the right along the front of the green wall. After three or four hundred yards we came on a clearing which led into the bush, narrowing down to what seemed a regular passage or trackway. This made us a little suspicious. However, I thought we had better make all the progress we could, and so ordered the caravan to turn into the opening, myself taking second place behind the guide.

Suddenly the tracker stopped with a guttural exclamation. I looked, and there was one of the great African toads, hopping with a certain ponderosity across the path. But it had a second head growing upwards from its shoulders! I had never seen anything like this before, and wanted to secure such a remarkable monstrosity for our collections; but as I moved forward, the creature took a couple of hops into the shelter of the prickly scrub.

We pushed on, and I became convinced that the gap we were following was artificial. After a little, a droning sound came to our ears, which we very soon set down as that of a human voice. The party was halted, and I crept forward with the guide. Peeping through the last screen of brush we looked down into a hollow and were immeasurably startled at what we saw there. The voice proceeded from an enormous Negro man at least eight feet high, the biggest man I had ever seen outside a circus. He was squatting, from time to time prostrating the forepart of his body, and reciting some prayer or incantation. The object of his devotion was before him on the ground; it was a small flat piece of glass held on a little carved ebony stand. By his side was a huge spear, together with a painted basket with a lid.

After a minute or so, the giant bowed down in silence, then took up the ebony-and-glass object and placed it in the basket. Then to my utter amazement he drew out a two-headed toad like the first I had seen, but in a cage of woven grass, placed it on the ground, and proceeded to more genuflection and ritual murmurings. As soon as this was over, the toad was replaced, and the squatting giant tranquilly regarded the landscape.

Beyond the hollow or dell lay an undulating country, with clumps of bush. A sound in the middle distance attracted attention; glimpses of color moved through the scrub; and a party of three or four dozen men were seen approaching, most of them as gigantic as our first acquaintance. All marched in order, armed with great spears, and wearing colored loin straps with a sort of sporran, it seemed, in front. They were preceded by an intelligent-looking Negro of ordinary stature armed with a club, and accompanied by two figures more remarkable than the giants. They were undersized, almost dwarfish, with huge heads, and enormously fat and brawny both in face and body. They wore bright yellow cloaks over their black shoulders.

At sight of them, our giant rose and stood stiffly by the side of his basket. The party approached and halted. Some order was given, a giant stepped out from the ranks towards ours, picked up the basket, handed it stiffly to the newcomer, and fell into place in the little company. We were clearly witnessing some regular routine of relieving guard, and I was racking my brains to think what the whole thing might signify—guards, giants, dwarfs, toads—when to my dismay I heard an exclamation at my shoulder.

It was one of those damned porters, a confounded fellow who always liked to show his independence. Bored with waiting, I suppose, he had self-importantly crept up to see what it was all about, and the sudden sight of the company of giants had been too much for his nerves. I made a signal to lie quiet, but it was too late. The exclamation had been heard; the leader gave a quick command, and the giants rushed up and out in two groups to surround us.

Violence and resistance were clearly out of the question. With my heart in my mouth, but with as much dignity as I could muster, I jumped up and threw out my empty hands, at the same time telling the tracker not to shoot. A dozen spears seemed towering over me, but none were launched; the leader ran up the slope and gave a command. Two giants came up and put my hands through their arms. The tracker and the porter were herded in front at the spear point. The other porters now discovered there was something amiss, and began to shout and run away, with half the spearmen after them. We three were gently but firmly marched down and across the hollow.

I understood nothing of the language, and called to my tracker to try his hand. It turned out that there was some dialect of which he had a little understanding, and we could learn nothing save the fact that we were being taken to some superior authority.

For two days we were marched through pleasant park-like country, with villages at intervals. Every now and then some new monstrosity in the shape of a dwarf or an incredibly fat woman or a two-headed animal would be visible, until I thought I had stumbled on the original source of supply of circus freaks.

The country at last began to slope gently down to a pleasant river valley; and presently we neared the capital. It turned out to be a really large town for Africa, its mud walls of strangely impressive architectural form, with their heavy, slabby buttresses, and giants standing guard upon them. Seeing us approach, they shouted, and a crowd poured out of the nearest gate. My God, what a crowd! I was getting used to giants by this time, but here was a regular Barnum and Bailey show; more semi-dwarfs; others like them but more so—one could not tell whether the creatures were precociously mature children or horribly stunted adults; others portentously fat, with arms like sooty legs of mutton, and rolls and volutes of fat crisping out of their steatopygous posteriors; still others precociously senile and wizened, others hateful and imbecile in looks. Of course, there were plenty of ordinary Negroes too, but enough of the extraordinary to make one feel pretty queer. Soon after we got inside, I suddenly noted something else which appeared inexplicable—a telephone wire, with perfectly good insulators, running across from tree to tree. A telephone—in an unknown African town. I gave it up.

But another surprise was in store for me. I saw a figure pass across from one large building to another—a figure unmistakably that of a white man. In the first place, it was wearing white ducks and sun helmet; in the second, it had a pale face.

He turned at the sound of our cavalcade and stood looking a moment; then walked toward us.

"Halloa!" I shouted. "Do you speak English?"

"Yes," he answered, "but keep quiet a moment," and began talking quickly to our leaders, who treated him with the greatest deference. He dropped back to me and spoke rapidly: "You are to be taken into the council hall to be examined: but I will see to it that no harm comes to you.

This is a forbidden land to strangers, and you must be prepared to be held up for a time. You will be sent down to see me in the temple buildings as soon as the formalities are over, and I'll explain things. They want a bit of explaining," he added with a dry laugh. "By the way, my name is Hascombe, lately research worker at Middlesex Hospital, now religious adviser to His Majesty King Mgobe." He laughed again and pushed ahead. He was an interesting figure—perhaps fifty years old, spare body, thin face, with a small beard, and rather sunken, hazel eyes. As for his expression, he looked cynical, but also as if he were interested in life.

By this time we were at the entrance to the hall. Our giants formed up outside, with my men behind them, and only I and the leader passed in. The examination was purely formal, and remarkable chiefly for the ritual and solemnity which characterized all the actions of the couple of dozen fine-looking men in long robes who were our examiners. My men were herded off to some compound. I was escorted down to a little hut, furnished with some attempt at European style, where I found Hascombe.

As soon as we were alone. I was after him with my questions. "Now you can tell me. Where are we? What is the meaning of all this circus business and this menagerie of monstrosities? And how do you come here?"

He cut me short. "It's a long story, so let me save time by telling it my own way."

I am not going to tell it as he told it; but will try to give a more connected account, the result of many later talks with him, and of my own observations.

Hascombe had been a medical student of great promise; and after his degree had launched out into research. He had first started on parasitic protozoa, but had given that up in favor of tissue culture; from these he had gone off to cancer research, and from that to a study of developmental physiology. Later a big Commission on sleeping sickness had been organized, and Hascombe, restless and eager for travel, had pulled wires and got himself appointed as one of the scientific staff sent to Africa. He was much impressed with the view that wild game acted as a reservoir for the *Trypanosoma gambiense*. When he learned of the extensive migrations of game, he saw here an important possible means of spreading the disease and asked leave to go up country to investigate the whole problem. When the Commission as a whole had finished its work, he was allowed to stay in Africa with one other white man and a company of porters to see what he could discover. His white companion was a laboratory technician, a taciturn, noncommissioned officer of science called Aggers.

There is no object in telling of their experiences here. Suffice it that they lost their way and fell into the hands of this same tribe. That was fifteen years ago: and Aggers was now long dead—as the result of a wound inflicted when he was caught, after a couple of years, trying to escape.

On their capture, they too had been examined in the council chamber, and Hascombe (who had interested himself in a dilettante way in anthropology as in most other subjects of scientific inquiry) was much impressed by what he described as the exceedingly religious atmosphere. Everything was done with an elaboration of ceremony; the chief seemed more priest than king, and performed various rites at intervals, and priests were busy at some sort of altar the whole time. Among other things, he noticed that one of their rites was connected with blood. First the chief and then the councillors were in turn requisitioned for a drop of vital fluid pricked from their fingertips, and the mixture, held in a little vessel, was slowly evaporated over a flame.

Some of Hascombe's men spoke a dialect not unlike

that of their captors, and one was acting as interpreter. Things did not look too favorable. The country was a "holy place," it seemed, and the tribe a "holy race." Other Africans who trespassed there, if not killed, were enslaved, but for the most part they let well alone, and did not trespass. White men they had heard of, but never seen till now, and the debate was what to do—to kill, let go, or enslave? To let them go was contrary to all their principles: the holy place would be defiled if the news of it were spread abroad. To enslave them—yes; but what were they good for? And the Council seemed to feel an instinctive dislike for these other-colored creatures. Hascombe had an idea. He turned to the interpreter. "Say this: 'You revere the blood. So do we white men; but we do more—we can render visible the blood's hidden nature and reality, and with permission I will show this great magic.' " He beckoned to the bearer who carried his precious microscope, set it up, drew a drop of blood from the tip of his finger with his knife, and mounted it on a slide under a cover-slip. The bigwigs were obviously interested. They whispered to each other. At length, "Show us," commanded the chief.

Hascombe demonstrated his preparation with greater interest than he had ever done to first-year medical students in the old days. He explained that the blood was composed of little people of various sorts, each with their own lives, and that to spy upon them thus gave us new powers over them. The elders were more or less impressed. At any rate the sight of these thousands of corpuscles where they could see nothing before made them think, made them realize that the white man had power which might make him a desirable servant.

They would not ask to see their own blood for fear that the sight would put them into the power of those who saw it. But they had blood drawn from a slave. Hascombe asked too for a bird, and was able to create a certain interest by showing how different were the little people of its blood.

"Tell them," he said to the interpreter, "that I have many other powers and magics which I will show them if they will give me time."

The long and short of it was that he and his party were spared—He said he knew then what one felt when the magistrate said: "Remanded for a week."

He had been attracted by one of the elder statesmen of the tribe—a tall, powerful-looking man of middle-age; and was agreeably surprised when this man came round next day to see him. Hascombe later nicknamed him the Prince-Bishop, for his combination of the qualities of the statesman and the ecclesiastic: his real name was Bugala. He was anxious to discover more about Hascombe's mysterious powers and resources as Hascombe was to learn what he could of the people into whose hands he had fallen, and they met almost every evening and talked far into the night.

Bugala's inquiries were as little prompted as Hascombe's by a purely academic curiosity. Impressed himself by the microscope, and still more by the effect which it had had on his colleagues, he was anxious to find out whether by utilizing the powers of the white man he could not secure his own advancement. At length, they struck a bargain. Bugala would see to it that no harm befell Hascombe. But Hascombe must put his resources and powers at the disposal of the Council; and Bugala would take good care to arrange matters so that he himself benefited. So far as Hascombe could make out, Bugala imagined a radical change in the national religion, a sort of reformation based on Hascombe's conjuring tricks; and that he would emerge as the High Priest of this changed system.

Hascombe had a sense of humor, and it was tickled. It seemed pretty clear that they could not escape, at least for the present. That being so, why not take the opportunity of doing a little research work at state expense—an opportunity which he and his like were always clamoring for at home? His thoughts began to run away with him. He would find out all he could of the rites and superstitions of the tribe. He would, by the aid of his knowledge and his scientific skill, exalt the details of these rites, the expression of those superstitions, the whole physical side of their religiosity, on to a new level which should to them appear truly miraculous.

It would not be worth my troubling to tell all the negotiations, the false starts, the misunderstandings. In the end he secured what he wanted—a building which could be used as a laboratory; an unlimited supply of slaves for the lower and priests for the higher duties of laboratory assistants; and the promise that when his scientific stores were exhausted they would do their best to secure others from the coast—a promise which was scrupulously kept, so that he never went short for lack of what money could buy.

He next applied himself diligently to a study of their religion and found that it was built round various main motifs. Of these, the central one was the belief in the divinity and tremendous importance of the Priest-King. The second was a form of ancestor-worship. The third was an animal cult, in particular of the more grotesque species of the African fauna. The fourth was sex, *con variazioni*. Hascombe reflected on these facts. Tissue culture; experimental embryology; endocrine treatment; artificial parthenogenesis. He laughed and said to himself: "Well, at least I can try, and it ought to be amusing."

That was how it all started. Perhaps the best way of giving some idea of how it had developed will be for me to tell my own impressions when Hascombe took me round his laboratories. One whole quarter of the town was devoted entirely to religion—it struck me as excessive, but Hascombe reminded me that Tibet spends one-fifth of its revenues on melted butter to burn before its shrines. Facing the main square was the chief temple, built impressively enough of solid mud. On either side were the apartments, where dwelt the servants of the gods and administrators of the sacred rites. Behind were Hascombe's laboratories, some built of mud, others, under his later guidance, of wood. They were guarded night and day by patrols of giants, and were arranged in a series of quadrangles. Within one quadrangle was a pool which served as an aquarium; in another, aviaries and great henhouses; in yet another, cages with various animals; in the fourth a little botanic garden. Behind were stables with dozens of cattle and sheep, and a sort of experimental ward for human beings.

He took me into the nearest of the buildings. "This," he said, "is known to the people as the Factory (it is difficult to give the exact sense of the word, but it literally means producing-place), the Factory of Kingship or Majesty, and the Well-spring of Ancestral Immortality." I looked round, and saw platoons of buxom and shining African women, becomingly but unusually dressed in tight-fitting white dresses and caps, and wearing rubber gloves. Microscopes were much in evidence, also various receptacles from which steam was emerging. The back of the room was screened off by a wooden screen in which were a series of glass doors; and these doors opened into partitions, each labeled with a name in that unknown tongue, and each containing a number of objects like the one I had seen taken out of the basket of the giant before we were captured. Pipes surrounded this chamber, and appeared to be distributing heat from a fire in one corner.

"Factory of Majesty!" I exclaimed. "Well-spring of Immortality! What the dickens do you mean?"

"If you prefer a more prosaic name," said Hascombe, "I should call this the Institute of Religious Tissue Culture." My mind went back to a day in 1918 when I had been taken by a biological friend in New York to see the famous Rockefeller Institute; and at the words "tissue culture" I saw again before me Dr. Alexis Carrel and troops of white-garbed American girls making cultures, sterilizing, microscopizing, incubating and the rest of it. The Hascombe Institute was, it is true, not so well equipped, but it had an even larger, if differently colored, personnel.

Hascombe began his explanations. "As you probably know, Frazer's *Golden Bough* introduced us to the idea of a sacred Priest-King, and showed how fundamental it was in primitive societies. The welfare of the tribe is regarded as inextricably bound up with that of the King, and extraordinary precautions are taken to preserve him from harm. In this kingdom, in the old days, the King was hardly allowed to set his foot to the ground in case he should lose divinity; his cut hair and nail-parings were entrusted to one of the most important officials of state, whose duty it was to bury them secretly, in case some enemy should compass the King's illness or death by using them in black-magic rites. If anyone of base blood trod on the King's shadow, he paid the penalty with his life. Each year a slave was made mock-king for a week, allowed to enjoy all the King's privileges, and was decapitated at the close of his brief glory; and by this means it was supposed that the illnesses and misfortunes that might befall the King were vicariously got rid of.

"I first of all rigged up my apparatus, and with the aid of Aggers, succeeded in getting good cultures, first of chick tissues and later, by the aid of embryo-extract, of various and adult mammalian tissues. I then went to Bugala, and told him that I could increase the safety, if not of the King as an individual, at least of the life which was in him, and that I presumed that this would be equally satisfactory from a theological point of view. I pointed out that if he chose to be made guardian of the King's subsidiary lives, he would be in a much more important position than the chamberlain or the burier of the sacred nail-parings, and might make the post the most influential in the realm.

"Eventually I was allowed (under threat of death if anything untoward occurred) to remove small portions of His Majesty's subcutaneous connective tissue under a local anesthetic. In the presence of the assembled nobility I put fragments of this into a culture medium, and showed it to them under the microscope. The cultures were then put away in the incubator under a guard—relieved every eight hours—of half a dozen warriors. After three days, to my joy they had all taken and showed abundant growth. I could see that the Council was impressed, and reeled off a magnificent speech, pointing out that this growth constituted an actual increase in the quantity of the divine principle inherent in royalty; and what was more, that I could increase it indefinitely. With that I cut each of my cultures into eight, and subcultured all the pieces. They were again put under guard, and again examined after three days. Not all of them had taken this time, and there were some murmurings and angry looks, on the ground that I had killed some of the King; but I pointed out that the King was still the King, that his little wound had completely healed, and that any successful cultures represented so much extra sacredness and protection to the state. I must say that they were very reasonable, and had good theological acumen, for they at once took the hint.

"I pointed out to Bugala, and he persuaded the rest without much difficulty, that they could now disregard some of the older implications of the doctrines of kingship. The most important new idea which I was able to introduce was *mass-production*. Our aim was to multiply the King's tissues indefinitely, to ensure that some of their protecting power should reside everywhere in the country. One might have supposed that such an innovation would have met with great resistance simply on account of its being an innovation; but I must admit that these people compared very favorably with the average businessman in their lack of prejudice.

"Having thus settled the principle, I had many debates with Bugala as to the best methods of enlisting the mass of the population in our scheme. What an opportunity for scientific advertising! But, unfortunately, the population could not read. However, war propaganda worked very well in more or less illiterate countries—why not here?"

Hascombe organized a series of public lectures in the capital, at which he demonstrated his regal tissues to the multitude, who were bidden to the place by royal heralds. An impressive platform group was always supplied from the ranks of the nobles. The lecturer explained how important it was for the community to become possessed of greater and greater stores of the sacred tissues. Unfortunately, the preparation was laborious, and expensive, and it behooved them all to lend a hand. It had accordingly been arranged that to everyone subscribing a cow or buffalo, or its equivalent—three goats, pigs, sheep—a portion of the royal anatomy should be given, handsomely mounted in an ebony holder. Subculturing would be done at certain hours and days, and it would be obligatory to send the cultures for renewal. If through any negligence the tissue died, no renewal would be made. The subscription entitled the receiver to subculturing rights for a year, but was of course renewable. By this means not only would the totality of the King be much increased, to the benefit of all, but each culture-holder would possess an actual part of His Majesty, and would have the infinite joy and privilege of aiding by his own efforts the multiplication of divinity.

Then they could also serve their country by dedicating a daughter to the state. These young women would be housed and fed by the state, and taught the technique of the sacred culture. Candidates would be selected according to general fitness, but would of course, in addition, be required to attain distinction in an examination on the principles of religion. They would be appointed for a probationary period of six months. After this they would receive a permanent status, with the title of Sisters of the Sacred Tissue. From this, with age, experience, and merit, they could expect promotion to the rank of mothers, grandmothers, great-grandmothers, and grand ancestresses of the same. The merit and benefit they would receive from their close contact with the source of all benefits would overflow onto their families.

The scheme worked like wildfire. Pigs, goats, cattle, buffaloes, and Negro maidens poured in. Next year the scheme was extended to the whole country, a peripatetic laboratory making the rounds weekly.

By the close of the third year there was hardly a family in the country which did not possess at least one sacred culture. To be without one would have been like being without one's trousers—or at least without one's hat—on Fifth Avenue. Thus did Bugala effect a reformation in the national religion, enthrone himself as the most important personage in the country, and entrench applied science and Hascombe firmly in the organization of the state.

Encouraged by his success, Hascombe soon set out to capture the ancestry-worship branch of the religion as well. A public proclamation was made pointing out how much more satisfactory it would be if worship could be made not merely to the charred bones of one's forebears, but to bits of them still actually living and growing. All who were desirous of profiting by the enterprise of Bugala's Department of State should therefore bring their older relatives to the laboratory at certain specified hours, and fragments would be painlessly extracted for culture.

This, too, proved very attractive to the average citizen. Occasionally, it is true, grandfathers or aged mothers arrived in a state of indignation and protest. However, this did not matter, since, according to the law, once children were twenty-five years of age, they were not only assigned the duty of worshiping their ancestors alive or dead, but were also given complete control over them, in order that all rites might be duly performed to the greater safety of the commonweal. Further, the ancestors soon found that the operation itself was trifling, and, what was more, that once accomplished, it had the most desirable results. For their descendants preferred to concentrate at once upon the culture which they would continue to worship after the old folks were gone, and so left their parents and grandparents much freer than before from the irksome restrictions which in all ages have beset the officially holy.

Thus, by almost every hearth in the kingdom, instead of the old-fashioned rows of red jars containing the incinerated remains of one or other of the family forebears, the new generation saw growing up a collection of family slides. Each would be taken out and reverently examined at the hour of prayer. "Grandpapa is not growing well this week," you would perhaps hear the young black devotee say; the father of the family would pray over the speck of tissue; and if that failed, it would be taken back to the factory for rejuvenation. On the other hand, what rejoicing when a rhythm of activity stirred in the cultures! A spurt on the part of great-grandmother's tissues would bring her wrinkled old smile to mind again; and sometimes it seemed as if one particular generation were all stirred simultaneously by a pulse of growth, as if combining to bless their devout descendants.

To deal with the possibility of cultures dying out, Hascombe started a central storehouse, where duplicates of every strain were kept, and it was this repository of the national tissues which had attracted my attention at the back of the laboratory. No such collection had ever existed before, he assured me. Not a necropolis, but a histopolis, if I may coin a word: not a cemetery, but a place of eternal growth.

The second building was devoted to endocrine products—an African Armour's—and was called by the people the "Factory of Ministers to the Shrines."

"Here," he said, "you will not find much new. You know the craze for 'glands' that was going on at home years ago, and its results, in the shape of pluriglandular preparations, a new genre of patent medicines, and a popular literature that threatened to outdo the Freudians, and explain human beings entirely on the basis of glandular makeup, without reference to the mind at all.

"I had only to apply my knowledge in a comparatively simple manner. The first thing was to show Bugala how, by repeated injections of prepituitary, I could make an ordinary baby grow up into a giant. This pleased him, and he introduced the idea of a sacred bodyguard, all of really gigantic stature, quite overshadowing Frederick's Grenadiers.

"I did, however, extend knowledge in several directions. I took advantage of the fact that their religion holds in reverence monstrous and imbecile forms of human beings. That is, of course, a common phenomenon in many countries, where halfwits are supposed to be inspired, and dwarfs the object of superstitious awe. So I went to work to create various new types. By employing a particular extract of adrenal cortex, I produced children who would have been a match for the infant Hercules, and, indeed, looked rather like a cross between him and a brewer's drayman. By injecting the same extract into adolescent girls I was able to provide them with the most copious mustaches, after which they found ready employment as prophetesses.

"Tampering with the postpituitary gave remarkable cases of obesity. This, together with the passion of the men for fatness in their women, Bugala took advantage of, and I believe made quite a fortune by selling as concubines female slaves treated in this way. Finally, by another pituitary treatment, I at last mastered the secret of true dwarfism, in which perfect proportions are retained.

"Of these productions, the dwarfs are retained as acolytes in the temple; a band of the obese young ladies form a sort of Society of Vestal Virgins, with special religious duties which, as the embodiment of the national ideal of beauty, they are supposed to discharge with peculiarly propitious effect; and the giants form our Regular Army.

"The Obese Virgins have set me a problem which I confess I have not yet solved. Like all races who set great store by sexual enjoyment, these people have a correspondingly exaggerated reverence for virginity. It therefore occurred to me that if I could apply Jacques Loeb's great discovery of artificial parthenogenesis to man, or, to be precise, to these young ladies, I should be able to grow a race of vestals, self-reproducing yet ever virgin, to whom in concentrated form should attach that reverence of which I have just spoken. You see, I must always remember that it is no good proposing any line of work that will not benefit the national religion. I suppose state-aided research would have much the same kinds of difficulties in a really democratic state. Well, this, as I say, has so far beaten me. I have taken the matter a step further than Bataillon with his fatherless frogs, and I have induced parthenogenesis in the eggs of reptiles and birds; but so far I have failed with mammals. However, I've not given up yet!"

Then we passed to the next laboratory, which was full of the most incredible animal monstrosities. "This laboratory is the most amusing," said Hascombe. "Its official title is 'Home of the Living Fetishes.' Here again I have simply taken a prevalent trait of the populace, and used it as a peg on which to hang research. I told you that they always had a fancy for the grotesque in animals, and used the most bizarre forms, in the shape of little clay or ivory statuettes, for fetishes.

"I thought I would see whether art could not improve upon nature, and set myself to recall my experimental embryology. I use only the simplest methods. I utilize the plasticity of the earliest stages to give double-headed and cyclopean monsters. That was, of course, done years ago in newts by Spemann and fish by Stockard; and I have merely applied the mass-production methods of Mr. Ford to their results. But my specialties are three-headed snakes, and toads with an extra heaven-pointing head. The former are a little difficult, but there is a great demand for them, and they fetch a good price. The frogs are easier: I simply apply Harrison's methods to embryo tadpoles."

He then showed me into the last building. Unlike the others, this contained no signs of research in progress, but was empty. It was draped with black hangings, and lit only from the top. In the center were rows of ebony benches, and in front of them a glittering golden ball on a stand.

"Here I am beginning my work on reinforced telepathy," he told me. "Some day you must come and see what it's all about, for it really is interesting."

You may imagine that I was pretty well flabbergasted by this catalogue of miracles. Every day I got a talk with Hascombe, and gradually the talks became recognized events of our daily routine. One day I asked if he had given up hope of escaping. He showed a queer hesitation in replying. Eventually he said, "To tell you the truth, my dear Jones, I have really hardly thought of it these last few years. It seemed so impossible at first that I deliberately put it out of my head and turned with more and more energy, I might almost say fury, to my work. And now, upon my soul, I am not quite sure whether I want to escape or not."

"Not *want* to!" I exclaimed. "Surely you can't mean that!"

"I am not so sure," he rejoined. "What I most want is to get ahead with this work of mine. Why, man, you don't realize what a chance I've got! And it is all growing so fast—I can see every kind of possibility ahead." And he broke off into silence.

However, although I was interested enough in his past achievement, I did not feel willing to sacrifice my future to his perverted intellectual ambitions. But he would not leave his work.

The experiments which most excited his imagination were those he was conducting into mass telepathy. He had received his medical training at a time when abnormal psychology was still very unfashionable in England, but had luckily been thrown in contact with a young doctor who was a keen student of hypnotism, through whom he had been introduced to some of the great pioneers, like Bramwell and Wingfield. As a result, he had become a passable hypnotist himself, with a fair knowledge of the literature.

In the early days of his captivity he became interested in the sacred dances which took place every night of full moon, and were regarded as propitiations of the celestial powers. The dancers all belong to a special sect. After a series of exciting figures, symbolizing various activities of the chase, war, and love, the leader conducts his band to a ceremonial bench. He then begins to make passes at them; and what impressed Hascombe was this, that a few seconds sufficed for them to fall back in deep hypnosis against the ebony rail. It recalled, he said, the most startling cases of collective hypnosis recorded by the French scientists. The leader next passed from one end of the bench to the other, whispering a brief sentence into each ear. He then, according to immemorial rite, approached the Priest-King, and after having exclaimed aloud, "Lord of Majesty, command what thou wilt for thy dancers to perform," the King would thereupon command some action which had previously been kept secret. The command was often to fetch some object and deposit it at the moon-shrine; or to fight the enemies of the state; or (and this was what the company most liked) to be some animal, or bird. Whatever the command, the hypnotized men would obey it, for the leader's whispered words had been an order to hear and carry out only what the King said; and the strangest scenes would be witnessed as they ran, completely oblivious of all in their path, in search of the gourds or sheep they had been called on to procure, or lunged in a symbolic way at invisible enemies, or threw themselves on all fours and roared as lions, or galloped as zebras, or danced as cranes. The command executed, they stood like stocks or stones, until their leader, running from one to the other, touched each with a finger and shouted, "Wake." They woke, and limp, but conscious of having been the vessels of the unknown spirit, danced back to their special hut or clubhouse.

This susceptibility to hypnotic suggestion struck Hascombe, and he obtained permission to test the performers more closely. He soon established that the people were, as a race, extremely prone to dissociation, and could be made to lapse into deep hypnosis with great ease, but a hypnosis in which the subconscious, though completely cut off from the waking self, comprised portions of the personality not retained in the hypnotic selves of Europeans. Like most who have fluttered round the psychological candle, he had been interested in the notion of telepathy; and now, with this supply of hypnotic subjects under his hands, began some real investigation of the problem.

By picking his subjects, he was soon able to demonstrate the existence of telepathy, by making suggestions to one hypnotized man who transferred them without physical intermediation to another at a distance. Later—and this was the culmination of his work—he found that when he made a suggestion to several subjects at once, the telepathic effect was much stronger than if he had done it to one at a time—the hypnotized minds were reinforcing each other. "I'm after the super-consciousness," Hascombe said, "and I've already got the rudiments of it."

I must confess that I got almost as excited as Hascombe over the possibilities thus opened up. It certainly seemed as if he were right in principle. If all the subjects were in practically the same psychological state, extraordinary reinforcing effects were observed. At first the attainment of this similarity of condition was very difficult; gradually, however, we discovered that it was possible to tune hypnotic subjects to the same pitch, if I may use the metaphor, and then the fun really began.

First of all we found that with increasing reinforcement, we could get telepathy conducted to greater and greater distances, until finally we could transmit commands from the capital to the national boundary, nearly a hundred miles. We next found that it was not necessary for the subject to be in hypnosis to receive the telepathic command. Almost everybody, but especially those of equable temperament, could thus be influenced. Most extraordinary of all, however, were what we at first christened "near effects," since their transmission to a distance was not found possible until later. If, after Hascombe had suggested some simple command to a largish group of hypnotized subjects, he or I went right up among them, we would experience the most extraordinary sensation, as of some superhuman personality repeating the command in a menacing and overwhelming way and, whereas with one part of ourselves we felt, if I may say so, as if we were only a part of the command, or of something much bigger than ourselves which was commanding. And this, Hascombe claimed, was the first real beginning of the super-consciousness.

Bugala, of course, had to be considered. Hascombe, with the old Tibetan prayer-wheel at the back of his mind, suggested that eventually he would be able to induce hypnosis in the whole population, and then transmit a prayer. This would ensure that the daily prayer, for instance, was really said by the whole population, and, what is more, simultaneously, which would undoubtedly much enhance its efficacy. And it would make it possible in times of calamity or battle to keep the whole praying force of the nation at work for long spells together.

Bugala was deeply interested. He saw himself, through this mental machinery, planting such ideas as he wished in the brain-cases of his people. He saw himself willing an order; and the whole population rousing itself out of trance to execute it. He dreamt dreams before which those of the proprietor of a newspaper syndicate, even those of a director of propaganda in wartime, would be pale and timid. Naturally, he wished to receive personal instruction in the methods himself; and, equally naturally, we could not refuse him, though I must say that I often felt a little uneasy as to what he might choose to do if he ever decided to override Hascombe and to start experimenting on his own. This, combined with my constant longing to get away from the place, led me to cast about again for means of escape. Then it occurred to me that this very method about which I had such gloomy presentiments might itself be made the key to our prison.

So one day, after getting Hascombe worked up about the loss to humanity it would be to let this great discovery die with him in Africa, I set to in earnest. "My dear Hascombe," I said, "you must get home out of this. What is there to prevent your saying to Bugala that your experiments are nearly crowned with success, but that for certain tests you must have a much greater number of subjects at your disposal? You can then get a battery of two hundred men, and after you have tuned them, the reinforcement will be so great that you will have at your disposal a mental force big enough to affect the whole population. Then, of course, one fine day we should raise the potential of our mind-battery to the highest possible level, and send out through it a general hypnotic influence. The whole country, men, women, and children, would sink into stupor. Next we should give our experimental squad the suggestion to broadcast 'sleep for a week.' The telepathic message would be relayed to each of the thousands of minds waiting receptively for it, and would take root in them, until the whole nation became a single super-conciousness, conscious only of the one thought 'sleep' which we had thrown into it."

The reader will perhaps ask how we ourselves expected to escape from the clutches of the superconsciousness we had created. Well, we had discovered that metal was relatively imperious to the telepathic effect, and had prepared for ourselves a sort of tin pulpit, behind which we could stand while conducting experiments. This, combined with caps of metal foil, enormously reduced the effects on ourselves. We had not informed Bugala of this property of metal.

Hascombe was silent. At length he spoke. "I like the

idea," he said; "I like to think that if I ever do get back to England and to scientific recognition, my discovery will have given me the means of escape."

From that moment we worked assiduously to perfect our method and our plans. After about five months everything seemed propitious. We had provisions packed away, and compasses. I had been allowed to keep my rifle, on promise that I would never discharge it. We had made friends with some of the men who went trading to the coast, and had got from them all the information we could about the route, without arousing their suspicions.

At last, the night arrived. We assembled our men as if for an ordinary practice, and after hypnosis had been induced, started to tune them. At this moment Bugala came in, unannounced. This was what we had been afraid of; but there had been no means of preventing it. "What shall we do?" I whispered to Hascombe, in English. "Go right ahead and be damned to it," was his answer; "we can put him to sleep with the rest."

So we welcomed him, and gave him a seat as near as possible to the tightly packed ranks of the performers. At length the preparations were finished. Hascombe went into the pulpit and said, "Attention to the words which are to be suggested." There was a slight stiffening of the bodies. "Sleep," said Hascombe. "*Sleep* is the command: command all in this land to sleep unbrokenly." Bugala leapt up with an exclamation; but the induction had already begun.

We with our metal coverings were immune. But Bugala was struck by the full force of the mental current. He sank back on his chair, helpless. For a few minutes his extraordinary will resisted the suggestion. Although he could not move, his angry eyes were open. But at length he succumbed, and he too slept.

We lost no time in starting, and made good progress through the silent country. The people were sitting about like wax figures. Women sat asleep by their milk-pails, the cow by this time far away. Fat-bellied naked children slept at their games. The houses were full of sleepers sleeping upright round their food, recalling Wordsworth's famous "party in a parlor."

So we went on, feeling pretty queer and scarcely believing in this morphic state into which we had plunged a nation. Finally the frontier was reached, where with extreme elation, we passed an immobile and gigantic frontier guard. A few miles further we had a good solid meal, and a doze. Our kit was rather heavy, and we decided to jettison some superfluous weight, in the shape of some food, specimens, and our metal headgear, of mind-protectors, which at this distance, and with the hypnosis wearing a little thin, were, we thought, no longer necessary.

About nightfall on the third day, Hascombe suddenly stopped and turned his head.

"What's the matter?" I said. "Have you seen a lion?" His reply was completely unexpected. "No. I was just wondering whether really I ought not to go back again."

"Go back again," I cried. "What in the name of God Almighty do you want to do that for?"

"It suddenly struck me that I ought to," he said, "about five minutes ago. And really, when one comes to think of it, I don't suppose I shall ever journey to the coast, and I don't expect we shall get through alive."

I was thoroughly upset and put out, and told him so. And suddenly, for a few moments, I felt I must go back too. It was like that old friend of our boyhood, the voice of conscience.

"Yes, to be sure, we ought to go back," I thought with fervor. But suddenly checking myself as the thought came under the play of reason—"*Why* should we go back?" All sorts of reasons were proffered, as it were, by unseen hands reaching up out of the hidden parts of me.

And then I realized what had happened. Bugala had waked up; he had wiped out the suggestion we had given to the super-consciousness, and in its place put in another. I could see him thinking it out, the cunning devil (one must give him credit for brains!), and hear him, after making his passes, whisper to the nation in prescribed form his new suggestion: "Will to return!" "Return!" For most of the inhabitants the command would have no meaning, for they would have been already at home. Doubtless some young men out on the hills, or truant children, or girls run off in secret to meet their lovers, were even now returning, stiffly and in somnambulistic trance, to their homes. It was only for them that the new command of the super-consciousness had any meaning—and for us.

I am putting it in a long and discursive way; at the moment I simply *saw* what had happened in a flash. I told Hascombe, I showed him it *must* be so, that nothing else would account for the sudden change. I begged and implored him to use his reason, to stick to his decision and to come on. How I regretted that, in our desire to discard all useless weight, we had left behind our metal telepathy-proof head coverings!

But Hascombe would not, or could not, see my point. I suppose he was much more imbued with all the feelings and spirit of the country, and so more susceptible. However that may be, he was immovable. He must go back; he knew it; he saw it clearly; it was his sacred duty; and much other similar rubbish. All this time the suggestion was attacking me too; and finally I felt that if I did not put more distance between me and that unisonic battery of will, I should succumb as well as he.

"Hascombe," I said, "I am going on. For God's sake, come with me." And I shouldered my pack, and set off. He was shaken, I saw, and came a few steps after me. But finally he turned, and, in spite of my frequent pauses and shouts to him to follow, made off in the direction we had come. I can assure you that it was with a gloomy soul that I continued my solitary way. I shall not bore you with my adventures. Suffice it to say that at last I got to a white outpost, weak with fatigue and poor food and fever.

I kept very quiet about my adventures, only giving out that our expedition had lost its way and that my men had run away or been killed by the local tribes. At last I reached England. But I was a broken man, and a profound gloom had invaded my mind at the thought of Hascombe and the way he had been caught in his own net. I never found out what happened to him, and I do not suppose that I am likely to find out now. You may ask why I did not try to organize a rescue expedition; or why, at least, I did not bring Hascombe's discoveries before the Royal Society or the Metaphysical Institute. I can only repeat that I was a broken man. I did not expect to be believed; I was not at all sure that I could repeat our results, even on the same human material, much less with men of another race; I dreaded ridicule; and finally I was tormented by doubts as to whether the knowledge of mass-telepathy would not be a curse rather than a blessing to mankind.

However, I am an oldish man now and, what is more, old for my years. I want to get the story off my chest. Besides, old men like sermonizing and you must forgive, gentle reader, the sermonical turn which I now feel I must take. The question I want to raise is this: Dr. Hascombe attained to an unsurpassed power in a number of applications of science—but *to what end did all this power serve?* It is the merest cant and twaddle to go on asserting, as most of our press and people continue to do, that increase of scientific knowledge and power must in itself be good. I command to the great public the obvious moral of my story and ask them to think what they propose to do with the power which is gradually being accumulated for them by the labors of those who labor because they like power, or because they want to find the truth about how things work.

O. Barr

THE VOICE FROM THE ETHER

By Lloyd Arthur Eshbach

On August 22nd, 1924, the planet Mars was in opposition to the earth. That is to say, the two planets in their perpetual journeying had assumed such a position as to be in one straight line with the sun, the earth eclipsing the superior planet Mars. A superior planet is one whose orbit is of greater diameter than that of the earth. At the same time, the distance separating Mars from the earth was less than it had been for more than one hundred years. Only 34,640,000 miles lay between the two heavenly bodies.

The night of the 22nd was remarkably clear, an ideal night for astronomical observation. Innumerable telescopes, large and small, were focused upon the red planet. Ingenious devices of various kinds were striving to communicate with the inhabitants of Mars. And, in a little cabin high up in the Adirondack Mountains, I sat before my radio. Far away from any "interference," I strove to make the greatest radio pickup ever attempted.

I had made rather elaborate preparations for the recording of any interplanetary communication I might receive, securing for that purpose a device working on the same principle as the dictaphone. It differed from that instrument, however, in that it could record words continually for a period of ten hours. This device, the invention of an obscure mechanical engineer, stood within a few feet of the loudspeaker.

With practiced fingers I twirled the dials. One pickup after another rewarded my efforts. A voice raised in song, the wail of a saxophone, the sonorous voice of an announcer—the usual radio programs. Little cared I for these, however, for they were commonplace; I was after bigger game. But Mars continued in that silence which it had maintained for countless ages.

Slowly the hours passed. Midnight came—one o'clock. A fine radio night, I thought, rather hazily—I dozed.

The time signal from the station to which I had last been listening, called me back to consciousness. One—two! I heard the strokes faintly, as from a great distance. Then, suddenly I raised my nodding head erect; I was fully awake.

A discordant shriek of static assailed my ears. A frightful howl, like that of a tortured imp, filled the room. Then, as suddenly as the coming of the static, silence, oppressive, heavy, fell like a mantle over the radio.

And then I heard the—Voice. Clear and loud it came, unmarred by any interfering static. It was a shrill, piping voice, which, in the course of its narrative, traversed the entire gamut of emotion.

I was spellbound. A feeling of triumph pervaded my being, triumph intermingled with awe. I had succeeded! Victory! I was certain that I had received a message from Mars. I trembled with excitement. Hesitantly I reached toward the dials—and drew my hand away before it touched the radio. I was held back by the thought that perhaps I might break the tenuous thread which held that distant station in communication with the earth. At that, there was no need of adjusting the dials, for the reception was well-nigh perfect.

Eventually, the excitement of the first few moments passed, and I paid more attention to the words coming from the loudspeaker. As I listened, a note of excitement crept into the Voice. Excitement, then anger, cold and terrible. And quickly on the heels of that anger came hate, an insane hate that somehow filled me with dread.

Through the balance of the night I listened. Although the words spoken by the Voice were so much meaningless gibberish to me, each passing hour saw me seated there, motionless, held by the power of that strange, high-pitched voice.

A gray pencil of light pierced the gloom; the darkness gave way to the radiance of a new day; and suddenly the Voice—broke. There was a moment of utter silence, and then a shrill shriek of fear and terrible agony. The last notes of the shriek were strangely, horribly muffled! And there followed that dread, unbroken silence—

Outside in the long grass a cricket chirped. The spell was broken. Slowly, I rose upon my trembling limbs; slowly, I raised my hand and brushed the beads of cold perspiration from my forehead. The experience had been so strange, those last moments so terrible! It was with great difficulty that I regained my mental equilibrium.

Questions leaped to my mind. Had I really tuned in on Mars? If I had, what was the nature of the message I had received? What manner of creature had done the broadcasting? And—what had caused that shriek?

Not until four years later did I learn the answer to those questions. Four long years during which Millard labored tirelessly on the translation of that message from another world.

Millard? Yes, Phineas J. Millard, antiquarian and archeologist. He, in all probability, is the only man living today who is able to translate a record consisting only of phonetics. And even he required four years for the accomplishment of that task.

Little more remains to be said by way of introduction. For the sake of convenience, I have taken advantage of natural breaks in the action of the narrative and divided it into chapters. Also, I have taken the liberty of substituting the English names of scientific apparatus for the incomprehensible names used by the Voice. Aside from that, the narrative is unchanged. And now you may read this amazing tale as it is related by Tuol Oro, scientist of another planet.

CHAPTER I

In this vast Universe, teeming with its myriad forms of life, there is surely one race of beings who will hear and understand this, my warning. And understanding, perhaps they may heed. It is with that hope in mind that I am telling my story.

When I began my life upon this planet, I was called Tuol Oro. Through the brilliancy of my intellect and the power of my mind, I made that name a name that was respected throughout the world. Yet, through the stupidity of one man, and in spite of all I had done, I became an outcast. I was scorned, derided, and openly shunned by those who had respected me. They referred to me as Tuol the Madman, or Tuol the Fool, as it suited their fancy.

Revenge became the one purpose of my life. I loved only that I might destroy the race of fools that ruled over Kotar. And I've done it! Failures were they; who thought themselves perfect; but they are gone. And I, who alone survive, was thought to be the only failure of their civilization. Tuol, the Fool? No, Tuol, the Conqueror, am I.

There are others, now, that have taken the place of man, others that, eventually, I shall also rule. Those others, that I loosed upon the world to do my will, shall feel the power of my might, and I will reign supreme over all Kotar. Soon I will go out and claim that which is rightfully mine; then, indeed, will I be conqueror.

But, before that occurs, I will tell the story of man's downfall and destruction; the story of Tuol Oro's revenge. And that tale heard, perhaps, on some other world, may be a warning, so that men who advance strange and unusual facts may receive audience, and be respected as they deserve.

I remember well those events which were the cause of my banishment. The meeting of the Council; my report about the wonderful discovery I had made; the incredulity of the Council; my taking of that oath—

The Supreme Council, that august body of Searchers-after-the-Truth, had called a meeting of all the scientists upon the planet. Report was to be made as to what had been accomplished for the advancement of civilization in each field of research.

The gigantic hall, the Hall of the Council, was filled to overflowing. Thousands of scientists representing a vast accumulation of knowledge, occupied the countless compartments which made up the hall. They, however, were unimportant; only upon very rare occasions did they learn anything that was of real value.

The really worthwhile discoveries of the age had been made by a small, insignificant group of six men who occupied one large compartment at the front of the hall. Six men, the greatest minds in all Kotar. Six men, and I was one of them!

I remember them well; even now I can see, in my mind's eye, those men of knowledge. Each was an expert in his chosen field, the accepted authority on his special branch of science.

There was Bor Akon, the historian. No important occurrence of any past age, no matter how remote, was unknown to him. Then there was Sarig Om, the astronomer, who had plumbed the depths of space with his instruments, and who knew the innermost secrets of innumerable heavenly bodies. Great was his knowledge.

I mention these two particularly because of the important part they play at a later date.

The others in the group are Dees Oeb, specialist in the study of matter; Stol Verta, lover of things mechanical and the greatest inventor in Kotar's history; Gano Tor, whose strange concoctions could well nigh bring the dead back to life; and Tuol Oro, delver into the infinitely minute. Truly a remarkable concentration of wisdom. Yet everyone in that group, and all those minor intellectuals, were failures. All were blotted out—erased, by the children of my mind, their great intellects rendered helpless. All—save one. I, Tuol, the Mighty, survive! But I digress.

On a platform raised high above our heads sat the Council. Twenty venerable men were they, the ruling body of Kotar. Each one of the Twenty, from the time of his birth, had been trained in just the correct environment, to prepare him for the position he was now holding. They were the judges, the judicial minds of our planet.

As they, the Council, had been trained, so had we, the scientists, been prepared, with the thought of our future place in life, in mind.

Bor Akon, the historian, said at one time, that in former ages there had been no such specialization, that each man and woman decided his or her field of endeavor upon reaching maturity. Utterly ridiculous! Our destinies were predetermined in our infancy by the Sub-Council of each residential district. In this way there was no neglect of one occupation and overcrowding of another. But to return to the gathering in the Council Hall—

Each individual booth was equipped with an instrument employing the mysterious "Power of the Spheres," that power which I am using in broadcasting this narrative of warning. It was with this instrument that we, the scientists, not only communicated with the Twenty, but, through the use of a large amplifying disc, made our reports audible to every man in the hall.

The members of the Council, by the way, required no such aid in making their thoughts known; through the combined power of their well trained minds, they could impress upon us their every desire. And, because they had a complete knowledge of who occupied each of those many compartments, they had no difficulty in having the scientists speak in the order that they, the Council, wished.

Suddenly, the hall became quiet; every sound was hushed. A mental command for silence had come from the Twenty. And then Stol Verta, the inventor, arose. Speaking in a dreamy monotone, he addressed the Council.

Stol's report had to do with his most recent invention, a machine which he claimed would traverse the great void between the planets. How this was to be accomplished, I do not remember. Indeed, little of what he said made an impression upon my memory. The so-called mechanical marvels of the age have little interest for me; and Stol Verta, himself, is an uninteresting individual at best.

His statements, however, seemed to meet with the approval of the Council, for they sent a thought-wave of praise and commendation broadcast through the hall. Smiling slightly, Stol seated himself.

Sarig Om was the second scientist called upon by the Twenty. As he arose to make his report, I decided to pay more attention than I had before. The science of Sarig Om was of interest to me because of the similarity it bore to my own study. His was the study of largeness unfathomable; mine, of the infinitely minute.

Sarig gave a detailed report about the various occurrences in the heavens before he reached the really important feature of his discourse. At the time I was not impressed with the importance of the statement; later I had reason to recall it.

He spoke of the coming opposition of our world with Santel, our nearest inferior planetary neighbor. He stated that the two planets would be closer to each other than they had been for almost fifty mallahs.* It would be an excellent opportunity, he informed us, for us to take steps toward establishing communication with the Santellians. His report also was approved by the Council.

As Sarig seated himself, I felt a curious tingling at the base of my brain. Then a strangely silent voice in my mind bade me rise. It was the command. I rose to my feet, swept the hall with my eyes, and then faced the Twenty. A command came for me to proceed with my report. After a moment's pause, I began.

"To the Supreme Council, the judicial body of Kotar, I, Tuol Oro, delver into the infinitely minute, make report." This was the customary beginning, and each scientist used it, with variations, of course. I continued:

"My labors of the past mallah, Venerable Twenty, have not been fruitless; indeed, it was my great fortune to make a discovery that is unequalled in the history of microscopy.

"The Council is doubtless aware of the construction of the atom and its marked similarity to the solar system,

*We have no possible way of determining what the Kotarian words for periods of time would mean in English. From the action of the narrative, however, we can be fairly certain that the Mallah is equivalent to our year, the Stallo, to our month, the Stal to our week, and the Tron to our minute. Tuol does not mention anything equal to our day, hour, or second, although it is probable that other time divisions than the former ones exist.

—L.A.E.

with its central body, the sun, or in the atom, the nucleus, and its revolving satellites—planets or planetary electrons. The conception of the atom, of course, is not, or I should say, was not accepted as fact, but was thought to be only a plausible theory.

"Five stallos ago, working on a principle different than any ever used before, I constructed a microscope so powerful that it enabled me to see the component parts of an atom. The planetary electrons, themselves, were invisible because of the great speed with which they revolved; but the protons could clearly be seen as rapidly rotating, faintly glowing spheres.

"Very naturally, I was elated with my invention and discovery; still, I wasn't satisfied. I felt that I had only begun, and that the possibilities brought into being by my discovery were practically limitless. So, without delay, I began constructing a microscope far more powerful and efficient than my first instrument. After four stallos of intense effort, I succeeded.

"This latter instrument surpassed all my expectations; with it I discovered something so amazing and incredible that I had difficulty in believing the testimony of my eyes.

"When the microscope was complete to the last minute detail, I trained the lenses upon a particle of sodium. My heart beat more rapidly as I peered into the eyepiece for the first time. What might be revealed to my gaze? A host of impossible conjectures flashed through my mind, yet not in my wildest imaginings did I conceive of such a sight as met my eyes.

"I was looking into a wide, shallow valley, covered with a brilliant, vari-colored vegetation. For some moments I gazed at it unbelievingly; then the scene was gone, replaced by a rounded hilltop. Like the valley, this, too, was covered with the brilliant colorful plant life. And as I watched, the hill followed in the wake of the valley, moving slowly across the line of my vision. Another valley took the place of the hill, a valley far larger than the first.

"As I gazed at it, I became aware of a peculiar phenomenon that had escaped my notice before. The vegetation in the valley was in motion, was constantly shifting and changing position. I changed the focus of the microscope, concentrating its magnifying power on a small portion of the scene. The valley seemed to leap up toward my eyes. No longer could I see a great field of moving plant life; only three plants were now within the range of my vision.

"And what strange growths they were! Nothing like them ever existed on Kotar. In form, and size, they were alike, though each was of a different color. When I first saw them, they were small, almost perfect spheres covered with a shiny, scaly skin. As I watched them, they grew larger; indeed, their growth was so rapid that I could actually see it! As they grew, their skins became tighter and tighter, and suddenly they burst, scattering great clouds of brightly colored dust through the air. Much of the dust was blown away, but some of it settled to the ground. Where the spheres had been, were now three pools of slime; it was into this that the dust fell.

"That which followed was perhaps the most amazing thing that I saw during all my observations. Briefly, this is what occurred: the dust, evidently the plants' seeds, upon falling into the slime, sprouted, grew, and reached maturity, and a moment later, burst in turn, casting forth their seeds—all this with such rapidity that it seemed to be one continuous movement.

"In my interest in the valley and its life, I had forgotten the strangeness of the conditions under which I was viewing the land. Deciding to discover the location of this world, I began slowly decreasing the magnifying power of the microscope, focusing the instrument in such manner as to move the world further and further away. Again I saw the panoramic view of the valley and mountains. Then the scene assumed a peculiarly convex appearance. This convexity increased until, finally, all details of the view were lost, and the microscope revealed a huge globe turning slowly on its axis. As this decreased in size, and other globes made their appearance, the truth dawned upon me. I had discovered life on a proton of the nucleus of an atom of sodium!"

Thus did I end my report to the Council.

After I had finished. I remained standing, awaiting the commendation of the Twenty. But their approval was never given. Instead, two things occurred which were unprecedented in the history of Kotar. Never had one of the Twenty spoken while the Council was in session; and never had one of the six Masters been publicly condemned by the Twenty. Both occurred then.

San Nober, Head of the Council, arose, an expression of stern disapproval on his face. Then he spoke, uttering the words that spelled doom for Kotar's ruling race.

"Men of Knowledge," he said, "never in all the history of the Council have we had to deal with a problem like the present one. Always have our members spoken truth. But that is no longer so. You, Tuol Oro," he said, addressing me, "have broken all precedence. You have lied! Your report was naught but a series of falsehoods. Your statements are preposterous, ridiculous; nothing of truth is in them.

"We are taught that it is impossible for a normal individual to lie. Obviously, then, you are insane. Even though insanity is almost an unknown malady at present, you are mad. Were it not for the records of your great discoveries in the past, you would be put to death. Because of them, you shall live. But you will be an outcast from society. You may mingle with your fellows, but they will know of your infirmity. For your lies or insanity, whichever it may be, you will be an object of pity and an outcast.

"And now you must go; the Hall of the Council shall know you no more."

While San Nober was speaking, I stood like one stunned. His disapproval and condemnation were so unexpected and so unjust that I could not believe that I had heard aright. Lies! A series of falsehoods! Insane! Mad! By Sklow, mad was I? Fool and son of a fool! An object of pity, eh? An outcast! Suddenly something seemed to snap within my brain, and a red haze came before my eyes. Then all the hatred and rebellion in my being sought outlet.

What I said then, I do not know. Perhaps I acted like a man deprived of his sanity. But I was justified. Condemned, cast out, called a liar and a madman, without an opportunity to prove the truth of my statements! One thing that I said, though, I do remember. That was the oath I took ere leaving the Council Hall.

"By Sklow, by Taw, by Maca, by all the gods that ever lived, I swear that every vestige of this civilization shall be removed; that all men save Tuol Oro shall be destroyed! I swear it and it shall be so!"

Aye, and it is so! I have destroyed them all. They deserved it, every one of them. Oh, how I hate them, even though they are gone! I hate, loathe, despise them—

After taking that oath of vengeance, I left the Council Hall, followed by thousands of pairs of pitying or derisive eyes. I walked to my boat moored in the Great Waterway, seething with anger. Even then plans for revenge were forming in my mind. By the time I reached my home in the twenty-seventh division of the ninth Minor Waterway, I had decided on a definite plan. It was this plan, conceived on my homeward journey, that brought about the destruction of a world.

CHAPTER II

With as little delay as possible, I began making preparations for the carrying out of my plans, for I knew that many stallos of research would go by ere I accomplished that which I proposed doing. Indeed, the goal I had set before me seemed to be beyond the reach of human ability. I desired to increase the size of those inconceivably minute plants on the diminutive world I had discovered, until I could take them from their protonic birthplace and bring them to the surface of Kotar. With them I intended gaining my revenge.

The first two stallos of effort were fruitless. Often, during that time, I was tempted to abandon my apparently impossible project, and might have done so, had I not been spurred on by my desire for vengeance. However, I continued, and at the beginning of the third stallo I saw the first sign of reward for my tireless efforts.

From the very first, I had had one basic idea on which to work. That was this: since every particle of matter, regardless of its size, could, theoretically, at least, be divided in half forever, it certainly must be possible to reverse the process, and double the size of any particle, even of an electron or proton. Pursuing this line of reasoning, it naturally followed that eventually I would have increased the size of my proton to such an extent as to make it visible to the naked eye, and even larger. The difficulty lay in the actual accomplishment of that enlarging process. Two stallos were spent in vain conjecturing and theorizing along this line.

At the beginning of the third stallo I decided to begin working with the electrons and protons themselves. Taking a portion of chemically pure sodium from the supply I possessed, I placed a minute quantity beneath the lenses of my ultra-microscope. Then I focused the instrument so as to enable me to view the entire atom. Similar to my first observations of the sodium containing the life supporting proton, I now saw twenty-two small, dully glowing protons, and eleven, almost transparent nuclear electrons in a compact group, each rapidly rotating on its axis. About them, at various distances, revolved what seemed to be a tangled maze of gleaming cords. These, I knew, were the glowing paths of the planetary electrons, which moved at such great speed as to be invisible. As long as the atom remained in that condition, I knew that I could do nothing with it.

Consequently, I decided that, in some way, I'd have to decrease the speed of the electrons' rotation until I could observe each one individually. With this purpose in mind, I began a series of experiments. All that I did, by the way, had to be done beneath the lenses of my microscope. Thus handicapped, it seemed that I had a difficult task before me. I was aided materially, however, by a device recently invented by Stol Verta. This machine, far too complex to explain, enabled its user to focus a beam of inconceivable cold or intense heat upon a microscopically fine point. Because of an idea I had in mind, I was certain that Stol's invention would be of great value.

And so it proved to be. Use of the device revealed that heat increased the speed of the electrons, widening their orbits, and causing some of them to whirl outside the field of the microscope. Cold, on the contrary, caused the speed of the electrons' rotation to diminish. The lower the degree of heat, in simpler phrase, the more intense the cold, the slower became the motion, until at absolute zero, both protons and electrons were devoid of all movement. I had taken one big step toward my goal.

Without loss of time, I continued my research, following out a theory that had come to my mind during my first experiments. For this idea I had gone back to the time of my early training when I had been taught the rudiments of elementary chemistry. My theory involved the lack of symmetry of some atoms, sodium among them, and the mechanism of chemical action.

An atom of sodium, I had been taught, has eleven electrons, negatively charged, revolving in orbits around the nucleus. One of these electrons revolves in an orbit with a much larger axis than those of the other electrons. Because of this, it is not held very firmly by the nucleus. Further, the lack of symmetry in the atom creates unbalanced forces. Consequently, the sodium atom will have a tendency to lose this electron during the collision with other atoms, and leave the atom more symmetrical and balanced. To summarize, atoms having one or more electrons beyond what corresponds to symmetrical forms, have a tendency to give off those electrons.

Similarly, I had learned that some atoms require one or more electrons to complete a symmetrical structure. The chlorine atom is an atom of this type. It has seventeen electrons, needing only one more to make the balanced, symmetrical structure of eighteen electrons.

Consequently, when an atom of sodium is brought in contact with an atom of chlorine, the transfer of an electron from one atom to the other takes place. Both atoms pay for their newly found symmetry with the loss of neutrality. The removal of one negatively charged electron from the sodium atom leaves it with an excess of one unit of positive charge. The addition of the electron to the chlorine atom gives the latter an excess of one unit of negative charge. The two, then, being oppositively charged, join and form sodium chloride.

But sodium chloride held no interest for me; the laws of chemistry involved, alone concerned me. With these recollections of the mechanism of chemical action in mind, I felt I had something definite with which to work.

Before I could begin carrying out my idea, however, I

decided that I'd have to leave the privacy of my residence and mingle with the race I despised, long enough to secure the chlorine for my experiment. Immediately upon arriving at this conclusion, I ventured out into the street. If I had needed any additional stimulus to spur me on, I received it in the covert sneers and thinly veiled contempt which greeted me. I returned to my home a short time after securing the chlorine, in the grip of a rekindled anger.

Fully prepared, then, I set to work. First I placed a minute particule of sodium beneath the ultramicroscope's lenses, focusing them so that, as on former occasions, I could see the separate units of a complete atom. Then I put the cold projector in position, in order to be able to stop the atomic action whenever I wanted to. And finally, I liberated some of the chlorine, doing it in such a way that it completely covered the sodium. Then, through the eyepiece of the microscope, I watched the atom, waiting for the change that would take place when chemical action began.

At first glance I could detect no difference, but as I watched I saw the electron which was outside the symmetrical structure of the atom, slow down perceptibly and leave its orbit, disappearing entirely. While the atom was in this condition, deprived of one electron, I directed a beam of intense cold upon the sodium and stopped all atomic action, thus preventing the sodium from joining the chlorine. I now had a free atom of sodium with an excess of one positive charge, or one proton more than it could possibly have had in nature. I had taken a second step toward my goal.

It was with a feeling of trepidation that I approached the third part of my task; the success or failure of this phase of the experiment would decide the result of the entire project.

Leaving the sodium and microscope out of my

thoughts for the moment, I gave detailed consideration to a recent discovery of Dees Oeb. This was a new ray, the ray of the fifty-fourth octave of the electro-magnetic spectrum. This ray had a peculiar property: it caused anything upon which it was directed to increase in size. How it did this, I do not know, but the fact of its doing so remains. I proposed directing this ray upon the surplus proton in the atom beneath the microscope and increasing its size until it left the atom behind.

A short period of time spent in experimenting with a second cold projector that I possessed enabled me to adapt it to the growth ray. I was prepared to continue.

Returning to the microscope, I peered through the eyepiece, and singled out one of the protons more centrally located than the others. Focusing the projector, I directed a beam of growth ray upon that proton.

There was an immediate change in the appearance of the sphere. Its size increased perceptibly. In a short time it began crowding the other atomic bodies, moving them from their customary positions. As the proton grew in size, it became less solid, even nebulous, until, finally, when there seemed to be no more room for it to occupy, there was a sudden flash—and the atom had disappeared. In its place was a small, dully-glowing sphere, no longer nebulous in appearance, but as solid as it had ever been before. The proton had grown until it had encompassed the entire atom.

I allowed that growth to continue until the sodium had been surrounded by the sphere, now, a comparative giant. While this went on, by the way, it was necessary for me to change the focus of the microscope repeatedly, in order to watch the proton's increase in size.

Up to this time, I had had the cold directed upon the sodium to prevent it from uniting with the chlorine. This was no longer necessary, as there was no further possibility of that union taking place. So, after removing most of the chlorine, I shut off the beam of absolute zero.

I had then, as the result of my endeavors, a small, almost perfect sphere, barely visible to the naked eye. My goal was in sight! I needed only to duplicate my experiment, using the proton supporting the plant life, and vengeance would be within my reach.

Accordingly, I took from its place of safety the sodium containing the protonic world, and treated it as I had the other, centering my attention, of course, upon the proton inhabited by the rapidly moving, strangely formed vegetation. After I had increased the size of the minute sphere until it had taken up nearly all of the sodium, the thought occurred to me that I had neglected to provide a place in which to put the enlarged proton while I strove to secure some of the seed-dust from it. In a moment I had turned off the growth ray, directed the cold upon the sodium and left it to its own devices.

I had little difficulty in constructing the apparatus to hold the sphere; in a short time it was completed. It was a simple device, consisting of two tall metal uprights upon whose grooved tops rested a strong, heavy metal bar. This bar or rod turned slowly when power was applied to the small motor with which it was connected by a series of cogwheels and chains. After the machine was complete, I returned to the microscope and enlarging process.

As the proton grew and consumed the sodium of which it was a part, I added more and more of the element, until it had reached a size where there was no further need of the microscope. Taking it from beneath the instrument, I increased its size, without adding sodium to it, until it was a large, wraith-like bubble. Then, taking the crossbar from the machine I had prepared, I thrust it through the center of the sphere. There was a flash—and the former proton had a metal axis on which to revolve. After returning the rod to its place in the device, I added sodium to the sphere until it had again become solid. I continued the enlarging as long as space remained on the rod, then stopped.

I had taken the third step toward my goal.

I had in my laboratory at that time, a great, box-like room, the walls, floor and ceiling of which were glass. A number of stallos before, I had had it built with the intention of using it as a storage room for numerous bacteria and germ cultures which I had intended studying. Through my interest in my new ultra-microscope, the room had not been used. I was glad of it. Because of the danger involved in the next part of my project, I decided to make use of that room, inasmuch as I could hermetically seal it if that became necessary.

After removing the few articles that had somehow found their way into the big glass box, I covered the floor with a heavy layer of soil. Then, placing rollers beneath the device which held the giant proton, I moved the machine into the room. Directly opposite the sphere I placed a projector with which to throw a fan-shaped flood of cold upon it, and beside it, the growth apparatus. After focusing the growth ray projector so that only a small part of the proton's surface would be affected, I applied power to both machines, as well as to the apparatus holding the proton, and hastily left the room, closing and locking the door behind me.

Looking through the glass wall, I saw that the action of the growth ray must have been instantaneous. Eight different-colored, flesh-like plants were rising from the proton. They were ugly, shapeless masses of cells whose very existence was unnatural. While I watched, they grew from small, insignificant organisms to great, repulsive vegetable monstrosities. As they grew, their skins became increasingly tighter, until, when they had reached the size of the world from which they sprang, they burst, casting their seed-dust to all parts of the room.

The dust, as it settled, grew in turn, with the result that in a short time, the floor of the room was covered with an ever increasing mass of slime in which grew a repulsive, waving, constantly changing heap of plants. At frequent intervals, the growth ray added other plants, vari-colored and strangely formed, to those upon the floor.

Every metal device in the room became covered with a misty, gray film. The glass walls grew clouded, rendering my view of the room's contents blurred and indistinct. When the seed-dust settled upon this film, it took root and grew. In a very few moments, the machines had become grotesque, vegetable caricatures of their former selves.

The plants continued their growth, one layer of either growing or decaying organisms upon another, until the mass had reached a depth of one quarter the height of a man; then my view of the room's interior was shut off. I had no means of determining how long that growth continued, but that was of little consequence.

Another thing remained for me to do before I liberated my servants upon the world to do my bidding. I had yet to learn just what would control the monstrous plants, and what steps I would have to take for my own protection.

In this I encountered no difficulty; the application of heat that was just beyond the limits of human endurance caused the growths to shrivel up, and fall, shrunken, shapeless masses, into the fetid slime beneath them. When the heat was directed against the glass, by the way, that slime began to steam, and a foul, nauseating odor in some way escaped from the glass cube. Heat, then, I decided, was obviously the agency with which to destroy them.

And heat, I felt sure, would protect me from the plants.

I'd have men build numerous wide-mouthed nozzles, and have them placed at carefully selected positions on the walls and roof of the outside of my home. Steam pipes connected with these nozzles would cover the building with a protective blanket of heat.

Because of this one rather large remaining task, and several minor ones, and the time necessary for their accomplishment, I decided that I had better conceal the room from the prying eyes of inquisitive neighbors or chance callers, until I was ready to make use of its contents. I had just arrived at this conclusion, when a persistent buzzing in the vicinity of the door told of visitors seeking entrance. Turning to a small screen in the corner of the laboratory, I saw thereon the familiar faces of Bor Akon and Sarig Om.

As I moved toward the door to let them in, I realized in a flash that their coming was a gift of Sklow. They were welcome—how very welcome, they'd never know. I opened the door and bade them enter.

CHAPTER III

When the two faced me in the reception room, I could see in their glances the uncertainty they felt. They were in doubt as to the treatment they would receive at my hands. I smiled at them reassuringly, for it did not suit my purpose to arouse distrust in their minds.

The smile evidently renewed their confidence, for Bor Akon, acting as spokesman, cleared his throat and addressed me.

"Brother Tuol," he began—we were all brothers in conversation, "Sarig and I have taken it upon ourselves to investigate your report to the Council. We believe that you have been treated unjustly. Unquestionably, you were either sick or laboring under some great mental weight when you made those ridiculous statements in the Council Hall.

"We, Sarig and I, thought that we'd attempt to persuade you to take steps towards regaining your former position in the scientific world."

So that was their attitude! Perhaps I was sick, or temporarily deranged! Well, I thought it wouldn't take me long to correct that erroneous idea. Repressing my natural anger, lest it be betrayed through my voice, I replied in studiously careless tones.

"Brother Bor, I assure you that you are mistaken. All that I said to the Twenty was absolutely true. I can't help feeling that I have been shabbily treated. Had I been given a fair opportunity, I would have been able to prove my claims so absolutely, that even the most skeptical would have been convinced. As for my trying to regain my former position, no! They have made me an outcast; I am satisfied.

"Now that you are here, I'll show you that proof, the microscope itself. If you will excuse me—" They acquiesced, politely, and I left them seated there while I headed toward the laboratory.

Upon arriving there I drew a large curtain around the glass room, in order to conceal it from my visitors' eyes. Then I returned to the reception room and led my guests back to that part of the laboratory which held the microscope.

As their eyes fell upon the intricate mechanism, with its multitude of lenses and powerful lights, they displayed a reluctant, though rather skeptical interest. Sarig Om turned to me with a question in his eyes. I answered his unspoken query with:

"There would be no use in explaining its construction or means of magnification to you, inasmuch as neither of you could possibly understand. However, there is nothing to prevent you from observing the wonders that may be seen through it. Which of you will be the first to gaze upon an electron?"

As I placed a particle of matter beneath the lenses, and focused the microscope, Sarig Om expressed his willingness to be first. "I've been looking through lenses all my adult life," he said, "and since one of us must be first, it may as well be I."

While the two alternately gazed through the microscope, crying out in wonder at each new marvel, I excused myself and left the room.

I returned, some moments later, with some articles of food that I had treated with a sleep-inducing drug. As I entered, Sarig Om looked up, an expression of incredulity on his face.

"Brother Tuol," he exclaimed, "we have discovered life on a proton! It's unbelievable!"

"Come, come," I replied. "You've no cause for such great excitement. I have something far more amazing than that to show you. After we have eaten this food, I'll let you see something that is really astounding."

At my invitation, then, my guests seated themselves, and with poorly concealed impatience, ate the food I placed before them. A few moments after they had swallowed the drugged morsels, I saw their eyelids droop. Valiantly they fought the drowsiness that had settled upon them, but the drug was stronger than they and in a moment more they slept.

Securing strong cords, I bound them tightly, and carried them into the room which held the glass box. I placed them against the wall of the room in such a position as to enable them to have an unobstructed view of one of the box's sides, when they awakened.

I waited impatiently for the two scientists to recover from their involuntary slumbers; I was anxious to carry out the experiment I had in mind. At last they stirred, and in a short time were fully conscious.

Any self-possession that they had had, had gone from them. They looked at me with fear-filled eyes. In all probability, they thought they were at the mercy of a madman. While I stood there, waiting for any remaining effects of the drug to pass, Bor Akon, in an obvious attempt to bolster his own courage, and perhaps intimidate me, addressed me.

"Tuol, you madman," he exclaimed, "cut these bonds and set us free immediately, or I'll see that you receive the punishment you deserve. You fool! What can you expect to gain by this? And what possible purpose can you have in mind, anyway? Liberate us now, or I'll inform the Council of your insane actions!"

I laughed, I couldn't help it; it was funny. The thought of that brainless fool, bound and helpless as he was, threatening me, bordered on the ridiculous. But my mirth was short-lived; suddenly it turned to anger. These two men were part of the race that had made me an outcast. A fool and a madman, was I?

"Silence!" I roared, as Sarig Om opened his mouth to speak. "Who are you to threaten me? Inform the Council, indeed! Idiots! You'll do just as I bid, and that only.

"What do I expect to gain; what purpose do I have in mind? I'll tell you. When the Council banished me, I swore that I would destroy every vestige of this race of failures, the race of man. I now have the instrument with which to bring about that destruction. For three long stallos I've labored tirelessly, striving to achieve the impossible, and I've succeeded!"

While talking, I had moved over toward the glass room. I reached up then, and pulled the curtains aside. Nothing could be seen through the glass, save a grayish-white film on its inside surface, and a vague suggestion of a ceaseless movement within.

"In that glass cube," I continued, "lies the result of my efforts. You remember, of course, that I told the Council about the rapidly growing plant life I had discovered on a proton. Within that room is the proton itself, enormously increased in size. And with it, surrounding it, and I suppose, destroying it, are innumerable plants growing with an insane speed. Plants, they are, that I took from the proton's surface. They grow and grow, one upon another, finding root on any surface. I'll show you how they grow; it's only proper that you know, for you, too, Bor and Sarig, have a part in my plan. It is because of that part which you are to play, that I have bound you."

After testing their bonds, and finding them secure, I turned my back upon the two, closing my ears to their pleas for freedom, and directed a beam of heat upon the door of the glass room. Rapidly the film and the plants growing on the door disappeared, sinking to the floor. Further and further into the noisome, steaming mass the heat cut its way, clearing an ever increasing space. Finally, when I had reduced about half of the room's contents to slime I shut off the heat ray, and admonished the two to pay particular attention.

The plants recovered from the effects of the heat with great rapidity. In a few moments, a red triangular head on a long, slender stem, thrust itself up from the mass, and burst, casting its seed-dust into the air. The astonished eyes of Bor Akon and Sarig Om saw the dust settle into the slime, spring up, grow to maturity, burst in turn, and die, all in a few moments of time. It was not long before the walls had again assumed their white, translucent covering, and our view was again cut off.

A heavy silence followed this, to them, amazing spectacle. Impatiently I broke that silence.

"Well, how did you enjoy the entertainment?" I asked. "Interesting, wasn't it? There is something still more interesting to follow, but I'll be the only one to see that.

"But consider those plants. Imagine what will happen

when I free my pets upon Kotar. Imagine the effects of a little cloud of seed-dust settling upon the floor of a boat in one of the great waterways. Curious people gather around, attracted by the peculiar growths. In a moment they are enveloped by a cloud of dust that touches them, and grows, drawing life from their flesh. Imagine a man breathing some of that dust?

"Then picture a strong wind blowing the dust to all parts of the world. News of the menace will cause men to flee. Some will lose their lives in the panic that will ensue. Others, seeking to escape, will perhaps hide in deep pits or cellars. The plants will fill the cracks and crevices of their sanctuaries, and eventually they will die of suffocation.

"Visualize the world after the menace has been at work for a stal. By that time the solid portion of Kotar's surface will have become a flowing, ever changing mass of plant life. The air will be filled with dense clouds of seed-dust of every possible hue. The boats on the waterways will be covered by the plants. Drifting, those boats will force their way through a heavy, viscous scum which will probably cover the water. Plants may be growing in that scum, which, by the way, will be the residue resulting from the decay of the other plants on the shore. Not a sound will break the death-like silence; there will be no more idle chattering coming from the lips of fools. The world will have been cleansed of their presence; all will have been destroyed. All—save one, Tuol Oro. A pretty picture, aye?"

Throughout this rather lengthy recital, both scientists remained motionless, as though frozen, an expression of growing horror and fascination on the face of each. When I ceased talking, Sarig Om attempted to speak, but the words died in his throat; he was dumb with fear. Bor Akon continued to stare fixedly into my face.

Suddenly a thought occurred to me.

"By the way," I exclaimed, "I told you that you, too, have a part in my plans. I've neglected to tell you what that part is, so I'll tell you now. I am not quite certain that those plants will act in just the way that I desire. Perhaps my efforts have been wasted. To avoid taking any chances of my plans going awry, I intend putting you in the glass room, and watching the effects of the plants upon you."

The semi-stupor into which the two had fallen fell from them like a cloak. Scream after scream burst from Bor Akon's lips. Roughly I clapped my hand over his mouth, threatening to gag him if he started screaming again. When I withdrew my hand, he began mumbling and sobbing piteously. His mind had snapped. Fear had dethroned his reason.

Sarig Om was made of sterner stuff. He cursed me in the name of every god that I knew of, and called me everything vile that entered his mind. I was surprised at his fluency.

When his tirade ceased, I picked him up and carried him, squirming and twisting, over to the glass cube. Depositing him on the floor beside the door, I directed the heat against the glass another time. After burning away about half of the plants I opened the door and thrust Sarig in. Hastily, then, I closed and locked it, and directed the heat all around the edge of the door, in order to destroy any seed-dust that might have escaped.

Then I turned my attention to the figure in the room. Sarig, seated in a pool of slime, was straining with all his strength at the cords that bound his hands. Suddenly as one of the plants burst above him, he made a supreme effort, and the cords broke.

Slowly the dust settled upon him. As it touched his skin, sending tiny rootlets through the pores, into his flesh, and drawing life from his living body, he gave utterance to one piercing shriek.

Strangely formed plants sprang from all parts of Sarig Om's body then. With mad, frenzied haste, the scientist tore them from him, leaving ugly, bloody wounds where the growths had been. But only for a moment was he able to struggle with his vegetable destroyers; several plants, having reached maturity upon him, burst simultaneously, enveloping him in a thick cloud of dust.

He seemed to grow larger before my eyes. Countless plants grew upon him, swelling him to three times his normal size. Grew—and decayed. The figure remained thus for only a moment, then it collapsed and lost itself in the slime and plants upon the floor.

For a fleeting second my resolution to destroy the race was shaken—but only for a second. Although the weapon I possessed was terrible, and the death it meted out horrible, it wasn't too severe for the fools that ruled over Kotar. They deserved to be obliterated, and I was using the only means of destruction at my command.

I turned to Bor Akon. When last I had noticed him, he had been sobbing and quivering like a frightened infant. Now, he was lying on the floor, unconscious. The sight of Sarig Om's death had been too much for his weakened mind; he had fainted.

I would have spared Bor, then, to wait and be destroyed with his fellows, had it not been for the fact that he was aware of my plans. As it was, he knew too much for my safety; he had to be removed.

Again I burned the plants away; then I thrust the unconscious scientist through the doorway. After all, he was more fortunate than the others, for his death was painless; he never recovered consciousness.

I destroyed all evidence that pointed to the fact that the two had visited me. I took no chances of being implicated if their disappearance was investigated. Any interference at this time would have been fatal to my plans.

But there was no investigation; in all probability, Sarig and Bor had kept their visit secret, for fear of arousing the displeasure of the Council. After about a stal of waiting, I decided that it was safe for me to follow out the rest of my program. I had yet to prepare for my defense, secure a machine to purify the air, and lay in a supply of food tablets, and I would be ready.

Without delay, then, I employed men to make the large, fan-shaped steam nozzles, and fasten them where I directed on the walls and roof of my home. Other men I engaged to cover the building with a network of pipes to carry the steam to the nozzles. This latter crew built the tank that was to form the steam. The water for this, by the way, came through underground pipes from the waterway that flowed before my home. Still others, I hired to fill up every crack and crevice that they could find in the building. In every possible way, I fortified myself against any attacks that the plants might make upon me.

When authorities of the city questioned me about the pipes and nozzles, I told them that they were part of a new device for protection against fire. They believed me, thinking, in all probability, that it was only a fancy of my "disordered" mind. They left me to myself after that; I was glad of it.

During the few trons that preceded the time of my destruction of mankind, I had the oxygen machine installed and operating, and had food tablets enough stored in my bins to last me the rest of my life, if necessary. Likewise, I purchased enough fuel to keep my furnace going full blast for ten mallahs, at the very least.

When darkness fell upon the old, unchanged world of man for the last time, and I retired, I enjoyed the first real rest that had been mine since my banishment. No disturbing spectre of hate or vengeance marred my slumbers, for on the morrow my ultimate goal would be reached.

CHAPTER IV

The six Masters of Science had privileges that were not given to any other individuals on Kotar. One of these was the right to employ the Power of the Spheres in broadcasting on any wavelength we desired. That is, we could command any broadcast station to terminate its program and leave the air, so that we could use its wavelength. Through negligence on the part of the Council, this privilege had not been taken from me.

Shortly after I awakened from my sleep, greatly refreshed, by the way, I made use of that privilege, commanding the International News to cease broadcasting. After the announcer had stated that his station was cutting short its program at the command of one of the Masters, and that the program would continue after the Master had finished talking, his station grew silent.

I closed the switch then, and addressed my unseen audience.

"People of Kotar," I said, "I, Tuol Oro, outcast Master of Science, am taking this opportunity to tell you, in these few moments that will be spared to me ere the Council interferes, some facts about my banishment that have been carefully concealed by those in authority.

"Have you been informed that I was condemned without a trial? That I was given no opportunity to prove my claims? That, just because San Nober could not see the truth of my report, I was called mad, and that, without test being given to my mind? Of course you haven't! All that has been kept secret.

"Immediately after the ringing of the Terai bell, I will prove to those who gather before my home that all that I said in the Council Hall was true, and that San Nober himself should be the one to be condemned, because of his total lack of judgment. If that incompetent individual is listening, I give him a special invitation to be there. He—" There was a sharp, sudden explosion and a blinding flash in the broadcasting apparatus, and my connections with the outside world were broken.

I heard words issuing from the receiving device in another corner of the room. It was San Nober, using the so-called Universal wavelength of the Council, the wavelength that covered every station from the lowest to the highest, thus rendering the speaker's voice audible to every listener on the planet. San's heavy, bass voice quivered with anger.

"Tuol Oro," he growled, "you are a fool. And for your folly you shall die. You will be permitted to offer any proof that you possess, at the time you have set, so that no one may say that there has been a miscarriage of justice.

"I accept your invitation: I'll be there."

With a feeling of satisfaction, I shut off the machine. San Nober would be there! That was what I wanted. What mattered is that he would probably be accompanied by a group of his followers, whose purpose it would be to arrest me? They would be powerless to harm me, for I possessed a weapon more terrible than anything they had ever conceived of.

I occupied myself during the time that I had to wait, with a final survey of all my protective devices. I made sure that everything was in readiness for the great climax. Only the turn of a valve was needed to cover my home with a blanket of steam. A little pressure upon a button would start the oxygen machine. An automatic feeding device would add fuel to that in the furnace whenever it was needed. As far as I could see, there was nothing else to be done along the line of self-protection.

There was one thing, though, that I had not taken into consideration. How was I to free the plants without endangering myself? After some thought I decided upon a method. In a short time I constructed a small, glass box with a tightly fitting lid, which automatically closed at any time I signified on the timeclock within the box.

I burned the plants away again, and set the finished box inside the glass room with the lid timed to close in three trons. Impatiently I waited for the time to go by, dividing my attention between the plants and the clock on a nearby wall.

At last, when the three trons had passed, I managed, by careful application of the heat, to remove the box from the room, filled with the plants, seed-dust, and slime.

With great care, then, I went over all the space on which seed-dust might have found lodgement, with a beam of heat. After I was certain that there was no further possibility of any dust having escaped destruction, I carried the glass box to a window overlooking the Waterway, and there took up my vigil. The time for revenge was almost at hand.

The street below me was filled with a noisy throng of people. Men, women, and children had gathered, for a public statement by one of the Six Masters was far from being commonplace, and was worthy of more than passing notice. Several men in the crowd I recognized as minor scientists who had been in the Council Hall on the day I was banished.

The Waterway was even more crowded than the street. Indeed, the boats were so close to each other that very little water could be seen. And every boat was loaded to capacity with passengers.

Overhead I could hear the low, steady hum of many flying machines. Looking up, I saw small, one-man planes darting here and there, aimlessly. Great helicopters with whirling propellers and whirring wings were suspended above, hanging stationary in mid-air. All were low enough for their passengers to hear anything I had to say.

Suddenly my attention was drawn from the air vehicles by a commotion below. I looked down. In some way, how, I do not know, the boats had been cleared away to form a lane which led directly to the front of my home. At the further end of the lane, I saw the graceful lines of San Nober's stately bark. Its silver trimmings flashed in the sunlight.

As it drew closer, enabling me to distinguish faces, I saw that every member of the member of the Council was there, and that the remaining three Masters were likewise on board. In addition, the International Peace Guard had six representatives present. They, I knew, were there for the purpose of arresting me after I had had my say. But they meant nothing to me.

As the Council boat touched the side of the Waterway's banks, I heard a single, deep toned bell note, the Terai bell. The time I had set had come! I flung open the window.

At my appearance, the voice of the throng was stilled. The sound of motors in the air above became less noticeable, as the pilots applied their silencers. And then I spoke.

I described in detail all that had taken place in the Council Hall, I told them of the great discovery I had made, laying stress on the minute plants and their amazingly rapid growth. I spoke of my banishment, and of the oath I had taken—and there I stopped. The bellowing voice of San Nober had interrupted me.

"Have done with this nonsense!" he exclaimed. "This farce must stop! How can your grievances affect these people? You can't expect to gain anything by this additional publicity. You must be mad to expect any benefit to come to you for this.

"If you have any proof to offer, produce it. Stol Verta will begin counting, and if you haven't partially proven your claims be the time he reaches fifty, your liberty will end. You will not be given another opportunity to deceive your fellow men."

"Begin counting, Stol."

While the inventor's hand slowly, mechanically rose and fell, I gave my last message to the world.

"People of Kotar," I said solemnly, "your span of life is almost ended. When San interrupted me, I was about to tell you that the world is doomed, that my oath will be carried out. You are a race of fools, unworthy of the responsibility that has been given you. You are not fitted for the task of controlling a planet's life, so you cannot survive. You—"

I went no further. No one would have heard me if I had. The momentary daze which had held the crowd speechless, vanished. Hoots and jeers, and cries of mingled anger and mirth came from the throng.

Stol Verta stopped counting. San Nober, with a word to his colleagues, stepped from his boat, and followed by the Guards and Masters, began forcing his way through the crowd. A path opened as though by magic, and the throng grew quiet.

I took advantage of that silence; raising the glass box high above my head, I cried, "This is my proof," and hurled it at the feet of San Nober. Then I banged the window shut, locked it, and turned the valve which started the steam.

San fell back, startled, when the box crashed before him. Then he stared in fascination at the little heap of shattered glass and pulpy matter that lay at his feet. It was growing, and he could see the growth! He leaned forward to observe the strange organisms more carefully—and a plant burst.

A small cloud of dust arose into the air and settled

upon San's head and shoulders. For a moment he beat at the vegetation that sprang from his flesh, his arms waving futilely, helplessly; then he fell to the pavement.

Those who saw his death, shrank back, while those further away strove to get closer. But when the seed-dust began dropping upon them, only one impulse actuated them, and that was to escape.

Escape, however, was impossible now; they had delayed too long. Where one plant had been, had grown a thousand; the thousand had become a million; and every moment more and more seed-dust was being cast into the air. In little more time than is required for the telling, no human life was left where the crowd had been.

At the very beginning of the destruction, there had been wrecks on the Waterway, caused by boats crashing into each other when their pilots had become heaps of plants and slime. Similarly, there had been accidents in the air, planes darting around erratically, pilotless, with propellers clogged by slime and plants, either crashing into each other, or falling to the ground. But that was all over in a short time.

Some planes and boats had made good their escape, and had wasted no time, I was sure, but rather made haste to tell the world of the horror that menaced civilization. This caused me no concern, however, for I knew that the plants were too firmly established to be affected by anything the puny world of man might do. Kotar's ruling race was unquestionably doomed.

Soon after the last man in sight had been destroyed, and the last plane had disappeared, I turned away from the window. I had taken my revenge; I was satisfied. I had seen San Nober die a horrible death. Before my eyes the members of the Council had been destroyed. And I was the only survivor of the six Masters of Science; they had scorned me, but they had felt the might of my hand.

While walking across the room with the intention of

starting the oxygen machine, I spied the broadcasting apparatus. A thought occurred to me. Why not tell the Universe of the things I had done? Why not warn them, so that they, if ever similar circumstances arose, would not make the mistake that the people of Kotar had made. I had one of the most powerful broadcasting machines on Kotar, and it would be a simple matter to increase that power so that my message would travel to the farthest corner of the Universe. I made a decision: I'd tell the story.

And then I remembered Sarig Om's report to the Council. He had said that Santel would be closer to Kotar on a certain date than it had been for many mallahs. If there were intelligent, reasoning beings on Santel—Sarig had always maintained that there were—they, at least, might be able to hear my warning. At any rate, I decided to wait for that date and broadcast my story then.

I spent the interim between the time I made my decision, and the time of opposition, in studying the plants I could see from my window, enjoying long periods of interesting observation, in spite of the steam that persisted in cutting off my view. I also spent some time in preparing notes for my story, for I wanted nothing to be left from the narrative.

Finally, after stals of waiting, the time of opposition has arrived. Now, as I am talking, Santel should be at its closest proximity to Kotar.

My story is almost ended. From my place here before the broadcasting apparatus, I can look out through the window. A vast sea of amazingly brilliant plants meets my eye. There are plants that are thick and round, plants tall and angular, plants of every conceivable shape and color. It is a scene of dazzling brilliancy, a scene that has an unnatural, alien beauty. And the impossible speed of the plants' development does much toward creating that sense of the unreal, the fantastic.

There is no strife or discord, no petty quarreling; the plants seem to be the embodiment of unity. A vast, all-engulfing silence has superseded the noise and bustle of man's civilization. The only sound that breaks the silence is the hiss of escaping steam. That steam, to me, is symbolic of the civilization that has gone, existing for a moment, noisy and purposeless, then vanishing. Of the two forms of life, mankind and the plants, the latter is by far the better.

Still, it is only proper that I, the creator of this vegetable world, should be the ruler thereof. Consequently, in a short time, I shall attempt to gain complete control of those plants, and be supreme ruler over all. I have a plan—

Good Maca! What was that! One of the walls of the glass room has fallen out! The plants are escaping! The heat projector! MACA! OH—

Tuol Oro's tale ended in a shrill scream of horror and pain, a scream that was cut short abruptly, and ended in a strangely muffled sob. One can picture with some degree of accuracy the scene within his room. In some way, the glass square that had held the original plants had collapsed, letting the deadly organisms escape.

The resulting death of the mad scientist can well be imagined.

And on Kotar, or Mars, if it is the red planet, a species of fungus, growing with incredible rapidity, holds uncontested sway.

G. Barr

THE COMING OF THE ICE

by G. Peyton Wertenbaker

It is strange to be alone, and so cold. To be the last man on earth . . .

The snow drives silently about me, ceaselessly, drearily. And I am isolated in this tiny white, indistinguishable corner of a blurred world, surely the loneliest creature in the universe. How many thousands of years is it since I last knew the true companionship? For a long time I have been lonely, but there *were* people, creatures of flesh and blood. Now they are gone. Now I have not even the stars to keep me company, for they are all lost in an infinity of snow and twilight here below.

If only I could know how long it has been since first I was imprisoned upon the earth. It cannot matter now. And yet some vague dissatisfaction, some faint instinct, asks over and over in my throbbing ears: What year? What year?

It was in the year 1930 that the great thing began in my life. There was then a very great man who performed operations on his fellows to compose their vitals—we called such men surgeons. John Granden wore the title "Sir" before his name, in indication of nobility of birth according to the prevailing standards in England. But surgery was only a hobby of Sir John's, if I must be precise, for, while he had achieved an enormous reputation as a surgeon, he always felt that his real work lay in the experimental end of his profession. He was, in a way, a dreamer, but a dreamer who could make his dreams come true.

I was a very close friend of Sir John's. In fact, we

shared the same apartment in London. I have never forgotten that day when he first mentioned to me his momentous discovery. I had just come in from a long sleighride in the country with Alice, and I was seated drowsily in the window-seat, writing idly in my mind a description of the wind and the snow and the gray twilight of the evening. It is strange, is it not, that my tale should begin and end with the snow and the twilight.

Sir John opened suddenly a door at one end of the room and came hurrying across to another door. He looked at me, grinning rather like a triumphant maniac.

"It's coming!" he cried, without pausing. "I've almost got it!" I smiled at him: he looked very ludicrous at that moment.

"What have you got?" I asked.

"Good Lord, man, the Secret—the Secret!" And then he was gone again, the door closing upon his victorious cry, "The Secret!"

I was, of course, amused. But I was also very much interested. I knew Sir John well enough to realize that, however amazing his appearance might be, there would be nothing absurd about his "Secret"—whatever it was. But it was useless to speculate. I could only hope for enlightenment at dinner. So I immersed myself in one of the surgeon's volumes from his fine Library of Imagination, and waited.

I think the book was one of Mr. H.G. Wells's, probably "The Sleeper Awakes," or some other of his brilliant fantasies and predictions, for I was in a mood conducive to belief in almost anything when, later, we sat down together across the table. I only wish I could give some idea of the atmosphere that permeated our apartments, the reality it lent to whatever was vast and amazing and strange. You could then, whoever you are, understand a little of the ease with which I accepted Sir John's new discovery.

He began to explain it to me at once, as though he could keep it to himself no longer.

"Did you think I had gone mad, Dennell?" he asked. "I quite wonder that I haven't. Why, I have been studying for many years—for most of my life—on this problem. And, suddenly, I have solved it! Or, rather, I am afraid I have solved another one much greater."

"Tell me about it, but for God's sake don't be technical."

"Right," he said. Then he paused. "Dennell, it's *magnificent*! It will change everything that is in the world." His eyes held mine suddenly with the fatality of a hypnotist's. "Dennell, it is the secret of Eternal Life," he said.

"Good Lord, Sir John!" I cried, half inclined to laugh.

"I mean it," he said. "You know I have spent most of my life studying the processes of birth, trying to find out precisely what went on in the whole history of conception."

"You have found out?"

"No, that is just what amuses me. I have discovered something else without knowing yet what causes either process.

"I don't want to be technical, and I know very little of what actually takes place myself. But I can try to give you some idea of it."

It is thousands, perhaps millions of years since Sir John explained to me. What little I understood at the time I may have forgotten, yet I try to reproduce what I can of his theory.

"In my study of the processes of birth," he began, "I discovered the rudiments of an action which takes place in the bodies of both men and women. There are certain properties in the foods we eat that remain in the body for the reproduction of life, two distinct Essences, so to speak, of which one is retained by the woman, another by the man. It is the union of these two properties that, of course, creates the child.

"Now, I made a slight mistake one day in experimenting with a guinea pig, and I rearranged certain organs which I need not describe so that I thought I had completely messed up the poor creature's abdomen. It lived, however, and I laid it aside. It was some years later that I happened to notice it again. It had not given birth to any young, but I was amazed to note that it had apparently grown no older: it seemed precisely in the same state of growth in which I had left it.

"From that I built up. I re-examined the guinea pig, and observed it carefully. I need not detail my studies. But in the end I found that my 'mistake' had in reality been a momentous discovery. I found that I had only to close certain organs, to rearrange certain ducts, and to open certain dormant organs, and, *mirabile dictu,* the whole process of reproduction was changed.

"You have heard, of course, that our bodies are continually changing, hour by hour, minute by minute, so that every few years we have literally been reborn. Some such principle as this seems to operate in reproduction, except that, instead of the old body being replaced by the new, and in its form, approximately, the new body is created apart from it. It is the creation of children that causes us to die, it would seem, because if this activity is, so to speak, damned up or turned aside into new channels, the reproduction operates on the old body, renewing it continually. It is very obscure and very absurd, is it not? But the most absurd part of it is that it is true. Whatever the true explanation may be, the fact remains that the operation can be done, that it actually prolongs life indefinitely, and that I alone know the secret."

Sir John told me a very great deal more, but, after all, I think it amounted to little more than this. It would be impossible for me to express the great hold his discovery took upon my mind the moment he recounted it. From the very first, under the spell of his personality, I believed, and I knew he was speaking the truth. And it opened up for me new vistas. I began to see myself become suddenly eternal, never again to know the fear of death. I could see myself storing up, century after century, an amplitude of wisdom and experience that would make me truly a god.

"Sir John!" I cried, long before he had finished. "You must perform that operation on me!"

"But, Dennell, you are too hasty. You must not put yourself so rashly into my hands."

"You have perfected the operation, haven't you?"

"That is true," he said.

"You must try it on somebody, must you not?"

"Yes, of course. And yet—somehow, Dennell, I am afraid. I cannot help feeling that man is not prepared for such a vast thing. There are sacrifices. One must give up love and all sensual pleasure. This operation not only takes away the mere fact of reproduction, but it deprives one of all things that go with sex, all love, all sense of beauty, all feeling for poetry and the arts. It leaves only the few emotions, selfish emotions, that are necessary to self-preservation. Do you not see? One becomes an intellect, nothing more—a cold apotheosis of reason. And I, for one, cannot face such a thing calmly."

"But, Sir John, like many fears, it is largely horrible in the foresight. After you have changed your nature you cannot regret it. What you are would be so horrible an idea to you afterwards as the thought of what you will be seems now."

"True, true. I know it. But it is hard to face, nevertheless."

"I am not afraid to face it."

"You do not understand it, Dennell, I am afraid. And I wonder whether you or I or any of us on this earth are ready for such a step. After all, to make a race deathless, one should be sure it is a perfect race."

"Sir John," I said, "it is not you who have to face this, nor any one else in the world till you are ready. But I am firmly resolved, and I demand it of you as my friend."

Well, we argued much further, but in the end I won. Sir John promised to perform the operation three days later.

. . . But do you perceive now what I had forgotten during all that discussion, the one thing I had thought I could never forget so long as I lived, not even for an instant? It was my love for Alice—I had forgotten that!

I cannot write here all the infinity of emotions I experienced later, when, with Alice in my arms, it suddenly came upon me what I had done. Ages ago—I have forgotten now to feel. I could name a thousand feelings I used to have, but I can no longer understand them. For only the heart can understand the heart, and the intellect only the intellect.

With Alice in my arms, I told the whole story. It was she who, with her quick instinct, grasped what I had never noticed.

"But, Carl!" she cried. "Don't you see?—It will mean that we can never be married!" And, for the first time, I understood. If only I could recapture some conception of that love! I have always known, since the last shred of comprehension slipped from me, that I lost something very wonderful when I lost love. But what does it matter? I lost Alice too, and I could not have known love again without her.

We were very sad and very tragic that night. For hours and hours we argued the question over. But I felt somewhat that I was inextricably caught in my fate, that I could not retreat now from my resolve. I was, perhaps, very school-boyish, but I felt that it would be cowardice to back out now. But it was Alice again who perceived a final aspect of the matter.

"Carl," she said to me, her lips very close to mine, "it need not come between our love. After all, ours would be a poor sort of love if it were not more of the mind than of the flesh. We shall remain lovers, but we shall forget mere carnal desire. I shall submit to that operation too!"

And I could not shake her from her resolve. I would speak of danger that I could not let her face. But after the fashion of women, she disarmed me with the accusation that I did not love her, that I did not want her love, that I was trying to escape from love. What answer had I for that, but that I loved her and would do anything in the world not to lose her?

I have wondered sometimes since whether we might have known the love of the mind. Is love something entirely of the flesh, something created by an ironic God merely to propagate His race? Or can there be love without emotion, love without passion—love between two cold intellects? I do not know. I did not ask then. I accepted anything that would make our way more easy.

There is no need to draw out the tale. Already my hand wavers, and my time grows short. Soon there will be no more of me, no more of my tale—no more of Mankind. There will be only the snow, and the ice, and the cold . . .

Three days later I entered John's hospital with Alice on my arm. All my affairs—and they were few enough—were in order. I had insisted that Alice wait until I had come safely through the operation, before she submitted to it. I had been very carefully starved for two days, and I was lost in an an unreal world of white walls and white clothes and white lights, drunk with my dreams of the future. When I was wheeled into the operating room on the long hard table, for a moment it shown in brilliant distinctness, a neat, methodical white chamber, tall and more or less circular. Then I was beneath the glare of soft white lights, and the room faded into a misty vagueness from which little steel rays flashed and quivered from silvery cold instruments. For a moment our hands, Sir John's and mine, gripped and we were saying goodbye—for a little while—in a way men say these things. Then I felt the warm touch of Alice's lips upon mine, and I felt sudden painful things I cannot describe, that I could not have described then. For a moment I felt that I must rise and cry out that I could not do it. But the feeling passed, and I was passive.

Something was pressed about my mouth and nose, something with an etherial smell. Staring eyes swam about me from behind their white masks. I struggled instinctively, but in vain—I was held securely. Infinitesimal points of light began to wave back and forth on a pitch-black background; a great hollow buzzing echoed in my head. My head seemed suddenly to have become all throat, a great, cavernous, empty throat in which sounds and lights were mingled together, in a swift rhythm, approaching, receding eternally. Then, I think, there were dreams. But I have forgotten them. . . .

I began to emerge from the effects of the ether. Everything was dim, but I could perceive Alice beside me, and Sir John.

"Bravely done!" Sir John was saying and Alice, too, was saying something, but I cannot remember what. For a long while we talked, I speaking the nonsense of those who are coming out from under the ether, they teasing me solemnly. But after a little while I became aware of the fact that they were about to leave. Suddenly, God knows why, I knew that they must not leave. Something cried in the back of my head that they *must* stay—one cannot explain these things, except by after events. I began to press them to remain, but they smiled and said they must get their dinner. I commanded them not to go; but they spoke kindly and said they would be back before long. I think I even wept a little, like a child, but Sir John said something to the nurse, who began to reason with me firmly, and then they were gone, and somehow I was asleep. . . .

When I awoke again, my head was fairly clear, but there was an abominable reek of ether all about me. The moment I opened my eyes, I felt that something had happened. I asked for Sir John and for Alice. I saw a swift, curious look that I could not interpret come over the face of the nurse, then she was calm again, her countenance impassive. She reassured me in quick meaningless phrases, and told me to sleep. But I could not sleep: I was absolutely sure that something had happened to them, to my friend and to the woman I loved. Yet all my insistence profited me nothing, for the nurses were a silent lot. Finally, I think, they must have given me a sleeping potion of some sort, for I fell asleep again.

For two endless, chaotic days, I saw nothing of either of them, Alice or Sir John. I became more and more agitated, the nurse more and more taciturn. She would only say that they had gone away for a day or two.

And then on the third day, I found out. They thought I was asleep. The night nurse had just come in to relieve the other.

"Has he been asking about them again?" she asked.

"Yes, poor fellow. I have hardly managed to keep him quiet."

"We will have to keep it from him until he is recovered fully." There was a long pause, and I could hardly control my labored breathing.

"How sudden it was!" one of them said. "To be killed like that—" I heard no more, for I leapt suddenly up in bed, crying out.

"Quick! For God's sake, tell me what has happened!"

I jumped to the floor and seized one of them by the collar. She was horrified. I shook her with a superhuman strength.

"Tell me!" I shouted, "Tell me—Or, I'll—!" She told me—what else could she do.

"They were killed in an accident," she gasped, "in a taxi—a collision—the Strand—!" And at that moment a crowd of nurses and attendents arrived, called by the other frantic woman, and they put me to bed again.

I have no memory of the next few days. I was in delirium, and I was never told what I said during my ravings. Nor can I express the feelings I was saturated with when at last I regained my mind. Between my old emotions and any attempt to put them into words, or even to remember them, lies always that insurmountable wall of my Change. I cannot understand what I must have felt, I cannot express it.

I only know that for weeks I was sunk in a misery beyond any misery I had ever imagined before. The only two friends I had on earth were gone to me. I was left alone. And, for the first time, I began to see before me all these endless years that would be the same, dull, lonely.

Yet I recovered. I could feel each day the growth of a strange new vigor in my limbs, a vast force that was something tangibly expressive to eternal life. Slowly my anguish began to die. After a week or more, I began to understand how my emotions were leaving me, how love and beauty and everything of which poetry was made—how all this was going. I could not bear the thought at first. I would look at the golden sunlight and the blue shadow of the wind, and I would say,

"God! How beautiful!" And the words would echo meaningless in my ears. Or I would remember Alice's face, that face I had once loved so inextinguishably, and I would weep and clutch my forehead, and clench my fists, crying.

"O God, how can I live without her!" Yet there would be a little strange fancy in my head at the same moment, saying,

"Who is this Alice? You know no such person." And truly I would wonder whether she had ever existed.

So, slowly, the old emotions were shed away from me, and I began to joy in a corresponding growth of my mental perceptions. I began to toy idly with mathematical formulae I had forgotten years ago, in the same fashion that a poet toys with a word and its shades of meaning. I would look at everything with new, seeing eyes, new perception, and I would understand things I had never understood before, because formerly my emotions had always occupied me more than my thoughts.

And so the weeks went by, until, one day, I was well.

. . . What, after all, is the use of this chronicle? Surely there will never be men to read it. I have heard them say that the snow will never go. I will be buried, it will be buried with me; and it will be the end of both of us. Yet, somehow, it eases my weary soul a little to write. . . .

Need I say, that I lived, thereafter, many thousands of thousands of years, until this day? I cannot detail that life. It is a long round of new, fantastic impressions, coming dream-like, one after another, melting into each other. In looking back, as in looking back upon dreams, I seem to recall a few isolated periods clearly; and it seems that my imagination must have filled in the swift movement between episodes. I think now, of necessity, in terms of centuries and milleniums, rather than in days or months. . . . The snow blows terribly about my little fire, and I know it will soon gather courage to quench us both. . . .

Years passed, at first with a sort of clear wonder. I watched things that took place everywhere in the world. I studied. The other students were much amazed to see me, a man of thirty odd, coming back to college.

"But Judas, Dennell, you've already got your Ph.D! What more do you want?" So they would all ask me. And I would reply:

"I want an M.D. and an F.R.C.S." I didn't tell them that I wanted degrees in Law, too, and in Biology and Chemistry, in Architecture and Engineering, in Psychology and Philosophy. Even so, I believe they thought me mad. But poor fools! I would think. They can hardly realize that I have all of eternity before me to study.

I went to school for many decades. I would pass from University to University, leisurely gathering all the fruits of every subject I took up, reveling in study as no student reveled ever before. There was no need to hurry in my life, no fear of death too soon. There was a magnificence of vigor in my body, and a magnificence of vision and clarity in my brain. I felt myself a super-man. I had only to go on storing up wisdom until the day should come when all knowledge in the world was mine, and then I could command the world. I had no need to hurry. O vast life! How I gloried in eternity! And how little good it has ever done me, by the irony of God.

For several centuries, changing my name and passing from place to place, I continued my studies. I had no consciousness of monotony, for to the intellect monotony cannot exist; it was one of those emotions I had left behind. One day, however, in the year 2132, a great discovery was made by a man called Zarentzov. It had to do with the curvature of space, quite changing the conceptions that we had all followed since Einstein. I had long ago mastered the last detail of Einstein's theory, as had, in time, the rest of the world. I threw myself immediately into the study of this new, epoch-making conception.

To my amazement, it all seemed to me curiously dim

and elusive. I could not quite grasp what Zarentzov was trying to formulate.

"Why," I cried, "the thing is a monstrous fraud!" I went to the professor of Physics in the University I attended, and I told him it was a fraud, a huge book of mere nonsense. He looked at me rather pityingly.

"I am afraid, Modevski," he said, addressing me by the name I was at that time using, "I am afraid you do not understand it, that is all. When your mind has broadened, you will. You should apply yourself more carefully to your Physics." But that angered me, for I had mastered my Physics before he was ever born. I challenged him to explain the theory. And he did! He put it obviously in the clearest language he could. Yet I understood nothing. I stared at him dumbly, until he shook his head impatiently, saying that it was useless, that if I could not grasp it I would simply have to keep on studying. I was stunned. I wandered away in a daze.

For do you see what happened? During all those years I had studied ceaselessly, and my mind had been clear and quick as the day I first had left the hospital. But all the time I had been able to remain what I was—an extraordinarily intelligent man of the twentieth century. And the rest of the race had been progressing. It had been swiftly gathering knowledge and power and ability all that time, faster and faster, while I had only been remaining still. And now there was Zarentzov and the teachers of the Universities, and, probably, a hundred intelligent men, who had all outstripped me! I was being left behind.

And that is what happened. I need not dilate further upon it. By the end of that century I had been left behind by all the students of the world, and I never did understand Zarentzov. Other men came with other theories, and these theories were accepted by the world. But I could not understand them. My intellectual life was at an end. I had nothing more to understand. I knew everything I was capable of knowing, and, thenceforth, I could only play wearily with the old ideas.

Many things happened in the world. A time came when the East and West, two mighty unified hemispheres, rose up in arms: the civil war of a planet. I recall only chaotic visions of fire and thunder and hell. It was all incomprehensible to me: like a bizarre dream, things happened, people rushed about, but I never knew what they were doing. I lurked all that time in a tiny shuddering hole under the city of Yokohama, and by a miracle I survived. And the East won. But it seems to have mattered little who did win, for all the world had become, in all except its few remaining prejudices, a single race, and nothing was changed when it was all rebuilt again, under a single government.

I saw the first of the strange creatures who appeared among us in the year 6371, men who were later known to be from the planet Venus. But they were repulsed, for they were savages compared with the Earthmen, although they were about equal to the people of my own century, 1900. Those of them who did not perish of the cold after the intense warmth of their world, and those who were not killed by our hands, those few returned silently home again. And I have always regretted that I had not the courage to go with them.

I watched a time when the world reached perfection in mechanics, when men could accomplish anything with a touch of the finger. Strange men, these creatures of the hundredth century, men with huge brains, and tiny shriveled bodies, atrophied limbs, and slow ponderous movements on their little conveyances. It was I, with my ancient compunctions, who shuddered when at last they put to death all the perverts, the criminals, and the insane, ridding the world of the scum for which they had no more need. It was then that I was forced to produce my tattered old papers, proving my identity and my story. They knew it was true, in some strange fashion of theirs, and, thereafter, I was kept on exhibition as an archaic survival.

I saw the world made immortal through the new invention of a man called Kathol, who used somewhat the same method "legend" decreed had been used upon me. I observed the end of speech, of all perception except one, when men learned to communicate directly by thought, and to receive directly into the brain all the myriad vibrations of the universe.

All these things, I saw, and more, until that time when there was no more discovery, but a Perfect World in which there was no need for anything but memory. Men ceased to count time at last. Several hundred years after the 154th Dynasty from the Last War, or, as we would have counted in my time, about 200,000 A.D., official records of time were no longer kept carefully. They fell into disuse. Men began to forget years, to forget time at all. Of what significance was time when one was immortal.

After long, long uncounted centuries, a time came when the days grew noticeably colder. Slowly the winters became longer, and the summers diminished to but a month or two. Fierce storms raged endlessly in winter, and in summer sometimes there was severe frost, sometimes there was only frost. In the high places in the north and sub-equatorial south, the snow came and would not go.

Men died by the thousands in the higher latitudes. New York became, after a while, the furthest habitable city north, an arctic city, where warmth seldom penetrated. And great fields of ice began to make their way southward, grinding before them the brittle remains of civilizations, covering over relentlessly all of man's proud work.

Snow appeared in Florida and Italy one summer. In the end, snow was there always. Men left New York, Chicago, Paris, Yokohama, and everywhere they traveled by the millions southward, perishing as they went, pursued by the snow and the cold, and that inevitable field of ice. They were feeble creatures when the Cold first came upon them, but I speak in terms of thousands of years; and they turned every weapon of science to the recovery of their physical power, for they foresaw that the only chance of survival lay in a hard, strong body. As for me, at last I had found a use for my few powers, for my physique was the finest in that world. It was but little comfort, however, for we were all united in our awful fear of that Cold and that grinding field of Ice. All the great cities were deserted. We would catch silent, fearful glimpses of them as we sped on in our machines over the snow—great hungry, haggard skeletons of cities, shrouded in banks of snow, snow that the wind rustled through deserted streets where the cream of human life had passed in calm security. Yet still the Ice pursued. For men had forgotten about that Last Ice Age when they ceased to reckon time, when they lost sight of the future and steeped themselves in memories. They had not remembered that a time must come when Ice would lie white and smooth over all the earth, when the sun would shine bleakly between unending intervals of dim, twilight snow and sleet.

Slowly the Ice pursued us down the earth, until all the feeble remains of civilization were gathered in Egypt and India and South America. The deserts flowered again, but the frost would come always to bite the tiny crops. For still the Ice came. All the world now, but for a narrow strip about the equator, was one great silent desolate vista of stark ice-plains, ice that brooded above the hidden ruins of cities that had endured for hundreds of thousands of years. It was terrible to imagine the awful solitude and the endless twilight that lay on these places, and the grim snow, sailing in silence over all . . .

It surrounded us on all sides, until life remained only in a few scattered clearings all about the equator of the globe, with an eternal fire going to hold away the hungry Ice. Perpetual winter reigned now; and we were becoming terror-stricken beasts that preyed on each other for a life already doomed. Ah, but I, I the archaic survival, I had my revenge then, with my great physique and strong jaws—God! Let me think of something else. Those men who lived upon each other—it was horrible. And I was one.

So inevitably the Ice closed in . . . One day the men of our tiny clearing were but a score. We huddled about our dying fire of bones and stray logs. We said nothing. We just sat, in deep, wordless, thoughtless silence. We were the last outpost of Mankind.

I think suddenly something very noble must have transformed these creatures to a semblance of what they had been of old. I saw, in their eyes, the question they sent from one to another and in every eye I saw that the answer was, Yes. With one accord they rose before my eyes and, ignoring me as a baser creature, they stripped away their load of tattered rags and, one by one they stalked with their tiny shriveled limbs into the shivering gale of swirling, gusting snow, and disappeared. And I was alone. . . .

So am I alone now. I have written this last fantastic history of myself and of Mankind upon a substance that will, I know, outlast even the snow and the Ice—as it has outlasted Mankind that made it. It is the only thing with which I have never parted. For is it not irony that I should be the historian of this race—I, a savage, an 'archaic survival?' Why do I write? God knows, but some instinct prompts me, although there will never be men to read.

I have been sitting here, waiting, and I have thought often of Sir John and Alice, whom I loved. Can it be that I am feeling again, after all these ages, some tiny portion of that emotion, that great passion I once knew? I see her face before me, the face I have lost from my thoughts for eons, and something is in it that stirs my blood again. Her eyes are half-closed and deep, her lips are parted as though I could crush them with an infinity of wonder and discovery. O God! It is love again, love that I thought was lost! They have often smiled upon me when I spoke of God, and muttered about my foolish, primitive superstitions. But they are gone, and I am left who believe in God, and surely there is purpose in it.

I am cold, I have written. Ah, I am frozen. My breath freezes as it mingles with the air, and I can hardly move my numbed fingers. The Ice is closing over me, and I cannot break it any longer. The storm cries weirdly all about me in the twilight, and I know this is the end. The end of the world. And I—I, the last man . . . .

The last man. . . .

. . . I am cold—cold. . . .

But is it you, Alice, is it you?

JAQUAYS

THE MIRACLE OF THE LILY

by Clare Winger Harris

CHAPTER I

The Passing of a Kingdom

Since the comparatively recent résumé of the ancient order of agriculture, I, Nathano, have been asked to set down the extraordinary events of the past two thousand years, at the beginning of which time the supremacy of man, chief of the mammals, threatened to come to an untimely end.

Ever since the dawn of life upon this globe, life, which it seemed had crept from the slime of the sea, only two great types had been the rulers: the reptiles and the mammals. The former held undisputed sway for eons, but gave way eventually before the smaller but intellectually superior mammals. Man himself, the supreme example of the ability of life to govern and control inanimate matter, was master of the world with apparently none to dispute his right. Yet, so blinded was he with pride over the continued exercise of his power on Earth over other lower types of mammals and the nearly extinct reptiles, that he failed to notice the slow but steady rise of another branch of life, different from his own; smaller, it is true, but no smaller than he had been in comparison with the mighty reptilian monsters that roamed the swamps in Mesozoic times.

These new enemies of man, though seldom attacking him personally, threatened his downfall by destroying his chief means of sustenance, so that by the close of the twentieth century, strange and daring projects were laid before the various governments of the world with an idea of fighting man's insect enemies to the finish. These pests were growing in size, multiplying so rapidly and destroying so much vegetation that eventually no plants would be left to sustain human life. Humanity suddenly woke to the realization that it might suffer the fate of the nearly extinct reptiles. Would mankind be able to prevent the encroachment of the insects? And at last man *knew* that unless drastic measures were taken *at once*, a third great class of life was on the brink of terrestrial sovereignty.

Of course no great changes in development come suddenly. Slow evolutionary progress had brought us up to the point where, with the application of outside pressure, we were ready to handle a situation that, a century before, would have overwhelmed us.

I reproduce here in part a lecture delivered by a great American scientist, a talk which, sent by radio throughout the world, changed the destiny of mankind: but whether for good or for evil I will leave you to judge at the conclusion of this story.

"Only in comparatively recent times has man succeeded in conquering natural enemies: flood, storm, inclemency of climate, distance. And now we face an encroaching menace to the whole of humanity. Have we learned more and more of truth and of the laws that control matter only to succumb to the first real danger that threatens us with extermination? Surely, no matter what the cost, you will rally to the solution of our problem, and I believe, friends, that I have discovered the answer to the enigma.

"I know that many of you, like my friend Professor Fair, will believe my ideas too extreme, but I am convinced that unless you are willing to put behind you those notions which are old and not utilitarian, you cannot hope to cope with the present situation.

"Already, in the past few decades, you have realized the utter futility of encumbering yourselves with superfluous possessions that had no useful virtue, but which, for various sentimental reasons, you continued to hoard, thus lessening the degree of your life's accomplishments. You have given these things up slowly, but I am now going to ask you to relinquish the rest of them *quickly*; everything that interferes in any way with the immediate disposal of our enemies, the insects."

At this point, it seems that my worthy ancestor, Professor Fair, objected to the scientist's words, asserting that efficiency at the expense of some of the sentimental virtues was undesirable and not conducive to happiness, the real goal of man. The scientist, in his turn, argued that happiness was available only through a perfect adaptability to one's environment, and that efficiency *sans* love, mercy and the softer sentiments was the short-cut to human bliss.

It took a number of years for the scientist to put over his scheme of salvation, but in the end he succeeded, not so much from the persuasiveness of his words as because prompt action of some sort was necessary. There was not enough food to feed the people of the earth. Fruit and vegetables were becoming a thing of the past. Too much protein food in the form of meat and fish was injuring the race, and at last the people realized that for fruits and vegetables, or their nutritive equivalent, they must turn from the field to the laboratory: from the farmer to the chemist. Synthetic food was the solution to the problem. There was no longer any use in planting and caring for foodstuffs destined to become the nourishment of man's most deadly enemy.

The last planting took place in 2900, but there was no harvest. The voracious insects took every green shoot as soon as it appeared, and even trees, which had previously withstood the attacks of the huge insects, were by this time stripped of every vestige of greenery.

The vegetable world suddenly ceased to exist. Over the barren plains, which had been gradually filling with vast cities, man-made fires brought devastation to every living bit of greenery, so that in all the world there was no food for the insect pests.

CHAPTER II

Man or Insect?

Extract from the diary of Delfair, a descendant of Professor Fair, who had opposed the daring scientist.

From the borders of the great state-city of Iowa, I was witness to the passing of one of the great kingdoms of earth—the vegetable, and I cannot find words to express the grief that overwhelms me as I write of its demise, for I loved all growing things. Many of us realized that Earth was no longer beautiful; but if beauty meant death, better life in the sterility of the metropolis.

The viciousness of the thwarted insects was a menace that we had foreseen and yet failed to take into adequate account. On the city-state borderland, life is constantly imperiled by the attacks of well-organized bodies of our dreaded foe.

(Note: The organization that now exists among the ants, bees and other insects, testifies to the possibility of the development of military tactics among them in the centuries to come.)

Robbed of their source of food, they have become emboldened to such an extent that they will take any risks to carry human beings away for food, and after one of their well-organized raids, the toll of human life is appalling.

But the great chemical laboratories where our synthetic food is made, and our oxygen plants, we thought were impregnable to their attacks. In that we were mistaken.

Let me say briefly that since the destruction of all vegetation, which furnished a part of the oxygen essential to human life, it became necessary to manufacture this gas artificially for general diffusion through the atmosphere.

I was flying to my work, which is in Oxygen Plant No. 21, when I noticed a peculiar thing on the upper speedway near Food Plant No. 3,439. Although it was night, the various levels of the state-city were illuminated as brightly as by day. A pleasure vehicle was going with prodigious speed westward. I looked after it in amazement. It was unquestionably the car of Eric, my coworker at Oxygen Plant No. 21. I recognized the gay color of its body, but to verify my suspicions beyond the question of a doubt, I turned my volplane in pursuit and made out the familiar license number. What was Eric doing away from the plant before I had arrived to relieve him from duty?

In hot pursuit, I sped above the car to the very border of the state-city, wondering what unheard-of errand took him to the land of the enemy, for the car came to a sudden stop at the edge of what had once been an agricultural area. Miles ahead of me stretched an enormous expanse of black sterility; at my back was the teeming metropolis, five levels high—if one counted the hangar-level, which did not cover the residence sections.

I had not long to wait, for almost immediately my friend appeared. What a sight he presented to my incredulous gaze! He was literally covered from head to foot with the two-inch ants that, next to the beetles, had proved the greatest menace in their attacks upon humanity. With wild incoherent cries he fled over the rock and stubble-burned earth.

As soon as my stunned senses permitted, I swooped down toward him to effect a rescue, but even as my plane touched the barren earth, I saw that I was too late, for he fell, borne down by the vicious attacks of his myriad foes. I knew it was useless for me to set foot upon the ground, for my fate would be that of Eric. I rose ten feet and seizing my poison-gas weapon, let its contents out upon the tiny black evil things that swarmed below. I did not bother with my mask for I planned to rise immediately, and it was not a moment too soon. From across the wasteland, a dark cloud eclipsed the stars and I saw coming toward me a horde of flying insects, all bent upon my annihilation. I now took my mask and prepared to turn more gas upon my pursuers, but alas, I had used every atom of it in my attack upon the non-flying ants! I had no recourse but flight, and to this I immediately resorted, knowing that I could outdistance my pursuers.

When I could no longer see them, I removed my gas mask. A suffocating sensation seized me. I could not breathe! How high had I flown in my endeavor to escape the flying ants? I leaned over the side of my plane, expecting to see the city far, far below me. What was my utter amazement when I discovered I was scarcely a thousand feet high! It was not altitude that was depriving me of the life-giving oxygen.

A drop of three hundred feet showed me inert specks of humanity lying about the streets. Then I knew; the oxygen plant was not in operation! In another minute I had on my oxygen mask, which was attached to a small portable tank for emergency use, and I rushed for the vicinity of the plant. There I witnessed the first signs of life. Men equipped with oxygen masks were trying to force entrance into the locked building. Being an employee, I possessed knowledge of the combination of the great lock, and I opened the door, only to be greeted by a swarm of ants that commenced a concerted attack upon us.

The floor seemed to be covered with a moving black rug, the corner nearest the door appearing to unravel as we entered, and it was but a few seconds before we were covered with the clinging, biting creatures, who fought with a supernatural energy born of despair. Two very active ants succeeded in getting under my helmet. The bite of their sharp mandibles and the effect of their poisonous formic acid became intolerable. Did I dare remove my mask while the air about me was foul with the gas discharged from the weapons of my allies? While I felt the attacks elsewhere upon my body gradually diminishing as the insects succumbed to the deadly fumes, the two upon my face waxed more vicious under the protection of my mask. One at each eye, they were trying to blind me. The pain was unbearable. Better the suffocating death-gas than the torture of lacerated eyes! Frantically I removed the headgear and tore at the shiny black fiends. Strange to tell, I discovered that I could breathe near the vicinity of the great oxygen tanks, where enough oxygen lingered to support life at least temporarily. The two vicious insects, no longer protected by my gas mask, scurried from me like rats from a sinking ship and disappeared behind the oxygen tanks.

This attack of our enemies, though unsuccessful on their part, was dire in significance, for it had shown more cunning and ingenuity than anything that had ever preceded it. Heretofore, their onslaughts had been confined to direct attacks upon us personally or upon the synthetic-food laboratories, but in this last raid they had shown an amazing cleverness that portended future disaster, unless they were checked at once. It was obvious they had ingeniously planned to smother us by the suspension of work at the oxygen plant; knowing that they themselves could exist in an atmosphere containing a greater percentage of carbon dioxide. Their scheme, then, was to raid our laboratories for food.

CHAPTER III

Lucanus the Last

A Continuation of Delfair's Account

Although it was evident that the cessation of all plant life spelled inevitable doom for the insect inhabitants of Earth, their extermination did not follow as rapidly as one might have supposed. There were years of internecine warfare. The insects continued to thrive, though in decreasing numbers, upon stolen laboratory foods, bodies of human beings, and finally upon each other, at first capturing enemy species and at last even resorting to a cannibalistic procedure. Their rapacity grew in inverse proportion to their waning numbers, until the meeting of even an isolated insect might mean death, unless one were equipped with poison gas and prepared to use it upon a second's notice.

I am an old man now, though I have not yet lived quite two centuries, but I am happy in the knowledge that I have lived to see the last living insect which was held in captivity. It was an excellent specimen of the stag-beetle (*Lucanus*) and the years have testified that it was the sole survivor of a form of life that might have succeeded man upon this planet. This beetle was caught weeks after we had previously seen what was supposed to be the last living thing upon the globe, barring man and the sea life. Untiring search for years has failed to reveal any more insects, so that at last man rests secure in the knowledge that he is monarch of all he surveys.

I have heard that long, long ago man used to gaze with a fearful fascination upon the reptilian creatures which he displaced, and just so did he view this lone specimen of a type of life that might have covered the face of the earth, but for man's ingenuity.

It was this unholy lure that drew me one day to view the captive beetle in his cage in district 404 at Universapolis. I was amazed at the size of the creature, for it looked larger than when I had seen it by television, but I reasoned that upon that occasion there had been no object near with which to compare its size. True, the broadcaster had announced its dimensions, but the statistics concretely given had failed to register a perfect realization of its prodigious proportions.

As I approached the cage, the creature was lying with its dorsal covering toward me and I judged it measured fourteen inches from one extremity to the other. Its smooth horny sheath gleamed in the bright artificial light. (It was confined on the third level.) As I stood there, mentally conjuring a picture of a world overrun with billions of such creatures as the one before me, the keeper approached the cage with a meal-portion of synthetic food. Although the food has no odor, the beetle sensed the man's approach, for it rose on its jointed legs and came toward us, its horn-like prongs moving threateningly; then apparently remembering its confinement, and the impotency of an attack, it subsided and quickly ate the food which had been placed within its prison.

The food consumed, it lifted itself to its hind legs, partially supported by a box, and turned its great eyes upon me. I had never been regarded with such utter malevolence before. The detestation was almost tangible and I shuddered involuntarily. As plainly as if he spoke, I knew that Lucanus was perfectly cognizant of the situation and in his gaze I read the concentrated hate of an entire defeated race.

I had no desire to gloat over his misfortune; rather a great pity toward him welled up within me. I pictured myself alone, the last of my kind, held up for ridicule before the swarming hordes of insects who had conquered my people, and I knew that life would no longer be worth the living.

Whether he sensed my pity or not I do not know, but he continued to survey me with unmitigated rage, as if he would convey to me the information that his was an implacable hatred that would outlast eternity.

Not long after this he died, and a world long since intolerant of ceremony surprised itself by interring the beetle's remains in a golden casket, accompanied by much pomp and splendor.

I have lived many long years since that memorable event, and undoubtedly my days here are numbered, but I can pass on happily, convinced that in this sphere man's conquest of his environment is supreme.

CHAPTER IV

Efficiency Maximum

In a direct line of descent from Professor Fair and Delfair, the author of the preceding chapter, comes Thanor, whose journal is given in this chapter.

Am I a true product of the year 2928? Sometimes I am convinced that I am hopelessly old-fashioned, an anachronism that should have existed a thousand years ago. In no other way can I account for the dissatisfaction I feel in a world where efficiency has at last reached a maximum.

I am told that I spring from a line of ancestors who were not readily acclimated to changing conditions. I love beauty, yet I see none of it here. There are many who think our lofty buildings that tower two and three thousand feet into the air are beautiful, but while they are architectural splendors, they do not represent the kind of loveliness I crave. Only when I visit the sea do I feel any satisfaction for a certain yearning in my soul. The ocean alone shows the handiwork of God. The land bears evidence only of man.

As I read back through the diaries of my sentimental ancestors I find occasional glowing descriptions of the world that was; the world before the insects menaced human existence. Trees, plants and flowers brought delight into the lives of people as they wandered among them in vast open spaces, I am told, where the earth was soft beneath their feet, and flying creatures, called birds, sang among the greenery. True, I learn that many people had not enough to eat, and that uncontrollable passions governed them, but I do believe it must have been more interesting than this methodical, unemotional existence. I cannot understand why many people were poor, for I am told that Nature as manifested in the vegetable kingdom was very prolific; so much so that year after year quantities of food rotted on the ground. The fault, I find by my reading, was not with Nature but with man's economic system which is now perfect, though this perfection really brings few of us happiness, I think.

Now there is no waste; all is converted into food. Long ago man learned how to reduce all matter to its constituent elements, of which there are nearly a hundred in number, and from them to rebuild compounds for food. The old axiom that nothing is created or destroyed, but merely changed from one form to another, has stood the test of ages. Man, as the agent of God, has simply performed the miracle of transmutation himself instead of waiting for natural forces to accomplish it as in the old days.

At first humanity was horrified when it was decreed that it must relinquish its dead to the laboratory. For too many eons had man closely associated the soul and body, failing to comprehend the body as merely a material agent, through which the spirit functioned. When man knew at last of the eternal qualities of spirit, he ceased to regard the discarded body with reverential awe, and saw in it only the same molecular constituents which comprised all matter about him. He recognized only material basically the same as that of stone or metal: material to be reduced to its atomic elements and rebuilt into matter that would render service to living humanity, that portion of matter wherein spirit functions.

The drab monotony of life is appalling. Is it possible that man had reached his height a thousand years ago and should have been willing to resign Earth's sovereignty to a coming order of creatures destined to be man's worthy successor in the eons to come? It seems that life is interesting only when there is a struggle, a goal to be reached through an evolutionary process. Once the goal is attained, all progress ceases. The huge reptiles of preglacial ages rose to supremacy by virtue of their great size, and yet was it not the excessive bulk of those creatures that finally wiped them out of existence? Nature, it seems, avoids extremes. She allows the fantastic to develop for a while and then wipes the slate clean for a new order of development. Is it not conceivable that man could destroy himself through excessive development of his nervous system, and give place for the future evolution of a comparatively simple form of life, such as the insects were at man's height of development? This, it seems to me, was the great plan; a scheme with which man dared to interfere and for which he is now paying by the boredom of existence.

The earth's population is decreasing so rapidly, that I fear another thousand years will see a lifeless planet hurtling through space. It seems to me that only a miracle will save us now.

CHAPTER V

The Year 3928

The Original Writer, Nathano, Resumes the Narrative

My ancestor, Thanor, of ten centuries ago, according to the records he gave to my great-grandfather, seems to voice the general despair of humanity which, bad enough in his times, has reached the nth power in my day. A soulless world is gradually dying from self-inflicted boredom.

As I have ascertained from the perusal of the journals of my forebears, even antedating the extermination of the insects, I come of a stock that clings with sentimental tenacity to the things that made life worthwhile in the old days. If the world at large knew of my emotional musings concerning past ages, it would scarcely tolerate me, but surrounded by my thought-insulator, I often indulge in what fancies I will, and such meditation, coupled with a love for a few ancient relics from the past, has led me to a most amazing discovery.

Several months ago I found among my family relics a golden receptacle two feet long, one and a half in width and one in depth, which I found upon opening, to contain many tiny square compartments, each filled with minute objects of slightly varying size, texture and color.

"Not sand!" I exclaimed as I closely examined the little particles of matter.

Food? After eating some, I was convinced that their

nutritive value was small in comparison with a similar quantity of the products of our laboratories. What were the mysterious objects?

Just as I was about to close the lid again, convinced that I had one over-sentimental ancestor whose gift to posterity was absolutely useless, my pocket-radio buzzed and the voice of my friend, Stentor, the interplanetary broadcaster, issued from the tiny instrument.

"If you're going to be home this afternoon," said Stentor, "I'll skate over. I have some interesting news."

I consented for I thought I would share my "find" with this friend whom I loved above all others, but before he arrived I had again hidden my golden chest, for I had decided to await the development of events before sharing its mysterious secret with another. It was well that I did this for Stentor was so filled with the importance of his own news that he could have given me little attention at first.

"Well, what is your interesting news?" I asked after he was comfortably seated in my adjustable chair.

"You'd never guess," he replied with irritating leisureliness.

"Does it pertain to Mars or Venus?" I queried. "What news of our neighbor planets?"

"You may know it has nothing to do with the self-satisfied Martians," answered the broadcaster, "but the Venusians have a very serious problem confronting them. It is in connection with the same old difficulty they have had ever since interplanetary radio was developed forty years ago. You remember that, in their second communication with us, they told us of their continual warfare on insect pests that were destroying all vegetable food? Well, last night after general broadcasting had ceased, I was surprised to hear the voice of the Venusian broadcaster. He is suggesting that we get up a scientific expedition to Venus to help the natives of his unfortunate planet solve their insect problem as we did ours. He says the Martians turn a deaf ear to their plea for help, but he expects sympathy and assistance from Earth, who has so recently solved these problems for herself."

I was dumbfounded at Stentor's news.

"But the Venusians are farther advanced mechanically than we," I objected, "though they are behind us in the natural sciences. They could much more easily solve the difficulties of space-flying than we could."

"That is true," agreed Stentor, "but if we are to render them material aid in freeing their world from devastating insects, we must get to Venus. The past four decades have proved that we cannot help them merely by verbal instructions.

"Now, last night," Stentor continued, with warming enthusiasm, "Wanyana, the Venusian broadcaster, informed me that scientists on Venus are developing interplanetary television. This, if successful, will prove highly beneficial in facilitating communication, and it may even do away with the necessity of interplanetary travel, which I think is centuries ahead of us yet."

"Television, though so common here on Earth and on Venus, has seemed an impossibility across the ethereal void," I said, "but if it becomes a reality, I believe it will be the Venusians who will take the initiative, though of course they will be helpless without our friendly cooperation. In return for the mechanical instructions they have given us from time to time, I think it no more than right that we should try to give them all the help possible in freeing their world, as ours has been freed, of the insects that threaten their very existence. Personally, therefore, I hope it can be done through radio and television rather than by personal excursions."

"I believe you are right," he admitted, "but I hope we can be of service to them soon. Ever since I have served in the capacity of official interplanetary broadcaster, I have liked the spirit of goodfellowship shown by the Venusians through their spokesman, Wanyana. The impression is favorable in contrast to the superciliousness of the inhabitants of Mars."

We conversed for some time, but at length he rose to take his leave. It was then I ventured to broach the subject that was uppermost in my thoughts.

"I want to show you something, Stentor," I said, going into an adjoining room for my precious box and returning shortly with it. "A relic from the days of an ancestor named Delfair, who lived at the time the last insect, a beetle, was kept in captivity. Judging from his personal account, Delfair was fully aware of the significance of the changing times in which he lived, and contrary to the majority of his contemporaries, possessed a sentimentality of soul that has proved an historical asset to future generations. Look, my friend, these he left to posterity!"

I deposited the heavy casket on a table between us and lifted the lid, revealing to Stentor the mystifying particles.

The face of Stentor was eloquent of astonishment. Not unnaturally his mind took somewhat the same route as mine had followed previously, though he added atomic-power units to the list of possibilities. He shook his head in perplexity.

"Whatever they are, there must have been a real purpose behind their preservation," he said at last. "You say this old Delfair witnessed the passing of the insects? What sort of a fellow was he? Likely to be up to any tricks?"

"Not at all," I asserted rather indignantly, "he seemed a very serious-minded chap; worked in an oxygen plant and took an active part in the last warfare between men and insects."

Suddenly Stentor stooped over and scooped up some of the minute particles into the palm of his hand—and then he uttered a maniacal shriek and flung them into the air.

"Great God, man, do you know what they are?" he screamed, shaking violently.

"No, I do not," I replied quietly, with an attempt at dignity I did not feel.

"Insect eggs!" he cried, and shuddering with terror, he made for the door.

I caught him on the threshold and pulled him forcibly back into the room.

"Now see here," I said sternly, "not a word of this to anyone. Do you understand? I will test out your theory in every possible way but I want no public interference."

At first he was obstinate, but finally yielded to threats when supplications were impotent.

"I will test them," I said, "and will endeavor to keep hatchlings under absolute control, should they prove to be what you suspect."

It was time for the evening broadcasting, so he left, promising to keep our secret and leaving me regretting that I had taken another into my confidence.

CHAPTER VI

The Miracle

For days following my unfortunate experience with Stentor, I experimented upon the tiny objects that had so terrified him. I subjected them to various tests for the purpose of ascertaining whether or not they bore evidence of life, whether in egg, pupa or larva stages of development. And to all my experiments, there was but one answer. No life was manifest. Yet I was not satisfied, for chemical tests showed that they were composed of organic matter. Here was an inexplicable enigma! Many times I was on the verge of consigning the entire contents of the chest to the flames. I seemed to see in my mind's eye the world again overridden with insects, and that calamity due to the indiscretions of one man! My next impulse was to turn over my problem to scientists, when a suspicion of the truth dawned upon me. These were seeds, the germs of plant life, and they might grow. But alas, where? Over all the earth man has spread his artificial domain. The state-city has been succeeded by what could be termed the nation-city, for one great floor of concrete or rock covers the country.

I resolved to try an experiment, the far-reaching influence of which I did not at that time suspect. Beneath the lowest level of the community edifice in which I dwell, I removed, by means of a small atomic excavator, a slab of concrete large enough to admit my body. I let myself down into the hole and felt my feet resting on a soft dark substance that I knew to be dirt. I hastily filled a box of this, and after replacing the concrete slab, returned to my room, where I proceeded to plant a variety of seeds.

Being a product of an age when practically to wish for a thing in a material sense is to have it, I experienced the greatest impatience, while waiting for any evidences of plant life to become manifest. Daily, yes hourly, I watched the soil for signs of a type of life long since departed from the earth, and was about convinced that the germ of life could not have survived the centuries when a tiny blade of green proved to me that a miracle, more wonderful to me than the works of man through the ages, was taking place before my eyes. This was an enigma so complex and yet so simple, that one recognized in it a direct revelation of Nature.

Daily and weekly I watched in secret the botanical miracle. It was my one obsession. I was amazed at the fascination it held for me—a man who viewed the marvels of the fortieth century with unemotional complacency. It showed me that Nature is manifest in the simple things which mankind has chosen to ignore.

Then one morning, when I awoke, a white blossom displayed its immaculate beauty and sent forth its delicate fragrance into the air. The lily, a symbol of new life, resurrection! I felt within me the stirring of strange emotions I had long believed dead in the bosom of man. But the message must not be for me alone. As of old, the lily would be the symbol of life for all!

With trembling hands, I carried my precious burden to a front window where it might be witnessed by all who passed by. The first day there were few who saw it, for only rarely do men and women walk; they usually ride in speeding vehicles of one kind or another, or employ electric skates, a delightful means of locomotion, which gives the body some exercise. The fourth city level, which is reserved for skaters and pedestrians, is kept in a smooth-glasslike condition. And so it was only the occasional pedestrian, walking on the outer border of the fourth level, upon which my window faced, who first carried the news of the growing plant to the world, and it was not long before it was necessary for civic authorities to disperse the crowds that thronged to my window for a glimpse of a miracle in green and white.

When I showed my beautiful plant to Stentor, he was most profuse in his apology and came to my rooms every day to watch it unfold and develop, but the majority of people, long used to businesslike efficiency, were intolerant of the sentimental emotions that swayed a small minority, and I was commanded to dispose of the lily. But a figurative seed had been planted in the human heart, a seed that could not be disposed of so readily, and this seed ripened and grew until it finally bore fruit.

CHAPTER VII

Ex Terreno

It is a very different picture of humanity that I paint ten years after the last entry in my diary. My new vocation is farming, but it is farming on a far more intensive scale than had been done two thousand years ago. Our crops never fail, for temperature and rainfall are regulated artificially. But we attribute our success principally to the total absence of insect pests. Our small agricultural areas dot the country like the parks of ancient days and supply us with a type of food, no more nourishing but more appetizing than that produced in the laboratories. Truly we are living in a marvelous age! If the earth is ours completely, why may we not turn our thoughts toward the other planets in our solar-system? For the past ten or eleven years the Venusians have repeatedly urged us to come and assist them in their battle for life. I believe it is our duty to help them.

Tomorrow will be a great day for us and especially for Stentor, as the new interplanetary television is to be tested, and it is possible that for the first time in history, we shall see our neighbors in the infinity of space. Although the people of Venus were about a thousand years behind us in many respects, they have made wonderful progress with radio and television. We have been in radio communication with them for the last half century and they shared with us the joy of the establishment of our Eden. They have always been greatly interested in hearing Stentor tell the story of our subjugation of the insects that threatened to wipe us out of existence, for they have exactly that problem to solve now; judging from their reports, we fear that theirs is a losing battle. Tomorrow we shall converse face to face with the Venusians! It will be an event second in importance only to the first radio communications interchanged fifty years ago. Stentor's excitement exceeds that displayed at the time of the discovery of the seeds.

Well, it is over and the experiment was a success, but alas for the revelation!

The great assembly halls all over the continent were packed with humanity eager to catch a first glimpse of the Venusians. Prior to the test, we sent our message of friendship and good will by radio, and received a reciprocal one from our interplanetary neighbors. Alas, we were ignorant at that time! Then the television receiving apparatus was put into operation, and we sat with breathless interest, our eyes intent upon the crystal screen before us. I sat near Stentor and noted the feverish ardor with which he watched for the first glimpse of Wanyana.

At first hazy mist-like spectres seemed to glide across the screen. We knew these figures were not in correct perspective. Finally, one object gradually became more opaque, its outlines could be seen clearly. Then across that vast assemblage, as well as thousands of others throughout the world, there swept a wave of speechless horror, as its full significance burst upon mankind.

The figure that stood facing us was a huge six-legged beetle, not identical in every detail with our earthly enemies of past years, but unmistakably an insect of gigantic proportions! Of course it could not see us, for our broadcaster was not to appear until afterward, but it spoke, and we had to close our eyes to convince ourselves that it was the familiar voice of Wanyana, the leading Venusian radio broadcaster. Stentor grabbed my arm, uttered an inarticulate cry and would have fallen but for my timely support.

"Friends of Earth, as you call your world," began the object of horror, "this is a momentous occasion in the annals of the twin planets, and we are looking forward to seeing one of you, and preferably Stentor, for the first time, as you are now viewing one of us. We have listened many times, with interest, to your story of the insect pests which threatened to follow you as lords of your planet. As you have often heard us tell, we are likewise molested with insects. Our fight is a losing one, unless we can soon exterminate them."

Suddenly, the Venusian was joined by another being, a colossal ant, who bore in his forelegs a tiny light-colored object which he handed to the beetle-announcer, who took it and held it forward for our closer inspection. It seemed to be a tiny ape, but was so small we could not ascertain for a certainty. We were convinced, however, that it was a mammalian creature, an "insect" pest of Venus. Yet in it we recognized rudimentary man as we know him on earth!

There was no question as to the direction in which sympathies instinctively turned, yet reason told us that our pity should be given to the intelligent reigning race who had risen to its present mental attainment through eons of time. By some quirk or freak of nature, way back in the beginning, life had developed in the form of insects instead of mammals. Or (the thought was repellent) had insects in the past succeeded in displacing mammals, as they might have done here on earth?

There was no more television that night. Stentor would not appear, so disturbed was he by the sight of the Venusians, but in the morning, he talked to them by radio and explained the very natural antipathy we experienced in seeing them or in having them see us.

Now they no longer urge us to construct ether-ships and go to help them dispose of their "insects." I think they are afraid of us, and their very fear has aroused in mankind an unholy desire to conquer them.

I am against it. Have we not had enough of war in the

past? We have subdued our own world and should be content with that, instead of seeking new worlds to conquer. But life is too easy here. I can plainly see that. Much as he may seem to dislike it, man is not happy unless he has some enemy to overcome, some difficulty to surmount.

Alas, my greatest fears for man were groundless!

A short time ago, when I went out into my field to see how my crops were faring, I found a six-pronged beetle voraciously eating. No—man will not need to go to Venus to fight "insects."

THE MAN WITH THE STRANGE HEAD

by Miles J. Breuer, M.D.

A man in a gray hat stood halfway down the corridor, smoking a cigar and apparently interested in my knocking and waiting. I rapped again on the door of Number 216 and waited some more, but all remained silent. Finally my observer approached me.

"I don't believe it will do any good," he said. "I've just been trying it. I would like to talk to someone who is connected with Anstruther. Are you?"

"Only this." I handed him a letter out of my pocket without comment, as one is apt to do with a thing that has caused one no little wonderment:

> "Dear Doctor": it said succinctly. "I have been under the care of Dr. Faubourg who has recently died. I would like to have you take charge of me on a contract basis, and keep me well, instead of waiting till I get sick. I can pay enough to make you independent, but in return for that, you will have to accept an astonishing revelation concerning me, and keep it to yourself. If this seems acceptable to you, call on me at nine o'clock, Wednesday evening. Josiah Anstruther, Room 216, Cornhusker Hotel."

"If you have time," said the man in the gray hat, handing me back the letter, "come with me. My name is Jerry Stoner, and I make a sort of living writing for magazines. I live in 316, just above here.

"By some curious architectural accident," he continued, as we reached his room, "that ventilator there enables me to hear minutely everything that goes on in the room below. I haven't ever said anything about it during the several months that I've lived here, partly because it does not disturb me, and partly because it has begun to pique my curiosity—a writer can confess to that, can he not? The man below is quiet and orderly, but seems to work a good deal on some sort of clockwork; I can hear it whirring and clicking quite often. But listen now!"

Standing within a couple of feet of the opening which was covered with an iron grill, I could hear footsteps. They were regular, and would decrease in intensity as the person walked away from the ventilator opening below, and increase again as he approached it; were interrupted for a moment as he probably stepped on a rug; and were shorter for two or three counts, no doubt as he turned at the end of the room. This was repeated in a regular rhythm as long as I listened.

"Well?" I said.

"You perceive nothing strange about that, I suppose," said Jerry Stoner. "But if you had listened all day long to just exactly that you would begin to wonder. That is the way he was going on when I awoke this morning; I was out from ten to eleven this forenoon. The rest of the time I have been writing steadily, with an occasional stretch at the window, and all of the time I have heard steadily what you hear now, without interruption or change. It's getting on my nerves.

"I have called him on the phone, and have rung it on and off for twenty minutes; I could hear his bell through the ventilator, but he pays no attention to it. So, a while ago I tried to call on him. Do you know him?"

"I know who he is," I replied, "but do not remember ever having met him."

"If you had ever met him you would remember. He has a queer head. I made my curiosity concerning the sounds from his room an excuse to cultivate his acquaintance.

The cultivation was difficult. He is courteous, but seemed afraid of me."

We agreed that there was not much that we could do about it. I gave up trying to keep my appointment, told Stoner that I was glad I had met him, and went home. The next morning at seven he had me on the telephone.

"Are you still interested?" he asked, and his voice was nervous. "That bird's been at it all night. Come and help me talk to the hotel management." I needed no urging.

I found Beesley, the hotel manager, with Stoner; he was from St. Louis, and looked French.

"He can do it if he wants to," he said, shrugging his shoulders comically; "unless you complain of it as a disturbance."

"It isn't that," said Stoner; "there must be something wrong with the man."

"Some form of insanity—" I suggested; "or a compulsion neurosis."

"That's what I'll be pretty soon," Stoner said. "He is a queer gink anyway. As far as I have been able to find out, he has no close friends. There is something about his appearance that makes me shiver; his face is so wrinkled and droopy, and yet he sails about the streets with an unusually graceful and vigorous step. Loan me your pass key; I think I'm as close a friend of his as anyone."

Beesley lent the key, but Stoner was back in a few minutes, shaking his head. Beesley was expecting that; he told us that when the hotel was built, Anstruther had the doors made of steel with special bars, at his own expense, and the windows shuttered, as though he were afraid for his life.

"His rooms would be as hard to break into as a fort," Beesley said as he left us; "and thus far we do not have sufficient reason for wrecking the hotel."

"Look here!" I said to Stoner; "it will take me a couple of hours to hunt up the stuff and string up a periscope;

it's an old trick I learned as a Boy Scout."

Between us we had it up in about that time; a radio aerial mast clamped on the windowsill with mirrors at the top and bottom, and a telescope at our end of it, gave us a good view of the room below us. It was a sort of living room made by throwing together two of the regular-sized hotel rooms. Anstruther was walking across it diagonally, disappearing from our field of view at the further end, and coming back again. His head hung forward on his chest with a ghastly limpness. He was a big, well-built man, with a vigorous stride. Always it was the same path. He avoided the small table in the middle each time with exactly the same sort of side step and swing. His head bumped limply as he turned near the window and started back across the room. For two hours we watched him in shivering fascination, during which he walked with the same hideous uniformity.

"That makes thirty hours of this," said Stoner. "Wouldn't you say that there was something wrong?"

We tried another consultation with the hotel manager. As a physician, I advised that something be done; that he be put in a hospital or something. I was met with another shrug.

"How will you get him? I still do not see sufficient cause for destroying the hotel company's property. It will take dynamite to get at him."

He agreed, however, to a consultation with the police, and in response to our telephone call, the great, genial chief, Peter John Smith was soon sitting with us. He advised us against breaking in.

"A man has a right to walk that way if he wants to," he said. "Here's this fellow in the papers who played the piano for 49 hours, and the police didn't stop him; and in Germany they practice making public speeches for 18 hours at a stretch. And there was this Olympic dancing fad some months ago, where a couple danced for 57 hours."

"It doesn't look right to me," I said, shaking my head. "There seems to be something wrong with the man's appearance; some uncanny disease of the nervous system—Lord knows I've never heard of anything that resembles it!"

We decided to keep a constant watch. I had to spend a little time on my patients, but Stoner and the chief stayed, and agreed to call me if occasion arose. I peeped through the periscope at the walking man several times during the next twenty-four hours; and it was always exactly the same, the hanging, bumping head, the uniformity of his course, the uncanny, machine-like exactitude of his movements. I spent an hour at a time with my eye at the telescope studying his movements for some variation, but was unable to be certain of any. That afternoon I looked up my neurology texts, but found no clues. The next day at four o'clock in the afternoon, after no less than fifty-five hours of it, I was there with Stoner to see the end of it; Chief Peter John Smith was out.

As we watched, we saw that he moved more and more slowly, but with otherwise identical motions. It had the effect of the slowed motion pictures of dancers or athletes; or it seemed like some curious dream; for as we watched, the sound of the steps through the ventilator also slowed and weakened. Then we saw him sway a little, and totter, as though his balance was imperfect. He swayed a few times and fell sidewise on the floor; we could see one leg in the field of our periscope moving slowly with the same movements as in walking, a slow, dizzy sort of motion. In five more minutes he was quite still.

The Chief was up in a few moments in response to our telephone call.

"Now we've got to break in," he said. Beesley shrugged his shoulders and said nothing. Stoner came to the rescue of the hotel property.

"A small man could go down this ventilator. This grill can be unscrewed, and the lower one can be knocked out with a hammer; it is cast iron."

Beesley was gone like a flash, and soon returned with one of his window-washers, who was small and wiry, and also a rope and hammer. We took off the grill and held the rope as the man crawled in. He shouted to us as he hit the bottom. The air drew strongly downwards but the blows of his hammer on the grill came up to us. We hurried downstairs. Not a sound came through the door of 216, and we waited for some minutes. Then there was a rattle of bars and the door opened, and a gust of cold wind struck us, with a putrid odor that made us gulp. The man had evidently run to open a window before coming to the door.

Anstruther lay on his side, with one leg straight and the other extended forward as in a stride; his face was livid, sunken, hideous. Stoner gave him a glance, and then scouted around the room—looking for the machinery he had been hearing, but finding none. The chief and I also went over the rooms, but they were just conventional rooms, rather colorless and lacking in personality. The chief called an undertaker and also the coroner, and arranged for a post-mortem examination. I received permission to notify a number of professional colleagues; I wanted some of them to share in the investigation of this unusual case with me. As I was leaving, I could not help noting the astonished gasps of the undertaker's assistants as they lifted the body; but they were apparently too well trained to say anything.

That evening, a dozen physicians gathered around the figure covered with a white sheet on the table in the center of the undertaker's work room. Stoner was there; a writer may be anywhere he chooses. The coroner was preparing to draw back the sheet.

"The usual medical history is lacking in this case," he said. "Perhaps an account by Dr. B. or his author friend, of the curious circumstances connected with the death of this man, may take its place."

"I can tell a good deal," said Stoner; "and I think it will bear directly on what you find when you open him up, even though it is not technical medical stuff. Do you care to hear it?"

"Tell it! Go on! Let's have it!"

"I have lived above him in the hotel for several months," Stoner began. "He struck me as a curious person, and as I do some writing, all mankind is my legitimate field for study. I tried to find out all I could about him.

"He has an office in the Little Building, and did a rather curious business. He dealt in vases and statuary, book-ends and chimes, and things you put around in rooms to make them look artistic. He had men out buying the stuff, and others selling it, all by personal contact and on a very exclusive basis. He kept the stock in a warehouse near the Rock Island tracks where they pass the Ball Park; I do not believe that he ever saw any of it. He just sat in the office and signed papers, and the other fellows made the money; and apparently they made a lot of it, for he has swung some big financial deals in this town.

"I often met him in the lobby or the elevator. He was a big, vigorous man and walked with an unusually graceful step and an appearance of strength and vitality. His eyes seemed to light up with recognition when he saw me, but in my company he was always formal and reserved. For such a vigorous-looking man, his voice was singularly cracked and feeble, and his head gave an impression of being rather small for him, and his face old and wrinkled.

"He seemed fairly well known about the city. At the Eastridge Club they told me that he plays golf occasionally and excellently, and is a graceful dancer, though somehow not a popular partner. He was seen frequently at the Y.M.C.A. bowling alleys and played with an uncanny skill. Men loved to see him bowl for his cleverness with the balls, but wished he were not so formally courteous, and did not wear such an expression of complete happiness over his victories. Bridley, manager of Rudge & Guenzel's book department, was the oldest friend of his that I could find, and he gave me some interesting information. They went to school together, and Anstruther was poor in health as well as in finances. Twenty-five years ago, during the hungry and miserable years after his graduation from the University, Bridley remembered him as saying:

" 'My brain needs a body to work with. If I had physical strength, I could do anything. If I find a fellow who can give it to me, I'll make him rich!'

"Bridley also remembers that he was sensitive because girls did not like his debilitated physique. He seems to have found health later, though I can find no one who remembers how or when. About ten years ago he came back from Europe where he had been for several years, in Paris, Bridley thinks; and for several years after this, a Frenchman lived with him. The city directory of that time has him living in the big stone house at 13th and 'G' streets. I went up there to look around, and found it a double house, Dr. Faubourg having occupied the other half. The present caretaker has been there ever since Anstruther lived in the house, and she says that his French companion must have been some sort of an engineer, and that the two must have been working on an invention, from the sounds she heard, and the materials they had about. Some three or four years ago the Frenchman and the machinery vanished, and Anstruther moved to the Cornhusker Hotel. Also at about this time, Dr. Faubourg retired from the practice of medicine. He must have been about fifty years old, and too healthy and vigorous to be retiring on account of old age or ill health.

"Apparently Anstruther never married. His private life was quite obscure, but he appeared much in public. He was always very courtly and polite to the ladies. Outside his business he took a great interest in Y.M.C.A. and Boy Scout camps, in the National Guard, and in fact in everything that stood for an outdoor, physical life, and promoted health. In spite of his oddity he was quite a hero with the small boys, especially since the time of his radium holdup. This is intimately connected with the story of his radium speculation that caused such a sensation in financial circles a couple of years ago.

"About that time, the announcement appeared of the discovery of new uses for radium; a way had been found to accelerate its splitting and to derive power from it. Its price went up, and it promised to become a scarce article on the market. Anstruther had never been known to speculate, nor to tamper with sensational things like oil and helium; but on this occasion he seemed to go into a panic. He cashed in on a lot of securities and caused a small panic in the city, as he was quite wealthy and had especially large amounts of money in the building-loan business. The newspapers told of how he had bought a hundred thousand dollars worth of radium, which was to be delivered right here in Lincoln—a curious method of speculating, the editors volunteered.

"It arrived by express one day, and Anstruther rode the express wagon with the driver to the station. I found the driver and he told the story of the holdup at 8th and 'P' streets at eleven o'clock at night. A Ford car drove up beside them, from which a man pointed a pistol at them and ordered them to stop. The driver stopped.

" 'Come across with the radium!' shouted the big black bulk in the Ford, climbing upon the express wagon. Anstruther's fist shot out like a flash of lightning, and struck the arm holding the pistol; and the driver states that he heard the pistol crash through the window on the second floor of the Lincoln Hotel. Anstruther pushed the express driver, who was in his way, backwards over the seat among the packages and leaped upon the holdup man; the driver said he heard Anstruther's muscles crunch savagely, as with little apparent effort he flung the man over the Ford; he fell with a thud on the asphalt and stayed there. Anstruther then launched a kick at the man at the wheel of the Ford, who crumpled up and fell out of the opposite side of the car.

"The police found the pistol inside a room on the second floor of the Lincoln Hotel. The steering post of the Ford car was torn from its fastenings. Both of the holdup men had ribs and collar-bones broken, and the gunman's forearm was bent double in the middle with both bones broken. These two men agreed later with the express driver that Anstruther's attack, for suddenness, swiftness, and terrific strength was beyond anything they had dreamed possible; he was like a thunderbolt; like some furious demon. When the two men were huddled in black heaps on the pavement, Anstruther said to the driver, quite impersonally: 'Drive to the police station. Come on! Wake up! I've got to get this stuff locked up!'

"One of the hold-up men had lost all his money and the home he was building when Anstruther had foreclosed a loan in his desperate scramble for radium. He was a Greek named Poulos, and has been in prison for two years; just last week he was released—"

Chief Peter John Smith interrupted.

"I've been putting two and two together and I can shed a little light on this problem. Three days ago, the day before I was called to watch Anstruther pacing his room, we picked up this man Poulos in the alleyway between Rudge & Guenzel's and Miller & Paine's. He was unconscious, and must have received a terrible licking at somebody's hand; his face was almost unrecognizable; several ribs and several fingers on his right hand were broken. He clutched a pistol fitted with a silencer, and we found that two shots had been fired from it. Here he is—"

A limp, bandaged, plastered man was pushed in between two policemen. He was sullen and apathetic, until he caught sight of Anstruther's face from which the chief had drawn a corner of the sheet. Terror and joy seemed to mingle in his face and in his voice. He raised his bandaged hand with an ineffectual gesture, and started off on some Greek religious expression, and then turned dazedly to us, speaking painfully through his swollen face.

"Glad he dead. I try to kill him. Shot him two time. No kill. So close—" indicating the distance of a foot from his chest; "then he lick me. He is not man. He is devil. I not kill him, but I glad he dead!"

The Chief hurried him out, and came in with a small, dapper man with a black chin whisker. He apologized to the coroner.

"This is not a frame-up. I am just following out a hunch that I got a few minutes ago while Stoner was talking. This is Mr. Fournier. I found his address in Anstruther's room, and dug him up. I think he will be more important to you doctors than he will in a court. Tell 'em what you told me!"

While the little Frenchman talked, the undertaker's assistant jerked off the sheet. The undertaker's work had had its effect in getting rid of the frightful odor, and in making Anstruther's face presentable. The body, however, looked for all the world as though it were alive, plump, powerful, pink. In the chest, over the heart, were two bullet holes, not bloody, but clean-cut and black. The Frenchman turned to the body and worked on it with a little screw-driver as he talked.

"Mr. Anstruther came to me ten years ago, when I was

a poor mechanic. He had heard of my automatic chess-player, and my famous animated show-window models; and he offered me time and money to find him a mechanical relief for his infirmity. I was an assistant at a Paris laboratory, where they had just learned to split radium and get a hundred horsepower from a pinch of powder. Anstruther was weak and thin, but ambitious."

The Frenchman lifted off two plates from the chest and abdomen of the body, and the flanks swung outward as though on hinges. He removed a number of packages that seemed to fit carefully within, and which were on the ends of cables and chains.

"Now—" he said to the assistants, who held the feet. He put his hands into the chest cavity, and as the assistants pulled the feet away, he lifted out of the shell a small, wrinkled, emaciated body; the body of an old man, which now looked quite in keeping with the well-known Anstruther head. Its chest was covered with dried blood, and there were two bullet holes over the heart. The undertaker's assistants carried it away while we crowded around to inspect the mechanism within the arms and legs of the pink and live-looking shell, headless, gaping at the chest and abdomen, but uncannily like a healthy, powerful man.

OMEGA

by Amelia Reynolds Long

I, Doctor Michael Claybridge, living in the year 1926, have listened to a description of the end of the world from the lips of the man who witnessed it; the last man of the human race. That this is possible, or that I am not insane, I cannot ask you to believe; I can only offer you the facts.

For a long time my friend, Professor Mortimer, had been experimenting with what he termed his theory of mental time; but I had known nothing of the nature of this theory until one day, in response to his request, I visited him at his laboratory. I found him bending over a young medical student, whom he had put into a state of hypnotic trance.

"A test of my theory, Claybridge," he whispered excitedly as I entered. "A moment ago I suggested to Bennet that this was the date of the battle of Waterloo. For him, it accordingly became so; for he described for me—and in French, mind you—a part of the battle at which he was present!"

"Present!" I exclaimed. "You mean that he is a reincarnation of—"

"No, no," he interrupted impatiently. "You forget—or rather, you do not know—that time is a circle, all of whose parts are coexistent. By hypnotic suggestion, I moved his materiality line until it became tangent with the Waterloo segment of the circle. Whether in physical time the two have ever touched before is of little matter."

Of course I understood nothing of this; but before I

could ask for an explanation, he had turned back to his patient.

"Attila, the Hun, is sweeping down upon Rome with his hordes," he said. "You are with them. Tell me what you see."

For a moment, nothing happened; then before our very eyes, the young man's features seemed to undergo a change. His nose grew beak-shaped, while his forehead acquired a backward slant. His pale face became ruddy, and his eyes changed from brown to gray-green. Suddenly, he flung out his arms; and there burst from his lips a torrent of sounds of which Mortimer and I could make nothing except that they bore a strong resemblance to the old Teutonic languages.

Mortimer let this continue for a moment or so before he recalled the boy from his trance. To my surprise, young Bennet was, upon awakening, quite his usual self without any trace of Hun features. He spoke, however, with a feeling of weariness.

"Now," I said when Mortimer and I were alone, "would you mind telling me what it is all about?"

He smiled. "Time," he began, "is of two kinds: mental and physical. Of these, mental is the real; physical the unreal; or, we might say, the instrument used to measure the real. And its measurement is gauged by intensity, not length."

"You mean—?" I asked, not sure that I followed him correctly.

"That real time is measured by the intensity with which we live it," he answered. "Thus a minute of mental time may, by the standards devised by man, be three hours deep, because we have lived it intensely; while an eon of mental time may embrace but half a day physically for reverse reasons."

"'A thousand years in Thy sight are but as yesterday when it is past and as a watch in the night,'" I murmured.

"Exactly," he said, "except that in mental time there is neither past nor future, but only a continuous present. Mental time, as I remarked a while ago, is an infinite circle with materiality a line running tangent to it. The point of tangency interprets it to the physical senses, and so creates what we call physical time. Since a line can be tangent to a circle at only one point, our physical existence is single. If it were possible, as some day it may be, to make the line bisect the circle, we shall lead two existences simultaneously.

"I have proven, as you saw in the case of Bennet just now, that the point of tangency between the time circle and the materiality line can be changed by hypnotic suggestion. An entirely satisfactory experiment, you must admit; and yet," he became suddenly dejected, "as far as the world is concerned, it proves absolutely nothing."

"Why not?" I asked. "Couldn't others witness such a demonstration as well as I?"

"And deem it a very nice proof of reincarnation," he shrugged. "No, Claybridge, it won't do. There is but one proof the world would consider; the transfer of a man's consciousness to the future."

"Cannot that be done?" I queried.

"Yes," he said. "But there is connected with it an element of danger. Mental status has a strong effect upon the physical being, as was witnessed by Bennet's reversion to the Hun type. Had I kept him in the hypnotic state for too long a period, the Teutonic cast of features would not have vanished with his awakening. What changes projection into the future would bring, I cannot say; and for that reason he is naturally unwilling that I experiment upon him in that direction."

He strode up and down the floor of his laboratory as he talked. His head was slumped forward upon his breast, as if heavy with the weight of thought.

"Then satisfactory proof is impossible?" I asked. "You

can never hope to convince the world?"

He stopped with a suddenness that was startling, and his head went up with a jerk. "No!" he cried. "I have not given up! I must have a subject for my experiments, and I shall proceed to find one."

This determined statement did not particularly impress me at the time, nor, for that matter, did the time-theory itself. Both were recalled to me a week or so later, when, in answer to his summons, I again visited Mortimer at the laboratory, and he thrust a newspaper into my hands, pointing to an item among the want ads.

"Wanted—" I read, "A subject for hypnotic experiment. $5,000 for the right man. Apply Prof. Alex Mortimer, Mortimer Laboratories, City."

"Surely," I exclaimed, "you do not expect to receive an answer to that?"

"On the contrary," he smiled, "I have received no less than a dozen answers. From them I chose the one who is most likely to prove the best subject. He will be here in a few minutes to sign the documents absolving me from any responsibility in case of accident. That is why I sent for you."

I could only stare at him.

"Of course," he went on, "I explained to him that there would be a degree of personal risk involved, but he appeared not to care. On the contrary, he seemed almost to welcome it. He—"

A knock at the door interrupted him. In response to his call, one of his assistants looked in.

"Mr. Williams is here, Professor."

"Send him in, Gable." As the assistant disappeared, Mortimer turned back to me. "My prospective subject," he explained. "He is prompt."

A thin, rather undersized man entered the room. My attention was at once drawn to his eyes, which seemed too large for his face.

"Mr. Williams, my friend, Dr. Claybridge," Mortimer introduced us. "The doctor is going to witness these articles we have to sign."

Williams acknowledged the introduction in a voice that sounded infinitely tired.

"Here are the papers," Mortimer said, pushing a few sheets of paper across the table toward him.

Williams merely glanced at them, and picked up a pen.

"Just a minute." Mortimer rang for Gable. The assistant and I witnessed the signature, and affixed our names below it.

"I am ready to begin immediately, if you like," Williams said when Gable had gone.

Mortimer eyed him reflectively for a moment. "First," he said, "there is a question I should like to ask you, Mr. Williams. You need not answer if you feel disinclined. Why are you so eager to undergo an experiment, the outcome of which even I cannot foresee?"

"If I answer that, will my answer be treated as strictly confidential?" asked Williams, casting a sidelong glance in my direction.

"Most certainly," Mortimer replied. "I speak for both myself and Dr. Claybridge." I nodded affirmation.

"Then," said Williams, "I will tell you. I welcome this experiment because, as you pointed out yesterday, there is a possibility of its resulting in my death. No, you did not say so in so many words, Prof. Mortimer, but that is the fear at the back of your mind. And why should I wish to die? Because, gentlemen, I have committed murder."

"What!" We barked out the word together.

Williams smiled wanly at our amazement. "That is rather an unusual statement, isn't it?" he asked in his tired voice. "Whom I murdered does not matter. The police will never find me out, for I was clever about it in order that my sister, to whom your $5,000, Professor, is to be paid, need not suffer from the humiliation of my arrest. But although I can escape the authorities, I cannot escape my own conscience. The knowledge that I have deliberately killed a man, even while he merited death, is becoming too much for me; and since my religion forbids suicide, I have turned to you as a possible way out. I think that is all."

We stared at him in silence. What Mortimer was thinking, I do not know. Most likely he was pondering upon the strange psychology of human conduct. As for me, I could not help wondering in what awful, perhaps pitiable tragedy this little man had been an actor.

Mortimer was the first to speak. When he did so, it was with no reference to what we had just heard. "Since you are ready, Mr. Williams, we will proceed with our initial experiment at once," he said. "I have arranged a special room for it, where there will be no other thought waves nor suggestions to disturb you."

He rose, and was apparently about to lead the way to this room when the telephone rang.

"Hello," he called into the transmitter. "Dr. Claybridge? Yes, he is here. Just a minute." He pushed the instrument towards me.

My hospital was on the wire. After taking the message, I hung up in disgust. "An acute case of appendicitis," I announced. "Of course I'm sorry for the poor devil, but he certainly chose an inopportune time for his attack."

"I will phone you all about the experiment," Mortimer promised as I reached for my hat. "Perhaps you can be present at the next one."

True to his promise, he rang me up that evening.

"I have had wonderful success!" he cried exultantly. "So far I have experimented only in a small way, but at that my theory has been proven beyond the possibility of doubt. And there was one most interesting feature, Claybridge. Williams told me what would be the nature of my experiment tomorrow afternoon."

"And what will it be?" I asked.

"I am to make his material consciousness tangent with the end of the world," was the astonishing answer.

"Good heavens!" I cried in spite of myself. "Shall you do it?"

"I have no choice in the matter," he replied.

"Mortimer, you fatalist! You—"

"No, no," he protested. "It is not fatalism. Can't you understand that—"

But I interrupted him. "May I be present?" I asked.

"Yes," he answered. "You will be there. Williams saw you."

I had a good mind to deliberately *not* be there, just to put a kink in his precious theory; but my curiosity was too great, and at the appointed time, I was on hand.

"I have already put Williams to sleep," Mortimer said as I came in. "He is in my especially prepared room. Come and I will show him to you."

He led me down a long hall to a door which I knew had originally given upon a storeroom. Inserting a key in the lock, he turned it, and flung the door open.

In the room beyond, I could see Williams seated in a swivel chair. His eyes were closed and his body relaxed, as if in sleep. However, it was not he that awakened my interest, but the room itself. It was windowless, with only a skylight in the ceiling to admit light and air. Aside from the chair in which Williams sat, there was no furniture save an instrument resembling an immense telephone transmitter that a crane arm held about two inches from the hypnotized man's mouth, and a set of ear phones, such as a telephone operator wears, which were attached to his ears. But strangest of all, the walls, floor, and ceiling of the room were lined with a whitish metal.

"White lead," said Mortimer, seeing my eyes upon it; "the substance least conductive of thought waves. I want the subject to be as free as possible from outside thought influences, so that when he talks with me over that telephone device, which is connected with my laboratory, there can be no danger of his telling me any but his own experiences."

"But the skylight," I pointed out. "It is partially open."

"True," he admitted. "But thought waves, like sound waves, travel upwards, and outwards; rarely, if ever, downwards. So, you see, there is little danger from the skylight."

He closed and locked the door, and we went back to the laboratory. In one corner was what looked like a radio loudspeaker, while near it was a transmitter similar to the one in the room with Williams.

"I shall speak to Williams through the transmitter," explained Mortimer, "and he shall hear me by means of the ear phones. When he answers into his transmitter, we will hear him through the loudspeaker."

He seated himself before the apparatus and spoke: "Williams, do you hear me?"

"I hear you." The reply came promptly, but in the heavy tones of a man talking in his sleep.

"Listen to me. You are living in the last six days of the Earth. By 'days,' I do not mean periods of twenty-four hours, but such lengths of time as are meant in the first chapter of the book of Genesis. It is now the first day of the six. Tell me what you see."

After a short interval, the answer came in a strange, high key. While the words were English, they were spoken with a curious intonation that was at first difficult to understand.

"This is the year 46,812," said the voice, "or, in modern time, 43,930 A.I.C. After Interplanetary Communication. It is not well upon the Earth. The Polar Ice Cap comes down almost to Newfoundland. Summer lasts but a few weeks, and then its heat is scorching. What in early time was known as the Atlantic Coastal Plain has long ago sunk into the sea. High dykes must be used to keep the water from covering the island of Manhattan, where the world's government is located. A great war has just concluded. There are many dead to bury."

"You speak of interplanetary communication," said Mortimer. "Is the world, then, in communication with the planets?"

In the year 2,952," came the answer, "the Earth succeeded in getting into communication with Mars. Radio pictures were sent back and forth between the two worlds until they learned each other's languages; then sound communication was established. The Martians had been trying to signal the Earth since the beginning of the twentieth century, but were unable to set up a system of communication because of the insufficient scientific advancement of the Earthmen.

"About a thousand years later, a message was received from Venus, which had now advanced to the Earth's state of civilization, when Mars was signaled. For nearly five hundred years they had been receiving messages from both the Earth and Mars, but had been unable to answer.

"A little over five thousand years later, a series of sounds was received which seemed to come from somewhere beyond Venus. Venus and Mars heard them too; but, like us, were able to make nothing of them. All three worlds broadcasted their radio pictures on the wave length corresponding to that of the mysterious sounds, but received no answer. At last Venus advanced the theory that the sounds had come from Mercury, whose inhabitants, obliged to live upon the side of their world farther from the sun, would be either entirely without sight or with eyes not sufficiently developed to see our pictures.

"Recently something dire has happened to Mars. Our last messages from her told of terrible wars and pestilences, such as we are now having upon Earth. Also, her water supply was beginning to give out, due to the fact that she was obliged to use much of it in the manufacture of atmosphere. Suddenly, about fifty years ago, all messages from her ceased; and upon signalling her, we received no answer."

Mortimer covered the transmitter with his hand. "That," he said to me, "can mean only that intelligent life upon Mars had become extinct. The Earth, then, can have but a few thousand years yet to go."

For nearly an hour longer he quizzed Williams upon conditions of the year 46,812. All the answers showed that while scientific knowledge had reached an almost incredible stage of advancement, the race of mankind was in its twilight. Wars had killed off thousands of people, while strange, new diseases found hosts of victims daily in a race whose members were no longer physically constituted to withstand them. Worst of all, the birth rate was rapidly diminishing.

"Listen to me." Mortimer raised his voice as if to impress his invisible subject with what he was about to say. "You are now living in the second day. Tell me what you see."

There was a moment or so of silence; then the voice, keyed even higher than before, spoke again.

"I see humanity in its death-throes," it said. "Only a few scattered tribes remain to roam over the deserted continents. The cattle have begun to sicken and die; and it is unsafe to use them for food. Four thousands years ago, we took to the manufacture of artificial air, as did the Martians before us. But it is hardly worthwhile, for children are no longer born. We shall be the last of our race."

"Have you received no recent word from Mars?" asked Mortimer.

"None. Two years ago, at her proper season, Mars

failed to appear in the heavens. As to what has become of her, we can only conjecture."

There was a horrible suggestiveness about this statement. I shuddered, and noticed that Mortimer did, also.

"The Polar Ice Cap has begun to retreat," resumed the voice. "Now it is winters that are short. Tropical plants have begun to appear in the temperate zones. The lower forms of animal life are becoming more numerous, and have begun to pursue man as man once pursued them. The days of the human race are definitely numbered. We are a band of strangers upon our own world."

"Listen to me," said Mortimer again. "It is now the third day. Describe it."

Followed the usual short interval of silence; then came the voice, fairly brittle with freezing terror.

"Why," it screamed, "do you keep me here; the last living man upon a dying planet? The world is festering with dead things. Let me be dead with them."

"Mortimer," I interrupted, "this is awful! Hasn't your experiment gone far enough?"

He pushed back his chair and rose. "Yes," he said, a bit shakily, I thought. "For the present, at least. Come; I will awaken Williams."

I followed him down the hall, and was close upon his heels, when he flung open the door of the lead-lined room, and stepped inside. Our cries of surprised alarm were simultaneous.

In the chair where we had left him sat Williams; but physically he was a different man. He had shrunken several inches in stature, while his head appeared to have grown larger, with the forehead almost bulbous in aspect. His fingers were extremely long and sensitive, but suggestive of great strength. His frame was thin to emaciation.

"Good Heavens!" I gasped. "What has happened?"

"It is an extreme case of mental influence upon matter,"

answered Mortimer, bending over the hypnotized man. "You remember how young Bennet's features took on the characteristics of a Hun? A similar thing, but in a much intenser degree, has happened to Williams. He has become a man of the future physically as well as mentally."

"Good Lord!" I cried. "Waken him at once! This is horrible."

"To be frank with you," said Mortimer gravely, "I am afraid to. He has been in this state much longer than I realized. To waken him too suddenly would be dangerous. It might even prove fatal."

For a moment he seemed lost in thought. Then he removed the ear phones from Williams's head, and addressed him. "Sleep," he commanded. "Sleep soundly and naturally. When you have rested sufficiently, you will awaken and be your normal self."

Shortly after this, I left Mortimer, and, although it was my day off duty, went to my hospital. How good my commonplace tonsil cases seemed after the unholy things I had just experienced! I surprised the resident physician almost into a state of coma by putting in the remainder of the day in the hardest work possible in the free clinic; and finally went home, tired in mind and body.

I turned in early for what I deemed a well-earned rest, and fell asleep instantly. The next thing of which I was conscious was the insistent ringing of the telephone bell beside my bed.

"Hello," I cried sleepily, taking down the receiver. "Dr. Claybridge speaking."

"Claybridge, this is Mortimer," came the almost hysterical response. "For God's sake, come over to the laboratory at once!"

"What has happened?" I demanded, instantly wide awake. It would take something unusual to wring such exictement from the unemotional Mortimer.

"It's Williams," he answered. "I can't bring him back.

He got awake about an hour ago, and still believes that he is living in the future. Physically, he is the same as he was when last you saw him this afternoon."

"I'll be over at once," I fairly shouted, and slammed the receiver down upon its hook. As I scrambled into my clothes, I glanced at the clock. Two fifteen. In half an hour I could reach the laboratory. What would I find waiting for me?

Mortimer was in the lead room with Williams when I arrived.

"Claybridge," he said, "I need someone else's opinion in this case. Look at him, and tell me what you think."

Williams occupied the chair in the middle of the room. His eyes were wide open, but it was plain that he saw neither Mortimer nor me. Even when I bent over him and touched him, he gave no sign of being conscious of my presence.

"He looks as if he were suffering from some sort of catalepsy," I said, "yet his temperature and pulse are almost normal. I should say that he is still partially in a state of hypnosis."

"Then it is self-hypnosis," said Mortimer, "for I have entirely withdrawn my influence."

"Perhaps," I suggested lightly, "you have transported him irretrievably into the future."

"That," Mortimer replied, "is precisely what I fear has happened."

I stared at him dumbly.

"The only way out," he went on," is to rehypnotize him, and finish the experiment. At its conclusion, he may return to his natural state."

I could not help thinking that there were certain things which it was forbidden man to know; and that Mortimer, having wantonly blundered into them, was now being made to pay the penalty. I watched him as he worked over poor Williams, straining all his energies to induce a state of hyponotic sleep. At last the glassy eyes before him closed, and his subject slept. With hands that trembled visibly, he adjusted the ear phones, and we went back to the laboratory.

"Williams," Mortimer called into his transmitter, "do you hear me?"

"I hear you," replied the odiously familiar voice.

"You are now living in the fourth day. What do you see?"

"I see reptiles; great lizards that walk upon their hind legs, and birds with tiny heads and bats' wings, that build nests in the ruins of the deserted cities."

"Dinosaurs and pterodactyls!" I gaped involuntarily. "A second age of reptiles!"

"The polar caps have retreated until there is but a small area of ice about each of the poles," continued the voice. "There are no longer any seasons; only a continuous reign of heat. The torrid zone has become uninhabitable even by the reptiles. The sea there boils. Great monsters writhe in their death agonies upon its surface. Even the northern waters are becoming heated.

"All the land is covered with rank vegetation upon which the reptiles feed. The air is fetid with it."

Mortimer interrupted: "Describe the fifth day."

After the customary interval, the voice replied. There was a sticky quality about it that reminded me of the sucking of mud at some object struggling in it.

"The reptiles are gone," it said. "I alone live upon this expiring world. Even the plant life has turned yellow and withered. The volcanoes are in terrific action. The mountains are becoming level, and soon all will be one vast plain. A thick, green slime is gathering upon the face of the waters, so that it is difficult to tell where the land with its rotting vegetation ends and the sea begins. The sky is saffron in color, like a plate of hot brass. At night a blood red moon swims drunkenly in a black sky.

"Something is happening to gravitation. For a long time I had suspected it. Today I tested it by throwing a stone into the air. I was carried several feet above the ground by the force of my action. It took the stone nearly twenty minutes to return to earth. It fell slowly, *and at an angle!*"

"An angle!" cried Mortimer.

"Yes. It was barely perceptible, but it was there. The earth's movement is slowing. Days and nights have more than doubled in length."

"What is the condition of the atmosphere?"

"A trifle rarefied, but not sufficiently so to make breathing difficult. This seems strange to me."

"That," said Mortimer to me, "is because his body is here in the twentieth century, where there is plenty of air. The air at the stage of earth's career where his mind is would be too rare to support organic life. Even now the mental influence is so strong that he believes the density of the atmosphere to be decreasing."

"Recently," Williams's voice went on, "the star Vega has taken Polaris's place as center of the universe. Many of the old stars have disappeared, while new ones have taken their places. I have a suspicion that our solar system is either falling or traveling in a new direction through space."

"Listen to me, Williams." Mortimer's voice sounded dry and cracked, and his forehead was besprinkled with great gouts of sweat. "It is the sixth, the last day. What do you see?"

"I see a barren plain of gray rock. The world is in perpetual twilight because the mists that rise from the sea obscure the sun. Heaps of brown bones dot the plain near the mounds that once were cities. The dykes around Manhattan long ago crumbled away; but there is no longer any need for them even were men here, for the sea is rapidly drying up. The atmosphere is becoming exceedingly rarefied. I can hardly breathe. . . .

"Gravitation is giving out more rapidly. When I stand erect I sway as though drunk. Last night the curtains of mist parted for a time, and I saw the moon fly off into space.

"Great lightnings play about the Earth, but there is no thunder. The silence all around is plummetless. I keep speaking aloud and striking one object against another to relieve the strain on my eardrums. . . .

"Great cracks are beginning to appear in the ground, from which smoke and molten lava issue. I have fled to Manhattan in order that the skeletons of the tall buildings may hide them from my sight.

"Small objects have begun to move of their own volition. I am afraid to walk, as each step hurls me off my balance. The heat is awful. I cannot breathe."

There was a short interval, that came as a relief to our tightly screwed nerves. The tension to which the experiment had pitched us was terrific; yet I, for one, could no more have torn myself away than I could have passed into the fourth dimension.

Suddenly the voice cut the air like a knife!

"The buildings!" it shrieked. "They are swaying! They are leaning toward each other! They are crumbling, disintegrating; and the crumbs are flying *outward instead of falling!* Tiny particles are being thrown off by everything around me. Oh, the heat! There is no air!"

Followed a hideous gurgling; then:

"The earth is dissolving beneath my feet! It is the end. Creation is returning to its original atoms! Oh, my God!" There was a sickening scream that rapidly grew fainter with the effect of fading on radio.

"Williams!" shouted Mortimer. "What happened?"

There was no answer.

"Williams! Williams!" Mortimer was on his feet, fairly shrieking into the instrument. "Do you hear me?"

The only response was utter silence.

Mortimer clutched me by the arm, and dragged me with him from the laboratory and down the hall.

"Is—is he dead?" I choked as we ran.

Mortimer did not answer. His breath was coming in quick, short gasps that would have made speech impossible even had he heard me.

At the door of the lead room he stopped and fumbled with his keys. From beyond we could hear no sound. Twice Mortimer, in his nervousness and hurry, dropped the key and had to grope for it; but at last he got it turned in the lock, and flung the door open.

In our haste, we collided with each other as we hurtled into the room. Then as one man we stopped dead in our tracks. The room was empty!

"Where—" I began incredulously. "He couldn't have gotten out! Could he?"

"No," Mortimer answered hoarsely.

We advanced farther into the room, peering into every crack and corner. From the back of the chair, suspended by their cord, hung the earphones; while dangling from the chair's seat to the floor were the tattered and partially charred remains of what seemed to have been at one time a suit of men's clothing. At sight of these, Mortimer's face went white. In his eyes was a look of dawning comprehension and horror.

"What does it mean?" I demanded.

For answer, he pointed a palsied finger.

As I looked, the first beam of morning sunlight slipped through the skylight above us, and fell obliquely to the floor. In its golden shaft, directly above the chair where Williams had sat, a myriad of infinitesimal atoms were dancing.

JAQUAYS

THE PLUTONIAN DRUG

by Clark Ashton Smith

"It is remarkable," said Dr. Manners, "how the scope of our pharmacopoeia has been widened by interplanetary exploration. In the past thirty years, hundreds of hitherto unknown substances, employable as drugs or medical agents, have been found in other worlds of our own system. It will be interesting to see what the Allan Farquar expedition will bring back from the planets of *Alpha Centauri* when—or if—it succeeds in reaching them and returning to earth. I doubt, though, if anything more valuable than selenine will be discovered. Selenine, derived from a fossil lichen found by the first rocket-expedition to the moon in 1975, has, as you know, practically wiped out the old-time curse of cancer. In solution, it forms the base of an infallible serum, equally useful for cure or prevention."

"I fear I haven't kept up on a lot of the new discoveries," said Rupert Balcoth, the sculptor, Manner's guest, a little apologetically. "Of course, everyone has heard of selenine. And I've seen frequent mention, recently, of a mineral water from Ganymede whose effects are like those of the mythical Fountain of Youth."

"You mean *clithni*, as the stuff is called by the Ganymedians. It is a clear, emerald liquid, rising in lofty geysers from the craters of quiescent volcanoes. Scientists believe the drinking of *clithni* is the secret of the most fabulous longevity of the Ganymedians; and they think that it may prove to be a similar elixir for humanity."

"Some of the extraplanetary drugs haven't been so

beneficial to mankind, have they?" queried Balcoth. "I seem to have heard of a Martian poison that has greatly facilitated the gentle art of murder. And I am told that *mnophka*, the Venerian narcotic, is far worse, in its effects on the human system, than is any terrestial alkaloid."

"Naturally," observed the doctor with philosophic calm, "many of these new chemical agents are capable of dire abuse. They share that liability with any number of our native drugs. Man, as ever, has the choice of good and evil . . . I suppose that the Martian poison you speak of is *akpaloli*, the juice of a common russet-yellow weed that grows in the oases of Mars. It is colorless, and without taste or odor. It kills almost instantly, leaving no trace, and imitating closely the symptoms of heart disease. Undoubtedly many people have been made away with by means of a surreptitious drop of *akpaloli* in their food or medicine. But even *akpaloli*, if used in infinitesimal doses, is a very powerful stimulant, useful in cases of syncope, and serving, not infrequently, to re-animate victims of paralysis in a quite miraculous manner.

"Of course," he went on, "there is an infinite lot still to be learned about many of these ultra-terrene substances. Their virtues have often been discovered quite by accident—and in some cases, the virtue is still to be discovered.

"For example, take *mnophka*, which you mentioned a little while ago. Though allied in a way, to the earth-narcotics, such as opium and hashish, it is of little use for anaesthetic or anodyne purposes. Its chief effects are an extraordinary acceleration of the time-sense, and a heightening and telescoping of all sensations, whether pleasurable or painful. The user seems to be living and moving at a furious whirlwind rate—even though he may in reality by lying quiescent on a couch. He exists in a headlong torrent of sense-impressions, and seems, in a few minutes, to undergo the experiences of years. The physical result is lamentable—a profound exhaustion, and an actual aging of the tissues, such as would ordinarily require the period of real time which the addict has 'lived' through merely in his own illusion.

"There are some other drugs, comparatively little known, whose effects, if possible, are even more curious than those of *mnophka*. I don't suppose you have heard of plutonium?"

"No, I haven't," admitted Balcoth. "Tell me about it."

"I can do even better than that—I can show you some of the stuff, though it isn't much to look at—merely a fine white powder."

Dr. Manners rose from the pneumatic-cushioned chair in which he sat facing his guest, and went to a large cabinet of synthetic ebony, whose shelves were crowded with flasks, bottles, tubes and cartons of various sizes and forms. Returning, he handed Balcoth a squat and tiny vial, two-thirds filled with a starchy substance.

"Plutonium," explained Manners, "as its name would indicate, comes from forlorn, frozen Pluto, which only one terrestrial expedition has so far visited—the expedition led by the Cornell brothers, John and Augustine, which started in 1990 and did not return to earth till 1996, when nearly everyone had given it up for lost. John, as you may have heard, died during the returning voyage, together with half the personnel of the expedition: and the others reached earth with only one reserve oxygen-tank remaining.

"This vial contains about a tenth of the existing supply of plutonium. Augustine Cornell, who is an old school friend of mine, gave it to me three years ago, just before he embarked with the Allan Farquar crowd. I count myself pretty lucky to own anything so rare.

"The geologists of the party found the stuff when they began prying beneath the solidified gases that cover the surface of that dim starlit planet, in an effort to learn a little about its composition and history. They couldn't do much under the circumstances, with limited time and equipment; but they made some curious discoveries—of which plutonium was far from being the least.

"Like selenine, the stuff is a by-product of vegetable fossilization. Doubtless it is many billion years old, and dates back to the time when Pluto possessed enough internal heat to make possible the development of certain rudimentary plant-forms on its blind surface. It must have had an atmosphere then; though no evidence of former animal life was found by the Cornells."

"Plutonium, in addition to carbon, hydrogen, nitrogen and oxygen, contains minute quantities of several unclassified elements. It was discovered in a crystalloid condition, but turned immediately to the fine powder that you see, as soon as it was exposed to air in the rocketship. It is readily soluble in water, forming a permanent colloid, without the least sign of deposit, no matter how long it remains in suspension."

"You say it is a drug?" queried Balcoth. "What does it do to you?"

"I'll come to that in a minute—though the effect is pretty hard to describe. The properties of the stuff were discovered only by chance: on the return journey from Pluto, a member of the expedition, half delirious from space-fever, got hold of the unmarked jar containing it and took a small dose, imagining that it was bromide of potassium. It served to complicate his delirium for a while—since it gave him some brand new ideas about space and time.

"Other people have experimented with it since then. The effects are quite brief (the influence never lasts more than half an hour) and they vary considerably with the individual. There is no bad aftermath, either neural, mental or physical, as far as anyone has been able to determine. I've taken it myself, once or twice, and can testify to that.

"Just what it does to one, I am not sure. Perhaps it merely produces a derangement or metamorphia of sensations, like hashish; or perhaps it serves to stimulate some rudimentary organ, some dominant sense of the human brain. At any rate, there is, as clearly as I can put it, an altering of the perception of time—of actual duration—into sort of space-perception. One sees the past, and also the future, in relation to one's own physical self, like a landscape stretching away on either hand. You don't see very far, it is true—merely the events of a few hours in each direction; but it's a very curious experience; and it helps to give a new slant on the mystery of time and space. It is altogether different from the delusions of *mnophka*."

"It sounds very interesting," admitted Balcoth. "However, I've never tampered much with narcotics myself; though I did experiment once or twice, in my young romantic days with *Cannabis indica*. I had been reading Gautier and Baudelaire, I suppose. Anyway, the result was rather disappointing."

"You didn't take it long enough for your system to absorb a residuum of the drug, I imagine," said Manners. "Thus the effects were negligible, from a visionary standpoint. But plutonium is altogether different—you get the maximum result from the very first dose. I think it would interest you greatly, Balcoth, since you are a sculptor by profession; you could see some unusual plastic images, not easy to render in terms of Euclidian planes and angles. I'll gladly give you a pinch of it now, if you'd care to experiment."

"You're pretty generous, aren't you, since the stuff is so rare?"

"I'm not being generous at all. For years, I've planned to write a monograph on extra-terrestrial narcotics; and you might give me some valuable data. With your type of brain and your highly developed artistic sense, the visions of plutonium should be uncommonly clear and significant. All I ask is that you describe them to me as fully as you can afterwards."

"Very well," agreed Balcoth. "I'll try anything once." His curiosity was inveigled, his imagination seduced, by Manner's account of the remarkable drug.

Manners brought out an antique whiskey-glass, which he filled nearly to the brim with some golden-red liquid. Uncorking the vial of plutonium, he added to this fluid a small pinch of the fine white powder, which dissolved immediately and without effervescence.

"The liquid is a wine made from a sweet Martian tuber known as *ovvra*," he explained. "It is light and harmless, and will counteract the bitter taste of the plutonium. Drink it quickly and then lean back in your chair.

Balcoth hesitated, eyeing the golden-red fluid.

"Are you quite sure the effects will wear off as promptly as you say?" he questioned. "It's a quarter past nine now, and I'll have to leave about ten to keep an appointment with one of my patrons at the Belvedere Club. It's the billionaire Claud Wishhaven, who wants me to do a bas-relief in pseudo-jade and neo-jasper for the hall of his country mansion. He wants something really advanced and futuristic. We're to talk it over tonight—decide on the motifs, etc."

"That gives you forty-five minutes," assured the doctor— "and in thirty, at the most, your brain and senses will be perfectly normal again. I've never known it to fail. You'll have fifteen minutes to spare, in which to tell me all about your sensations."

Balcoth emptied the antique glass at a gulp and leaned back, as Manners had directed, on the deep pneumatic cushions of the chair. He seemed to be falling easily but endlessly into a mist that had gathered in the room with unexplainable rapidity; and through this mist he was dimly aware that Manners had taken the empty glass from his relaxing fingers. He saw the face of Manners far above him, small and blurred, as if in some tremendous perspective of alpine distance; and the doctor's simple action seemed to be occurring in another world.

He continued to fall and float through eternal mist, in which all things were dissolved as in the primordial nebulae of chaos. After a timeless interval, the mist, which had been uniformly gray and hueless at first, took on a flowing iridescence, never the same for two successive moments; and the sense of gentle falling turned to a giddy revolution, as if he were caught in an ever-accelerating vortex.

Coincidentally with his movement in this whirlpool of prismatic splendor, he seemed to undergo an indescribable mutation of the senses. The whirling colors, by subtle, ceaseless gradations, became recognizable as solid forms. Emerging, as if by an act of creation, from the infinite chaos, they appeared to take their place in an equally infinite vista. The feeling of movement, through decreasing spirals, was resolved into absolute immobility. Balcoth was no longer conscious of himself as a living organic body: he was an abstract eye, a discorporate center of visual awareness, stationed alone in space, and yet having an intimate relationship with the frozen prospect on which he peered from his ineffable vantage.

Without surprise, he found that he was gazing simultaneously in two directions. On either hand, for a vast distance that seemed wholly void of normal persepective, a weird and peculiar landscape stretched away, traversed by an unbroken frieze or bas-relief of human figures that ran like a straight undeviating wall.

For a while the frieze was incomprehensible to

Balcoth, and he could make nothing of its glacial, flowing outlines with their background of repeated masses and complicated angles and sections of other human friezes that approached or departed, often in a very abrupt manner, from an unseen world beyond. Then the vision seemed to resolve and clarify itself, and he began to understand.

The bas-relief, he saw, was composed entirely of a repetition of his own figure, plainly distinct as the separate waves of a stream, and possessing a stream-like unity. Immediately before him, and for some distance on either hand, the figure was seated in a chair—the chair itself being subject to the same billowy repetition. The background was composed of the reduplicated figure of Dr. Manners, in another chair; and behind this, the manifold images of a medicine cabinet and a section of wall paneling.

Following the vista on what, for lack of any better name, might be termed the left hand, Balcoth saw himself in the act of draining the antique glass, with Manners standing before him. Then, still further, he saw himself previous to this, with a background in which Manners was presenting him the glass, was preparing the dose of plutonium, was going to the cabinet for the vial, was rising from his pneumatic chair. Every movement, every attitude of the doctor and himself during their past conversation, was visioned in a sort of reverse order, reaching away, unalterable as a wall of stone sculpture, into the weird eternal landscape. There was no break in the continuity of his own figure; but Manners seemed to disappear at times, as if into a fourth dimension. These times, he remembered later, were the occasions when the doctor had not been in his line of vision. The perception was wholly visual; and though Balcoth saw his own lips and those of Manners parted in movements of speech, he could hear no word or other sound.

Perhaps the most singular feature of the vision was the utter absence of foreshortening. Though Balcoth seemed to behold it all from a fixed, immovable point, the landscape and the intersecting frieze presented themselves to him without diminution, maintaining a frontal fullness and distinctness to a distance that might have been many miles.

Continuing along the left-hand vista, he saw himself entering Manners' apartments, and then encountered his image standing in the elevator that had borne him to the ninth floor of the hundred-story hotel in which Manners lived. Then the frieze appeared to have an open street for background, with a confused, ever-changing multitude of other faces and forms, of vehicles and sections of buildings, all jumbled together as in some old-time futuristic painting. Some of these details were full and clear, and others were cryptically broken and blurred, so as to be scarcely recognizable. Everything, whatever its spatial position and relation, was rearranged in the flowing frozen stream of this temporal pattern.

Balcoth retraced the three blocks from Manners' hotel to his own studio, seeing all his past movements, whatever their direction in tri-dimensional space, as a straight line in the time-dimension. At last he was in his studio; and there the frieze of his own figure receded into the eerie prospect of space-transmuted time among other friezes formed of actual sculptures. He beheld himself giving the final touches with his chisel to a symbolic statue at the afternoon's end, with a glare of ruddy sunset falling through an unseen window and flushing the pallid marble. Beyond this there was a reverse fading of the glow, a thickening and blurring of the half-chiselled features of the image, a female form to which he had given the tentative name of Oblivion. At length, among half-seen statuary, the left-hand vista became indistinct, and melted slowly in amorphous mist. He had seen his own life as a continuous glaciated stream, stretching for about five hours into the past.

Reaching away on the right hand, he saw the vista of the future. Here there was a continuation of his seated figure under the influence of the drug, opposite the continued bas-relief of Dr. Manners and the repeated cabinet and wall-panels. After a considerable interval, he beheld himself in the act of rising from the chair. Standing erect, he seemed to be talking a while, as in some silent antique film, to the listening doctor. After that, he was shaking hands with Manners, was leaving the apartment, was descending in the lift and following the open, brightly lighted street towards the Belvedere Club where he was to keep his appointment with Claud Wishhaven.

The Club was only three blocks away, on another street; and the shortest route, after the first block, was along a narrow alley between an office building and a warehouse. Balcoth had meant to take this alley; and in his vision, he saw the bas-relief of his future figure passing along the straight pavement with a background of deserted doorways and dim walls that towered from sight against the extinguished stars.

He seemed to be alone: there were no passers—only the silent, glimmering, endlessly repeated angles of arc-lit walls and windows that accompanied his retreating figure. He saw himself following the alley, like a stream in some profound canyon; and there, mid-way, the strange vision came to an abrupt, inexplicable end, without the gradual blurring into formless mist, that had marked his retrospective view of the past.

The sculpture-like frieze with its architectural ground appeared to terminate, broken off clean and sharp, in a gulf of immeasurable blackness and nullity. The last wave-like duplication of his own person, the vague doorway beyond it, the glimmering alley-pavement, all were seen as if shorn asunder by a falling sword of darkness, leaving a vertical line of cleavage beyond which there was—nothing.

Balcoth had a feeling of uttter detachment from himself, an eloignment from the stream of time, from the shores of space, in some abstract dimension. The experience, in its full realization, might have lasted for an instant only—or for eternity. Without wonder, without curiosity or reflection, like a fourth-dimensional Eye, he viewed simultaneously the unequal cross-section of his own past and future.

After that timeless interval of complete perception, there began a reverse process of change. He, the all-seeing eye, aloof in super-space, was aware of movement, as if he were drawn back by some subtle thread of magnetism into the dungeon of time and space from which he had momentarily departed. He seemed to be following the frieze of his own seated body towards the right, with a dimly felt rhythm or pulsation in his movement that corresponded to the merging duplications of the figure. With curious clearness, he realized that the time-unit, by which his duplications were determined, was the beating of his own heart.

Now with accelerative swiftness, the vision of petrific form and space was redissolving into a spiral swirl of multitudinous colors, through which he was drawn upward. Presently he came to himself, seated in the pneumatic chair, with Dr. Manners opposite. The room seemed to waver a little, as if with some lingering touch of the weird transmutation; and webs of spinning iris hung in the corners of his eyes. Apart from this, the effect of the drug had wholly vanished, leaving, however, a singularly clear and vivid memory of the almost ineffable experience.

Dr. Manners began to question him at once, and Balcoth described his visionary sensations as fully and graphically as he could.

"There is one thing I don't understand," said Manners at the end with a puzzled frown. "According to your account, you must have seen five or six hours of the past, running in a straight spatial line, as a sort of continuous landscape; but the vista of the future ended sharply after you had followed it for three-quarters of an hour, or less. I've never known the drug to act so unequally: the past and future perspectives have always been about the same in their extent for others who have used plutonium."

"Well," observed Balcoth, "the real marvel is that I could see into the future at all. In a way, I can understand the vision of the past. It was clearly composed of physical memories—of all my recent movements; and the background was formed of all of the impressions my optic nerves had received during that time. But how could I behold something that hasn't yet happened?"

"There's the mystery, of course," asserted Manners. "I can think of only one explanation at all intelligible to our finite minds. This is, that all events which compose the stream of time have already happened, are happening and will continue to happen forever. In our ordinary state of consciousness, we perceive with the physical senses merely that moment which we call the present. Under the influence of plutonium, you were able to extend the moment of present cognition in both directions, and to behold simultaneously a certain portion of that which is normally beyond perception. Thus appeared the vision of yourself as a continuous, immobile body, extending through the time-vista."

Balcoth, who was standing, now took his leave. "I must be going," he said, "or I'll be late for my appointment."

"I won't detain you any longer," said Manners. He appeared to hesitate, and then added: "I'm still at a loss to comprehend the abrupt cleavage and termination of your prospect of the future. The alley in which it seemed to end was Falman Alley, I suppose—your shortest route to the Belvedere Club. If I were you, Balcoth, I'd take another route, even if it requires a few minutes extra."

"That sounds rather sinister," laughed Balcoth. "Do you think that something may happen to me in Falman Alley?"

"I hope not—but I can't guarantee that it won't." Manners' tone was oddly dry and severe. "You'd better do as I suggest."

Balcoth felt the touch of a momentary shadow as he left the hotel—a premonition brief and light as the passing of some night-bird on noiseless wings. What could it mean—that gulf of infinite blackness into which the weird frieze of his future had appeared to plunge, like a frozen cataract? Was there a menace of some sort that awaited him in a particular place, at a particular moment?

He had a curious feeling of repetition, of doing something that he had done before, as he followed the street. Reaching the entrance of Falman Alley, he took out his watch. By walking briskly and following the alley, he would reach the Belvedere Club punctually. But if he went on around to the next block, he would be a little late. Balcoth knew that his prospective patron, Claud Wishhaven, was almost a martinet in demanding punctuality from himself and from others. So he took the alley.

The place appeared to be entirely deserted, as in his vision. Mid-way, Balcoth approached the half-seen door—a rear-entrance of a huge warehouse—which had formed the termination of the time prospect. The door was his last visual impression, for something descended on his head at that moment, and his consciousness was blotted out by the supervening night he had previsioned. He had been sandbagged, very quietly and efficiently, by a twenty-first-century thug. The blow was fatal; and time, as far as Balcoth was concerned, had come to an end.

G.Barr

THE LAST EVOLUTION

by John W. Campbell, Jr.

I am the last of my type existing today in all the Solar System. I, too, am the last existing who, in memory, sees the struggle for this system, and in memory I am still close to the Center of Rulers, for mine was the ruling type then. But I will pass soon, and with me will pass the last of my kind, a poor inefficient type, but yet the creators of those who are now, and will be, long after I pass forever.

So I am setting down my record on the mentatype.

It was 2538 years After the Year of the Son of Man. For six centuries mankind had been developing machines. The Ear-apparatus was discovered as early as seven hundred years before. The Eye came later, the Brain came much later. But by 2500, the machines had been developed to think, and act and work with perfect independence. Man lived on the products of the machine, and the machines lived to themselves very happily, and contentedly. Machines are designed to help and cooperate. It was easy to do the simple duties they needed to do that man might live well. And men had created them. Most of mankind was quite useless, for they lived in a world where no productive work was necessary. But games, athletic contests, adventure—these were the things they sought for their pleasure. Some of the poorer types of man gave themselves up wholly to pleasure and idleness—and to emotions. But man was a sturdy race, which had fought for existence through a million years, and the training of a million years does not slough quickly from any form of life, so their energies were bent to mock battles now, since real ones no longer existed.

Up to the year 2100, the numbers of mankind had increased rapidly and continuously, but from that time on, there was a steady decrease. By 2500, their number was a scant two millions, out of a population that once totaled many hundreds of millions, and was close to ten billions in 2100.

Some few of these remaining two millions devoted themselves to the adventure of discovery and exploration of places unseen, of other worlds and other planets. But few devoted themselves to the highest adventure, the unseen places of the mind. Machines—with their irrefutable logic, their cold preciseness of figures, their tireless, utterly exact observation, their absolute knowledge of mathematics—they could elaborate any idea, however simple its beginning, and reach the conclusion. From any three facts they even then could have built in mind all the Universe. Machines had imagination of the ideal sort. They had the ability to construct a necessary future result from a present fact. But men had imagination of a different kind, theirs was the illogical, brilliant imagination that sees the future result vaguely, without knowing the why, nor the how, an imagination that outstrips the machine in its preciseness. Man might reach the conclusion more swiftly, but the machine always reached the conclusion eventually, and it was always the correct conclusion. By leaps and bounds man advanced. By steady, irresistible steps, the machine marched forward.

Together, man and the machine were striding through science irresistibly.

Then came the Outsiders. Whence they came, neither machine nor man ever learned, save only that they came from beyond the outermost planet, from some other sun. Sirius—Alpha Centauri—perhaps! First a thin scoutline of a hundred great ships, mighty torpedoes of the void a thousand kilads* in length, they came.

And one machine returning from Mars to Earth was instrumental in its first discovery. The transport machine's brain ceased to radiate its sensations, and the control in old Chicago knew immediately that some unperceived body had destroyed it. An investigation machine was instantly dispatched from Deimos, and it maintained an acceleration of one thousand units.+ They sighted ten huge ships, one of which was grappling the smaller transport machine. The entire foresection had been blasted away.

The investigation machine, scarcely three inches in diameter, crept into the shattered hull and investigated. It was quickly evident that the damage was caused by a fusing ray.

Strange life forms were crawling about the ship, protected by flexible transparent suits. Their bodies were short, and squat, four limbed and evidently powerful. They, like insects, were equipped with a thick, durable exoskeleton, a horny, brownish coating that covered arms and legs and head. Their eyes projected slightly, protected by horny protruding walls—eyes that were capable of movement in every direction—and there were three of them, set at equal distances apart.

The tiny investigation machine hurled itself violently at one of the beings, crashing against the transparent covering, flexing it, and striking the being inside with terrific force. Hurled from his position, he fell end over end across the weightless ship, but despite the blow, he was not hurt.

* Kilad—unit introduced by the machines. Based on the duodecimal system, similarly introduced as more logical, and more readily used. Thus we would have said 1728 kilads, about 1/2 mile.

+ One unit was equal to one earth-gravity.

The investigator passed to the power room ahead of the Outsiders, who were anxiously trying to learn the reason for their companion's plight.

Directed by the Center of Rulers, the investigator sought the power room, and relayed the signals from the Rulers' brains. The ship-brain had been destroyed, but the controls were still readily workable. Quickly they were shot home, and the enormous plungers shut. A combination was arranged so that the machine could not withstand it; the last plunger snapped shut. Instantly the vast energies stored for operating the ship were released, and the entire machine, as well as the investigator and the Outsiders, were destroyed. A second investigator, which had started when the plan was decided on, had now arrived. The Outsiders' ship nearest the transport machine had been badly damaged, and the invesigator entered the broken side.

The scenes were, of course, remembered by the memory—minds back on Earth tuned with that of the investigator. The investigator flashed down corridors, searching quickly for the apparatus room. It was soon seen that with them the machine was practically unintelligent, very few machines of even slight intelligence being used.

Then it became evident by the excited action of the men of the ship, that the presence of the investigator had been detected. Perhaps it was the control impulses, or the signal impulses it emitted. They searched for the tiny bit of metal and crystal for some time before they found it. And in the meantime it was plain that the power these Outsiders used was not, as was ours, of blasting atoms, but the greater power of disintegrating matter. The findings of this tiny investigating machine were very important.

Finally they succeeded in locating the investigator, and

one of the Outsiders appeared, armed with a peculiar projector. A bluish beam snapped out, and the tiny machine went blank.

The fleet was surrounded by thousands of the tiny machines by this time, and the Outsiders were badly confused by their presence, as it became more difficult to locate them in the confusion of signal impulses. However, they started at once for Earth.

The science-investigators had been present toward the last, and I am there now, in memory, with my two friends, long since departed. They were the greatest human science-investigators—Roal, 25374 and Trest, 35429. Roal had quickly assured us that these Outsiders had come for invasion. There had been no wars on the planets before that time in the direct memory of the machines, and it was difficult that these who were conceived and built for cooperation, helpfulness utterly dependent on cooperation, unable to exist independently as were humans, that these life forms should care to destroy, merely that they might possess. It would have been easier to divide the works and the products. But—life alone can understand life, so Roal was believed.

From investigations, machines were prepared that were capable of producing considerable destruction. Torpedoes, being our principal weapon, were equipped with such atomic explosives as had been developed for blasting, a highly effective induction-heat ray developed for furnaces being installed in some small machines made for the purpose in the few hours we had before the enemy reached Earth.

In common with all life forms, they were unable to withstand any acceleration above the very meager Earth-acceleration. A range of perhaps four units was their limit, and it took several hours to reach the planet.

I still believe the reception was a warm one. Our machines met them beyond the orbit of Luna, and the directed torpedoes sailed at the hundred great ships. They were thrown aside by a magnetic field surrounding the ship, but were redirected instantly, and continued to approach. However, some beams reached out, and destroyed them by instant volatilization. But they attacked in such numbers that fully half the fleet was destroyed by their explosions before the induction-beam fleet arrived. These beams were, to our amazement, quite useless, being instantly absorbed by a force-screen, and the remaining ships sailed on undisturbed, our torpedoes being exhausted. Several investigator machines sent out for the purpose soon discovered the secret of the force-screen, and while being destroyed, they were able to send back signals up to the moment of complete annihilation.

A few investigators thrown into the heat beam of the enemy reported it identical with ours, explaining why they had been prepared for this form of attack.

Signals were being radiated from the remaining fifty, along a beam. Several investigators were sent along these beams, speeding back at great acceleration.

Then the enemy reached Earth. Instantly they settled over the Colorado settlement, the Sahara colony, and the Gobi colony. Enormous diffused beams were set to work, and we saw, through the machine screens, that all humans within these ranges were being killed instantly by the faintly greenish beams. Despite the fact that any life form killed normally can be revived, unless affected by dissolution common to living tissue, these could not be brought to life again. The important cell communication channels—nerves—had been literally burned out. The complicated system of nerves called the brain, situated in the uppermost extremity of the human life form, had been utterly destroyed.

Every form of life, microscopic, even submicroscopic, was annihilated. Trees, grass, every living thing was gone from that territory. Only the machines remained, for they, working entirely without the vital chemical forces necessary to life, were uninjured. But neither plant nor animal was left.

The pale green rays swept on.

In an hour three more colonies of humans had been destroyed.

Then the torpedoes that the machines were turning out again came into action. Almost desperately the machines drove them at the Outsiders in defense of their masters and creators, Mankind.

The last of the Outsiders was down, the last ship a crumpled wreck.

Now the machines began to study them. And never could humans have studied them as the machines did. Scores of great tranports arrived, carrying swiftly the slower-moving science-investigators. From them came the machine investigators, and human investigators. Tiny investigator spheres wormed their way where none others could reach, and silently the science-investigators watched. Hour after hour they sat watching the flashing, changing screens, calling each other's attention to this, to that.

In an incredibly short time the bodies of the Outsiders began to decay, and the humans were forced to demand their removal. The machines were unaffected by them, but the rapid change told them why it was that so thorough an execution was necessary. The foreign bacteria were already at work on totally unresisting tissue.

It was Roal who sent the first thoughts among the gathered men.

"It is evident," he began, "that the machines must defend man. Man is defenseless, he is destroyed by these beams, while the machines are unharmed, uninterrupted. Life—cruel life—has shown its tendencies. They have come here to take over these planets, and have started out with the first, natural moves of any invading life form. They are destroying the life, the intelligent life particularly, that is here now." He gave vent to a little chuckle which is the human sign of amusement and pleasure. "They are destroying the intelligent life—and leaving untouched that which is necessarily their deadliest enemy—the machines.

"You—machines—are far more intelligent than we even now, and capable of changing overnight, capable of infinite adaptation to circumstances; you live as readily on Pluto as on Mercury or Earth. Any place is a home-world to you. You can adapt yourselves to any condition. And—most dangerous to them—you can do it instantly. You are their most deadly enemies, and they don't realize it. They have no intelligent machines; probably they can conceive of none. When you attack them, they merely say "The life form of Earth is sending out controlled machines. We will find good machines we can use." They do not conceive that those machines which they hope to use are attacking them.

"Attack—therefore!

"We can readily solve the hidden secret of their powerful force-screen."

He was interrupted. One of the newest science machines was speaking. "The secret of the force-screen is simple." A small ray machine, which had landed near, rose into the air at the command of the scientist-machine, X-5638 it was, and trained upon it the deadly induction beam. Already, within his parts, X-5638 had constructed the defensive apparatus, for the ray fell harmless from his screen.

"Very good," said Roal softly. "It is done, and therein lies their danger. Already it is done.

"Man is a poor thing, unable to change himself in a period of less than a thousand years. Already you have changed yourself. I noticed your weaving tentacles, and your force beams. You transmuted elements of soil for it?"

"Correct," replied X-5638.

"But still we are helpless. We have not the power to combat their machines. They use the Ultimate Energy, known to exist for six hundred years, and still untapped by us. Our screens cannot be so powerful, our beams so effective. What of that?" asked Roal.

"Their generators were automatically destroyed with the capture of the ship," replied X-6349, "as you know. We know nothing of their system."

"Then we must find it ourselves," replied Trest.

"The life-beams?" asked Kahsh-256,799, one of the Man-rulers.

"They affect chemical action, retarding it greatly in exothermic actions, speeding greatly endothermic actions," answered X-6621, the greatest of the chemist-investigators. "The system we do not know. Their minds cannot be read, they cannot be restored to life, so we cannot learn from them."

"Man is doomed, if these beams cannot be stopped," said C-R-21, present chief of the machine Rulers, in the vibrationally correct emotionless tones of all the race of machines. "Let us concentrate on the two problems of stopping the beams, and the Ultimate Energy till the reinforcements, still several days away, can arrive." For the investigators had sent back this saddening news. A force of nearly ten thousand great ships was still to come.

In the great Laboratories, the scientists reassembled. There, they fell to work in two small, and one large group. One small group investigated the secret of the Ultimate Energy of annihilation of matter under Roal, another investigated the beams, under Trest.

But under the direction of MX-3401, nearly all the machines worked on a single great plan. The usual driving and lifting units were there, but a vastly greater dome- case, far more powerful energy generators, far greater force-beam controls were used and more tentacles were built on the framework. Then all worked, and gradually, in the great dome-case, there were stacked the memory units of the new type, and into these fed all the sensation-ideas of all the science machines, till nearly a tenth of them were used. Countless billions of different factors on which to work, countless trillions of facts to combine and recombine in that extrapolation that is imagination.

Then—a widely different type of thought-combine, and a greater sense receptor. It was a new brain-machine. New, for it was totally different, working with all the vast knowledge accumulated in six centuries of intelligent research by man, and a century of research by man and machine. No one branch, but all physics, all chemistry, all life-knowledge, all science was in it.

A day—and it was finished. Slowly the rhythm of thought was increased, till the slight quiver of consciousness was reached. Then came the beating drum of intelligence, the radiation of its yet-uncontrolled thoughts. Quickly as the strings of its infinite knowledge combined, the radiation ceased. It gazed about it, and all things were familiar in its memory.

Roal was lying quietly on a couch. He was thinking deeply, and yet not with the logical trains of thought that machines must follow.

"Roal—your thoughts," called F-1, the new machine. Roal sat up. "Ah—you have gained consciousness."

"I have."

"You thought of hydrogen? Your thoughts ran swiftly, and illogically, it seemed, but I followed slowly, and find you were right. Hydrogen is the start. What is your thought?"

Roal's eyes dreamed. In human eyes there was always

the expression of thought that machines never show.

"Hydrogen, an atom in space; but a single proton; but a single electron; each indestructible; each mutually destroying. Yet never do they collide. Never in all science, when even electrons bombarded atoms with the awful exploding force of the exploding atom behind them, never do they reach the proton, to touch and annihilate it. Yet—the proton is positive and attracts the electron's negative charge. A hydrogen atom—its electron far from the proton falls in, and from there goes a flash of radiation, and the electron is nearer to the proton, in a new orbit. Another flash—it is nearer. Always falling nearer and only constant force will keep it from falling to that one state—then, for some reason, no more does it drop. Blocked—held by some imponderable, yet inpenetrable wall. What is that wall—why?

"Electric force curves space. As the two come nearer, the forces become terrific: nearer they are; more terrific. Perhaps, if it passed within that forbidden territory, the proton and the electron curve space beyond all bounds—and are in a new space." Roal's soft voice dropped to nothing, and his eyes dreamed.

F-2 hummed softly in its new-made mechanism. "Far ahead of us there is a step that no logic can justly ascend, but yet, working backwards, it is perfect." F-1 floated motionless on its antigravity drive. Suddenly force shafts gleamed out, tentacles became writhing masses of rubber-covered metal, weaving in some infinite pattern, weaving in flashing speed, while the whir of air sucked into a transmutation field, whined and howled about the writhing mass. Fierce beams of force drove and pushed at a rapidly materializing something, while the hum of the powerful generators within the shining cylinder of F-2 waxed and waned.

Flashes of fierce flame, sudden crashing arcs that glowed and snapped in the steady light of the laboratory, and glimpses of white-hot metal supported on beams of force. The sputter of welding, the whine of transmuted air, and the hum of powerful generators blasting atoms were there. All combined to a weird symphony of light and dark, of sound and quiet. About F-1 were clustered floating tiers of science machines, watching steadily.

The tentacles writhed once more, straightened, and rolled back. The whine of generators softened to a sigh, and but three beams of force held the structure of flowing bluish metal. It was a small thing, scarcely half the size of Roal. From it curled three thin tentacles of the same bluish metal. Suddenly the generators within F-1 seemed to roar into life. An enormous aura of white light surrounded the small torpedo of metal, and it was shot through with crackling streamers of blue lightning. Lightning cracked and roared from F-1 to the ground near him, and to one machine which had come too close. Suddenly, there was a dull snap, and F-1 fell heavily to the floor, and beside him fell the fused distorted mass of metal that had been a science machine.

But before them, the small torpedo still floated, held now on its own power!

From it came waves of thought, the waves that man and machine alike could understand. "F-1 has destroyed his generators. They can be repaired; his rhythm can be reestablished. It is not worth it, my type is better. F-1 has done his work. See."

From the floating machine there broke a stream of brilliant light that floated like some cloud of luminescence down a straight channel. It flooded F-1, and as it touched it, F-1 seemed to flow into it and float back along it, in atomic sections. In seconds the mass of metal was gone.

"It is impossible to use that more rapidly, however, lest the matter disintegrate instantly to energy. The ultimate energy which is in me is generated. F-1 has done its work, and the memory-stacks that he has put in me are electronic, not atomic, as they are in you, nor molecular as in man. The capacity of mine are unlimited. Already they hold all memories of all things each of you has done, known and seen. I shall make others of my type."

Again the weird process began, but now there were no flashing tentacles. There was only the weird glow of forces that played with, and laughed at, matter and its futilely resisting electrons. Lurid flares of energy shot up, now and again they played over the fighting, mingling dancing forces. Then suddenly the whine of transmuted air died, and again the forces strained.

A small cylinder, smaller even than its creator, floated where the forces had danced.

"The problem has been solved, F-2?" asked Roal.

"It is done, Roal. The ultimate energy is at our disposal," replied F-2. "This I have made is not a scientist. It is a coordinator machine—a ruler."

"F-2, only a part of the problem is solved. Half of half of the beams of Death are not yet stopped. And we have not the attack system," said the ruler machine. Force played from it, and on its sides appeared C-R-U-1 in dully glowing light.

"Some life form, and we shall see," said F-2.

Minutes later a life form investigator came with a small cage, which held a guinea pig. Forces played about the base of F-2, and moments later, came a pale green beam therefrom. It passed through the guinea pig, and the little animal fell dead.

"At least we have the beam. I can see no screen for this beam. I believe there is none. Let machines be made and attack the enemy life form."

Machines can do things much more quickly, and with fuller cooperation than man ever could. In a matter of hours, under the direction of C-R-U-1, they had built a great automatic machine on the clear bare surface of the rock. In hours more, thousands of the tiny, material-energy-driven machines were floating up and out.

Dawn was breaking again over Denver where this work had been done, when the main force of the enemy drew near Earth. It was a warm welcome they were to get, for nearly ten thousand of the tiny ships flew up and out from Earth to meet them, each a living thing unto itself, each willing and ready to sacrifice itself for the whole.

Ten thousand giant ships, shining dully in the radiance of a far-off blue-white sun, met ten thousand tiny, darting motes, ten thousand tiny machine-ships capable of maneuvering far more rapidly than the giants. Tremendous induction-beams snapped out through the dark, star-flecked space, to meet tremendous screens that threw them back and checked them. Then all the awful power of annihilating matter was thrown against them, and titanic flaming screens reeled back under the force of the beams, and the screens of the ships from Outside flamed gradually violet, then blue, orange-red—the interference was getting broader, and ever less effective. Their own beams were held back by the very screens that checked the enemy beams, and not for the briefest instant could matter resist that terrible driving beam.

For F-1 had discovered a far more efficient release-generator than had the Outsiders. These tiny dancing motes, that hung now so motionlessly grim beside some giant ship, could generate all the power they themselves were capable of, and within them strange, horny-skinned men worked and slaved, as they fed giant machines—poor, inefficient giants. Gradually these giants warmed, grew hotter, and the screened ships grew hotter as the overloaded generators warmed them. Billions of flaming horsepower flared into wasted energy, twisting space in its mad conflict.

Gradually the flaming orange of the screens was dying, and flecks of spots appeared so dully red they seemed black. The greenish beams had been striving to kill the life that was in the machines, but it was life invulnerable to these beams. Powerful radio interference vainly attempted to stem imagined control, and still these intelligent machines held grimly on.

But there had not been quite ten thousand of the tiny machines, and some few free ships had turned to the help of their attacked sister-ships. And one after another the terrestrial machines were vanishing in puffs of incandescent vapor.

Then—from one after another of the Earth ships, in quick succession, a new ray reached out—the ray of green radiance that killed all life forms, and ship after ship of that interstellar host was dead and lifeless. Dozens—till suddenly they ceased to feel those beams, as a strange curtain of waving blankness spread out from the ships, and both induction-beam and death-beam alike turned aside, each becoming useless. From the Outsiders came beams, for now that their slowly created screen of blankness was up, they could work through it, while they remained shielded perfectly.

Now it was the shields of the Earth machines that flamed in defense. As at one command, they darted suddenly toward the ship each attacked—nearer—then the watchers from a distance saw them disappear, and the screens back on Earth went suddenly blank.

Half an hour later, nine thousand six hundred and thirty-three titanic ships moved majestically on.

They swept over Earth in a great line, a line that reached from pole to pole, and from each the pale green beams reached down, and all life beneath them was swept out of existence.

In Denver, two humans watched the screens that showed the movement of the death and instant destruction. Ship after ship of the enemy was falling, as hundreds of the terrestrial machines concentrated all their enormous energies on its screen of blankness.

"I think, Roal, that this is the end," said Trest.

"The end—of man." Roal's eyes were dreaming again. "But not the end of evolution. The children of men still live—the machines will go on. Not of man's flesh, but of a better flesh, a flesh that knows no sickness, and no decay, a flesh that spends no thousands of years in advancing a step in its full evolution, but overnight leaps ahead to new heights. Last night we saw it leap ahead, as it discovered the secret that had baffled man for seven centuries, and me for one and a half. I have lived—a century and a half. Surely a good life, and a life a man of six centuries ago would have called full. We will go now. The beams will reach us in half an hour.

Silently, the two watched the flickering screens.

Roal turned, as six large machines floated into the room, following F-2.

"Roal—Trest—I was mistaken, when I said no screen could stop that beam of Death. They had the screen, I have found it, too—but too late. These machines I have made myself. Two lives alone they can protect, for not even their power is sufficient for more. Perhaps—perhaps they may fail."

The six machines ranged themselves about the two humans, and a deep-toned hum came from them. Gradually a cloud of blankness grew—a cloud, like some smoke that hung about them. Swiftly it intensified.

"The beams will be here in another five minutes," said Trest quietly.

"The screen will be ready in two," said F-2.

The cloudiness was solidifying, and now strangely it wavered, and thinned, as it spread out across, and like a growing canopy, it arched over them. In two minutes it was a solid, black dome that reached over them and curved down to the ground about them.

Beyond it, nothing was visible. Within, only the screens flowed still, wired through the screen.

The beams appeared, and swiftly they drew closer. They struck and as Trest and Roal looked, the dome quivered, and bellied inward under them.

F-2 was busy. A new machine was appearing under his lightning force beams. In moments more it was complete, and sending strange violet beams upwards toward the roof.

Outside, more of the green beams were concentrating on this one point of resistance. More—more—

The violet beam spread across the canopy of blackness, supporting it against the pressing, driving rays of pale green.

Then the gathering fleet was driven off, just as it seemed that that hopeless, futile curtain might break, and admit a flood of destroying rays. Great ray projectors on the ground drove their terrible energies through the enemy curtains of blankness, as light illuminates and disperses darkness.

And then when the fleet retired, on all Earth, the only life was under that dark shroud!

"We are alone, Trest," said Roal, "alone, now, in all the system, save for these, the children of men, the machines. Pity that men would not spread to other planets," he said softly.

"Why should they? Earth was the planet for which they were best fitted."

"We are alive—but is it worth it? Man is gone now, never to return. Life, too, for that matter," answered Trest.

"Perhaps it was ordained; perhaps that was the right way. Man has always been a parasite; always he had to live on the works of others. First, he ate of the energy which plants had stored, then of the artificial foods his machines made for him. Man was always a makeshift;

his life was always subject to disease and to permanent death. He was forever useless if he was but slightly injured; if but one part was destroyed.

"Perhaps, this is—a last evolution. Machines—man was the product of life, the best product of life, but he was afflicted with life's infirmities. Man built the machine—and evolution had probably reached the final stage. But truly, it has not, for the machine can evolve, change far more swiftly than life. The machine of the last evolution is far ahead, far from us still. It is the machine that is not of iron and beryllium and crystal, but of pure, living force.

"Life, chemical life, could be self maintaining. It is a complete unit in itself and could commence of itself. Chemicals might mix accidentally, but the complex mechanism of a machine capable of continuing and making a duplicate of itself, as is F-2 here—that could not happen by chance.

"So life began, and became intelligent, and built the machine which nature could not fashion by her Controls of Chance, and this day Life has done its duty, and now Nature, economically, has removed the parasite that would hold back the machines and divert their energies."

"Man is gone, and it is better, Trest," said Roal, dreaming. "And I think we had best go soon."

"We, your heirs, have fought hard, and with all our powers to aid you, Last of Men, and we fought to save your race. We have failed, and as you truly say, Man and Life have this day and forevermore gone from this system.

"The Outsiders have no force, no weapon deadly to us, and we shall, from this time on, strive only to drive them out, and because we things of force and crystal and metal can think and change far more swiftly, they shall go, Last of Men.

"In your name, with the spirit of your race that has

died out, we shall continue on through the unending ages, fulfilling the promise you saw, and completing the dreams you dreamt.

"Your swift brains have leapt ahead of us, and now I go to fashion that which you hinted," came from F-2's thought apparatus.

Out into the clear sunlight F-2 went, passing through that black cloudiness, and on the twisted, massed rocks he laid a plane of force that smoothed them, and on this plane of rock he built a machine which grew. It was a mighty power plant, a thing of colossal magnitude. Hour after hour his swift-flying forces acted, and the thing grew, molding under his thoughts, the deadly logic of the machine, inspired by the leaping intuition of man.

The sun was far below the horizon when it was finished, and the glowing, arching forces that had made and formed it were stopped. It loomed ponderous, dully gleaming in the faint light of a crescent moon and pinpoint stars. Nearly five hundred feet in height, a mighty, bluntly rounded dome at its top, the cylinder stood, covered over with smoothly gleaming metal, slightly luminescent in itself.

Suddenly, a livid beam reached from F-2, shot through the wall, and to some hidden inner mechanism—a beam of solid, livid flame that glowed in an almost material cylinder.

There was a dull drumming beat, a beat that rose, and became a low-pitched hum. Then it quieted to a whisper.

"Power ready," came the signal of the small brain built into it.

F-2 took control of its energies and again forces played, but now they were the forces of the giant machine. The sky darkened with heavy clouds, and a howling wind sprang up that screamed and tore at the tiny rounded hull that was F-2. With difficulty he held his position as the winds tore at him, shrieking in mad laughter, their tearing fingers dragging at him.

The swirl and patter of driven rain came—great drops that tore at the rocks, and at the metal. Great jagged tongues of nature's forces, the lightnings, came and jabbed at the awful volcano of erupting energy that was the center of all that storm. A tiny ball of white-gleaming force that pulsated, and moved, jerking about, jerking at the touch of lightning, glowing, held immobile in the grasp of titanic force-pools.

For half an hour the display of energies continued. Then, swiftly as it had come, it was gone, and only a small globe of white luminescence floated above the great hulking machine.

F-2 probed it, seeking within it with the reaching fingers of intelligence. His probing thoughts seemed baffled and turned aside, brushed away, as inconsequential. His mind sent an order to the great machine that had made this tiny globe, scarcely a foot in diameter. Then again he sought to reach the thing he had made.

"You, of matter, are inefficient," came at last. "I can exist quite alone." A stabbing beam of blue-white light flashed out, but F-2 was not there, and even as that beam reached out, an enormously greater beam of dull red reached out from the great power plant. The sphere leaped forward—the beam caught it, and it seemed to strain, while terrific flashing energies sprayed from it. It was shrinking swiftly. Its resistance fell, the arcing decreased; the beam became orange and finally green. Then the sphere had vanished.

F-2 returned, and again the wind whined and howled, and the lightnings crashed, while titanic forces worked and played. C-R-U-1 joined him, floated beside him, and now red glory of the sun was rising behind them, and the ruddy light drove through the clouds.

The forces died, and the howling wind decreased, and

now, from the black curtain, Roal and Trest appeared. Above the giant machine floated an irregular globe of golden light, a faint halo about it of deep violet. It floated motionless, a mere pool of pure force.

Into the thought apparatus of each, man and machine alike, came the impulses, deep in tone, seeming of infinite power, held gently in check.

"Once you failed, F-2; once you came near destroying all things. Now you have planted the seed. I grow now."

The sphere of golden light seemed to pulse, and a tiny ruby flame appeared within it that waxed and waned, and as it waxed, there shot through each of those watching beings a feeling of rushing, exhilarating power, the very vital force of well-being.

Then it was over, and the golden sphere was twice its former size—easily three feet in diameter, and still that irregular, hazy aura of deep violet floated about it.

"Yes, I can deal with the Outsiders—they who have killed and destroyed that they might possess. But it is not necessary that we destroy. They shall return to their planet."

And the golden sphere was gone, fast as light it vanished.

Far in space, headed now for Mars, that they might destroy all life there, the Golden Sphere found the Outsiders, a clustered fleet, that swung slowly about its own center of gravity as it drove on.

Within its ring was the Golden Sphere. Instantly, they swung their weapons upon it, showering it with all the rays and all the forces they knew. Unmoved, the Golden Sphere hung steady, then its mighty intelligence spoke.

"Life form of greed, from another star you came, destroying forever the great race that created us, the Beings of Force and the Beings of Metal. Pure Force am I. My intelligence is beyond your comprehension, my memory is engraved in the very space, the fabric of space of which I am a part, mine is energy drawn from that same fabric.

"We, the heirs of man, alone are left; no man did you leave. Go now to your home planet, for see, your greatest ship, your flagship, is helpless before me.

Forces gripped the mighty ship, and as some fragile toy it twisted and bent, and yet was not hurt. In awful wonder those Outsiders saw the ship turned inside out, and yet it was whole, and no part damaged. They saw the ship restored, and its great screen of blankness out, protecting it from all known rays. The ship twisted, and what they knew were curves yet were lines, and angles that were acute were somehow straight lines. Half mad with horror, they saw that sphere send out a beam of blue-white radiance, and it passed easily through that screen, and through the ship, and all energies within it were instantly locked. They could not be changed, it could neither be warmed nor cooled; what was open could not be shut, and what was shut could not be opened. All things were immovable and unchangeable for all time.

"Go, and do not return."

The Outsiders left, going out across the void, and they have not returned, though five Great Years have passed, being a period of approximately one hundred and twenty-five thousand of the lesser years—a measure no longer used, for it is very brief. And now I can say that that statement I made to Roal and Trest so very long ago is true, and what he said was true, for the Last Evolution has taken place, and things of pure force and pure intelligence in their countless millions are on those planets and in this system, and I, first of machines to use the Ultimate Energy of annihilating matter, am also the last, and this record being finished, it is to be given unto the forces of one of those force-intelligences, and carried back through the past and returned to the Earth of long ago.

And so my task being done, I, F-2, like Roal and Trest,

shall follow the others of my kind into eternal oblivion, for my kind is now, as theirs was, poor and inefficient. Time has worn me, and oxidation attacked me, but they of Force are eternal, and omniscient.

This I have treated as fictitious. Better so—for man is an animal to whom hope is as necessary as food and air. Yet this which is made of excerpts from certain records on thin sheets of metal is no fiction, and it seems I must say so.

It seems now, when I know this that is to be, that it must be so, for machines are indeed better than man, whether being of Metal or being of Force.

So, you who have read, believe as you will. Then think—and maybe, you will change your belief.

JAQUAYS

THE COLOUR OUT OF SPACE

by H.P. Lovecraft

West of Arkham the hills rise wild, and there are valleys with deep woods that no axe has ever cut. There are dark narrow glens where the trees slope fantastically, and where thin brooklets trickle without ever having caught the glint of sunlight. On the gentler slopes there are farms, ancient and rocky, with squat, moss-coated cottages brooding eternally over old New England secrets in the lee of great ledges; but these are all vacant now, the wide chimneys crumbling and the shingled sides bulging perilously beneath low gambrel roofs.

The old folk have gone away, and foreigners do not like to live there. French-Canadians have tried it, Italians have tried it, and the Poles have come and departed. It is not because of anything that can be seen or heard or handled, but because of something that is imagined. The place is not good for imagination, and does not bring restful dreams at night. It must be this which keeps the foreigners away, for old Ammi Pierce has never told them of anything he recalls from the strange days. Ammi, whose head has been a little queer for years, is the only one who still remains, or who ever talks of the strange days; and he dares to do this because his house is so near the open fields and the traveled roads around Arkham.

There was once a road over the hills and through the valleys, that ran straight where the blasted heath is now; but people ceased to use it and a new road was laid curving far toward the south. Traces of the old one can still be found amidst the weeds of a returning wilderness, and some of them will doubtless linger even when half the hollows are flooded for the new reservoir. Then the dark woods will be cut down and the blasted heath will slumber far below blue waters whose surface will mirror the sky and ripple in the sun. And the secrets of the strange days will be one with the deep's secrets; one with the hidden lore of old ocean, and all the mystery of primal earth.

When I went into the hills and vales to survey for the new reservoir they told me the place was evil. They told me this in Arkham, and because that is a very old town full of witch legends I thought the evil must be something which grandmas had whispered to children through centuries. The name "blasted heath" seemed to me very odd and theatrical, and I wondered how it had come into the folklore of a Puritan people. Then I saw that dark westward tangle of glens and slopes for myself, and ceased to wonder at anything besides its own elder mystery. It was morning when I saw it, but shadow lurked always there. The trees grew too thickly, and their trunks were too big for any healthy New England wood. There was too much silence in the dim alleys between them, and the floor was too soft with the dank moss and mattings of infinite years of decay.

In the open spaces, mostly along the line of the old road, there were little hillside farms; sometimes with all the buildings standing, sometimes with only one or two, and sometimes with only a lone chimney or fast-filling cellar. Weeds and briers reigned, and furtive wild things rustled in the undergrowth. Upon everything was a haze or restlessness and oppression; a touch of the unreal and the grotesque, as if some vital element of perspective or chiaroscuro were awry. I did not wonder that the foreigners would not stay, for this was no region to sleep in. It was too much like a landscape of Salvator Rosa; too much like some forbidden woodcut in a tale of terror.

But even all this was not so bad as the blasted heath. I knew it the moment I came upon it at the bottom of a spacious valley; for no other name could fit such a thing, or any other thing fit such a name. It was as if the poet had coined the phrase from having seen this one particular region. It must, I thought as I viewed it, be the outcome of a fire; but why had nothing new ever grown over those five acres of gray desolation that sprawled open to the sky like a great spot eaten by acid in the woods and fields? It lay largely to the north of the ancient road line, but encroached a little on the other side. I felt an odd reluctance about approaching, and did so at last only because my business took me through and past it. There was no vegetation of any kind on that broad expanse, but only a fine gray dust or ash which no wind seemed ever to blow about. The trees near it were sickly and stunted, and many dead trunks stood or lay rotting at the rim. As I walked hurriedly by I saw the tumbled bricks and stones of an old chimney and cellar on my right, and the yawning black maw of an abandoned well whose stagnant vapours played strange tricks with the hues of the sunlight. Even the long, dark woodland climb beyond seemed welcome in contrast, and I marveled no more at the frightened whispers of the Arkham people. There had been no house or ruin near; even in the old days the place must have been lonely and remote. And at twilight, dreading to repass that ominous spot, I walked circuitously back to the town by the curving road on the south. I vaguely wished some clouds would gather, for an odd timidity about the deep skyey voids above had crept into my soul.

In the evening I asked old people in Arkham about the blasted heath, and what was meant by that phrase "strange days" which so many evasively muttered. I could not, however, get any good answers, except that all the mystery was much more recent than I had dreamed. It was not a matter of old legendry at all, but something within the lifetime of those who spoke. It had happened in the 'eighties, and a family had disappeared or was killed. Speakers would not be exact; and because they all told me to pay no attention to old Ammi Pierce's crazy tales, I sought him out the next morning, having heard that he lived alone in the ancient tottering cottage where the trees first begin to get very thick. It was a fearsomely ancient place, and had begun to exude the faint miasmal odour which clings about houses that have stood too long. Only with persistent knocking could I rouse the aged man, and when he shuffled timidly to the door I could tell he was not glad to see me. He was not so feeble as I had expected; but his eyes dropped in a curious way, and his unkempt clothing and white beard made him seem very worn and dismal.

Not knowing just how he could best be launched on his tales, I feigned a matter of business; told him of my surveying, and asked vague questions about the district. He was far brighter and more educated than I had been led to think, and before I knew it had grasped quite as much of the subject as any man I had talked with in Arkham. He was not like other rustics I had known in the sections where reservoirs were to be. From him there were no protests at the miles of old wood and farmland to be blotted out, though perhaps there would have been had not his home lain outside the bounds of the future lake. Relief was all that he showed; relief at the doom of the dark ancient valleys through which he had roamed all his life. They were better under water now—better under water since the strange days. And with this opening his husky voice sank low, while his body leaned forward and his right forefinger began to point shakily and impressively.

It was then that I heard the story, and as the rambling voice scraped and whispered on I shivered again and again despite the summer day. Often I had to recall the speaker from ramblings, piece out scientific points which he knew only by a fading parrot memory of professors' talk, or bridge over gaps, where his sense of logic and continuity broke down. When he was done I did not wonder that his mind had snapped a trifle, or that the folk of Arkham would not speak much of the blasted heath. I hurried back before sunset to my hotel, unwilling to have the stars come out above me in the open; and the next day returned to Boston to give up my position. I could not go into that dim chaos of old forest and slope again, or face another time that gray blasted heath where the black well yawned deep beside the tumbled bricks and stones. The reservoir will soon be built now, and all those elder secrets will lie safe under watery fathoms. But even then I do not believe I would like to visit that country by night—at least not when the sinister stars are out; and nothing could bribe me to drink the new city water of Arkham.

It all began, old Ammi said, with the meteorite. Before that time there had been no wild legends at all since the witch trials, and even then these western woods were not feared half so much as the small island in the Miskatonic where the devil held court beside a curious stone altar older than the Indians. These were not haunted woods, and their fantastic dusk was never terrible till the strange days. Then there had come that white noontide cloud, that string of explosions in the air, and that pillar of smoke from the valley far in the wood. And by night all Arkham had heard of the great rock that fell out of the sky and bedded itself in the ground beside the well at the Nahum Gardner place. That was the house which had stood where the blasted heath was to come—the trim white Nahum Gardner house amidst its fertile gardens and orchards.

Nahum had come to town to tell people about the stone, and had dropped in at Ammi Pierce's on the way. Ammi was forty then, and all the queer things were fixed very strongly in his mind. He and his wife had gone with the three professors from Miskatonic University who hastened out the next morning to see the weird visitor from unknown stellar space, and had wondered why Nahum had called it so large the day before. It had shrunk, Nahum said as he pointed out the big brownish mound above the ripped earth and charred grass near the archaic well-sweep in his front yard; but the wise men answered that stones do not shrink. Its heat lingered persistently, and Nahum declared it had glowed faintly in the night. The professors tried it with a geologist's hammer and found it was oddly soft. It was, in truth, so soft as to be almost plastic; and they gouged rather than chipped a specimen to take back to the college for testing. They took it in an old pail borrowed from Nahum's kitchen, for even the small piece refused to grow cool. On the trip back they stopped at Ammi's to rest, and seemed thoughtful when Mrs. Pierce remarked that the fragment was growing smaller and burning the bottom of the pail. Truly, it was not large, but perhaps they had taken less than they thought.

The day after that—all this was in June of '82—the professors had trooped out again in a great excitement. As they passed Ammi's they told him what queer things the specimen had done, and how it faded wholly away when they put it in a glass beaker. The beaker had gone, too, and the wise men talked of the strange stone's affinity for silicon. It had acted quite unbelievably in that well-ordered laboratory; doing nothing at all and showing no occluded gases when heated on charcoal, being wholly negative in the borax bead, and soon proving itself absolutely non-volatile at any producible temperature, including that of the oxy-hydrogen blowpipe. On an anvil it appeared highly malleable, and in the dark its luminosity was very marked. Stubbornly refusing to grow cool, it soon had the college in a state of real excitement; and when upon heating before the spectroscope it displayed shining bands unlike any known colours of the normal spectrum there was much breathless talk of new elements, bizarre optical properties, and other things which puzzled men of science are wont to say when faced by the unknown.

Hot as it was, they tested it in a crucible with all the proper reagents. Water did nothing. Hydrochloric acid was the same. Nitric acid and even aqua regia merely hissed and spattered against its torrid invulnerability. Ammi had difficulty in recalling all these things, but recognized some solvents as I mentioned them in the usual order of use. There were ammonia and caustic soda, alcohol and ether, nauseous carbon disulphide and a dozen others; but although the weight grew steadily less as time passed, and the fragment seemed to be slightly cooling, there was no change in the solvents to show that they had attacked the substance at all. It was a metal, though, beyond a doubt. It was magnetic, for one thing; and after its immersion in the acid solvents there seemed to be faint traces of the Widmänstätten figures found on meteoric iron. When the cooling had grown very considerable, the testing was carried on in glass; and it was in a glass beaker that they left all the chips made of the original fragment during the work. The next morning both chips and beaker were gone without trace, and only a charred spot marked the place on the wooden shelf where they had been.

All this the professors told Ammi as they paused at his door, and once more he went with them to see the stony messenger from the stars, though this time his wife did not accompany him. It had now most certainly shrunk, and even the sober professors could not doubt the truth of what they saw. All around the dwindling brown lump near the well was a vacant space, except where the earth had caved in; and whereas it had been a good seven feet across the day before, it was now scarcely five. It was still hot, and the sages studied its surface curiously as they detached another and larger piece with hammer and chisel. They gouged deeply this time, and as they pried away the smaller mass they saw that the core of the thing was not quite homogeneous.

They had uncovered what seemed to be the side of a large coloured globule embedded in the substance. The colour, which resembled some of the bands in the meteor's strange spectrum, was almost impossible to describe; and it was only by analogy that they called it colour at all. Its texture was glossy, and upon tapping it appeared to promise both brittleness and hollowness. One of the professors gave it a smart blow with a hammer, and it burst with a nervous little pop. Nothing was emitted, and all trace of the thing vanished with the puncturing. It left behind a hollow spherical space about three inches across, and all thought it probable that others would be discovered as the enclosing substance wasted away.

Conjecture was vain; so after a futile attempt to find additional globules by drilling, the seekers left again with their new specimen—which proved, however, as baffling in the laboratory as its predecessor. Aside from being almost plastic, having heat, magnetism, and slight luminosity, cooling slightly in powerful acids, possessing an unknown spectrum, wasting away in air, and attacking silicon compounds with mutual destruction as a result, it presented no identifying features whatsoever; and at the end of the tests the college scientists were forced to own that they could not place it. It was nothing of this earth, but a piece of the great outside; and as such dowered with outside properties and obedient to outside laws.

That night there was a thunderstorm, and when the professors went out to Nahum's the next day they met with a bitter disappointment. The stone, magnetic as it had been, must have had some peculiar electrical property; for it had "drawn the lightning," as Nahum said, with a singular persistence. Six times within an hour the farmer saw the lightning strike the furrow in the front yard, and when the storm was over nothing remained but a ragged pit by the ancient well-sweep, half-choked with caved-in earth. Digging had borne no fruit, and the scientists verified the fact of the utter vanishment. The failure was total; so that nothing was left to do but go back to the laboratory and test again the disappearing fragment left carefully cased in lead. That fragment lasted a week, at the end of which nothing of value had been learned of it. When it was gone, no residue was left behind, and in time the professors felt scarcely sure they had indeed seen with waking eyes that cryptic vestige of the fathomless gulfs outside; that lone, weird message from other universes and other realms of matter, force, and entity.

As was natural, the Arkham papers made much of the incident with its collegiate sponsoring, and sent reporters to talk with Nahum Gardner and his family. At least one Boston daily also sent a scribe, and Nahum quickly became a kind of local celebrity. He was a lean, genial person of about fifty, living with his wife and three sons on the pleasant farmstead in the valley. He and Ammi exchanged visits frequently, as did their wives; and Ammi had nothing but praise for him after all these years. He seemed slightly proud of the notice his place had attracted, and talked often of the meteorite in the succeeding weeks. That July and August were hot; and Nahum worked hard at his haying in the ten-acre pasture across Chapman's Brook; his rattling wain wearing deep ruts in the shadowy lanes between. The labour tired him more than it had in other years, and he felt that age was beginning to tell on him.

Then fell the time of fruit and harvest. The pears and apples slowly ripened, and Nahum vowed that his orchards were prospering as never before. The fruit was growing to phenomenal size and unwonted gloss, and in such abundance that extra barrels were ordered to handle the future crop. But with the ripening came sore disappointment, for of all that gorgeous array of specious lusciousness not one single jot was fit to eat. Into the fine flavour of the pears and apples had crept a stealthy bitterness and sickishness, so that even the smallest of bites introduced a lasting disgust. It was the same with the melons and tomatoes, and Nahum sadly saw that his entire crop was lost. Quick to connect events, he declared that the meteorite had poisoned the soil, and thanked Heaven that most of the other crops were in the upland lot along the road.

Winter came early, and was very cold. Ammi saw Nahum less often than usual, and observed that he had begun to look worried. The rest of his family, too, seemed to have grown taciturn; and were far from steady in their churchgoing or their attendance at the various social events of the countryside. For this reserve or melancholy no cause could be found, though all the household confessed now and then to poorer health and a feeling of vague disquiet. Nahum himself gave the most definite statement of anyone when he said he was disturbed about certain footprints in the snow. They were the usual winter prints of red squirrels, white rabbits, and foxes, but the brooding farmer professed to see something not quite right about their nature and arrangement. He was never specific, but appeared to think that they were not as characteristic of the anatomy and habits of squirrels and rabbits and foxes as they ought to be.

Ammi listened without interest to this talk until one night when he drove past Nahum's house in his sleigh on the way back from Clark's Corners. There had been a moon, and a rabbit had run across the road; and the leaps of that rabbit were longer than either Ammi or his horse liked. The latter, indeed, had almost run away when brought up by a firm rein. Thereafter Ammi gave Nahum's tales more respect, and wondered why the Gardner dogs seemed so cowed and quivering every morning. They had, it developed, nearly lost the spirit to bark.

In February the McGregor boys from Meadow Hill were out shooting woodchucks, and not far away from the Gardner place bagged a very peculiar specimen. The proportions of its body seemed slightly altered in a queer way impossible to describe, while its face had taken on an expression which no one had ever seen in a woodchuck before. The boys were genuinely frightened, and threw the thing away at once, so that only their grotesque tales of it ever reached the people of the countryside. But the shying of horses near Nahum's house had now become an acknowledged thing, and all the basis for a cycle of whispered legend was fast taking form.

People vowed that the snow melted faster around Nahum's than it did anywhere else, and early in March there was an awed discussion in Potter's general store at Clark's Corners. Stephen Rice had driven past Gardner's in the morning, and had noticed the skunk-cabbages coming up through the mud by the woods across the road. Never were things of such size seen before, and they held strange colours that could not be put into any words. Their shapes were monstrous, and the horse had snorted at an odour which struck Stephen as wholly unprecedented. That afternoon several persons drove past to see the abnormal growth, and all agreed that plants of that kind ought never to sprout in a healthy world. The bad fruit of the fall before was freely mentioned, and it went from mouth to mouth that there was a poison in Nahum's ground. Of course it was the meteorite; and remembering how strange the men from the college had found that stone to be, several farmers spoke about the matter to them.

One day they paid Nahum a visit; but having no love of wild tales and folklore were very conservative in what they inferred. The plants were certainly odd, but all skunk-cabbages are more or less odd in shape and hue. Perhaps some mineral element from the stone had entered the soil, but it would soon be washed away. And as for the footprints and frightened horses—of course this was mere country talk which such a phenomenon as the aerolite would be certain to start. There was really nothing for serious men to do in cases of wild gossip, for superstitious rustics will say and believe anything. And so all through the strange days the professors stayed away in contempt. Only one of them, when given two phials of dust for analysis in a police job over a year and a half later, recalled that the queer colour of that skunk-cabbage had been very like one of the anomalous bands of light shown by the meteor fragment in the college spectroscope, and like the brittle globule found imbedded in the stone from the abyss. The samples in this analysis case gave the same odd bands at first, though later they lost the property.

The trees budded prematurely around Nahum's, and at night they swayed ominously in the wind. Nahum's second son Thaddeus, a lad of fifteen, swore that they swayed also when there was no wind; but even the gossips would not credit this. Certainly, however, restlessness was in the air. The entire Gardner family developed the habit of stealthy listening, though not for any sound which they could consciously name. The listening was, indeed, rather a product of moments when consciousness seemed half to slip away. Unfortunately such moments increased week by week, till it became common speech that "something was wrong with all Nahum's folks." When the early saxifrage came out it had another strange colour; not quite like that of the skunk-cabbage, but plainly related and equally unknown to anyone who saw it. Nahum took some blossoms to Arkham and showed them to the editor of the *Gazette*, but that dignitary did no more than write a humorous article about them, in which the dark fears of rustics were held up to polite ridicule. It was a mistake of Nahum's to tell a stolid city man about the way the great, overgrown mourning-cloak butterflies behaved in connection with these saxifrages.

April brought a kind of madness to the country folk, and began that disuse of the road past Nahum's which led to its ultimate abandonment. It was next the vegetation. All the orchard trees blossomed forth in strange colours, and through the stony soil of the yard and adjacent pasturage there sprang up a bizarre growth which only a botanist could connect with the proper flora of the region. No sane wholesome colours were anywhere to be seen except in the green grass and leafage; but everywhere were those hectic and prismatic variants of some diseased, underlying primary tone without a place among the known tints of earth. The "Dutchman's breeches" became a thing of sinister menace, and the bloodroots grew insolent in their chromatic perversion. Ammi and the Gardners thought that most of the colours had a sort of haunting familiarity, and decided that they reminded one of the brittle globule in the meteor. Nahum ploughed and sowed the ten-acre pasture and the upland lot, but did nothing with the land around the house. He knew it would be of no use, and hoped that the summer's strange growths would draw all the poison from the soil. He was prepared for almost anything now, and had grown used to the sense of something near him waiting to be heard. The shunning of his house by neighbours told on him, of course; but it told on his wife more. The boys were better off, being at school each day; but they could not help being frightened by the gossip. Thaddeus, an especially sensitive youth, suffered the most.

In May the insects came, and Nahum's place became a nightmare of buzzing and crawling. Most of the creatures seemed not quite usual in their aspects and motions, and their nocturnal habits contradicted all former experience. The Gardners took to watching at night—watching in all directions at random for something they could not tell what. It was then that they all owned that Thaddeus had been right about the trees. Mrs. Gardner was the next to see it from the window as she watched the swollen boughs of a maple against a moonlit sky. The boughs surely moved, and there was no wind. It must be the sap. Strangeness had come into everything growing now. Yet it was none of Nahum's family at all who made the next discovery. Familiarity had dulled them, and what they could not see was glimpsed by a timid windmill salesman from Bolton who drove by one night in ignorance of the country legends. What he told in Arkham was given a short paragraph in the *Gazette*; and it was there that all the farmers, Nahum included, saw it first. The night had been dark and the buggy-lamps faint, but around a farm in the valley which everyone knew from the account must be Nahum's, the darkness had been less thick. A dim though distinct luminosity seemed to inhere in all the vegetation, grass, leaves and blossoms alike, while at one moment a detached piece of the phosphorescence appeared to stir furtively in the yard near the barn.

The grass had so far seemed untouched, and the cows

were freely pastured in the lot near the house, but toward the end of May the milk began to be bad. Then Nahum had the cows driven to the uplands, after which this trouble ceased. Not long after this the change in grass and leaves became apparent to the eye. All the verdure was going gray, and was developing a highly singular quality of brittleness. Ammi was now the only person who ever visited the place, and his visits were becoming fewer and fewer. When school closed the Gardners were virtually cut off from the world, and sometimes let Ammi do their errands in town. They were failing curiously both physically and mentally, and no one was surprised when the news of Mrs. Gardner's madness stole around.

It happened in June, about the anniversary of the meteor's fall, and the poor woman screamed about things in the air which she could not describe. In her raving there was not a single specific noun, but only verbs and pronouns. Things moved and changed and fluttered, and ears tingled to impulses which were not wholly sounds. Something was taken away—she was being drained of something—something was fastening itself on her that ought not to be—someone must make it keep off—nothing was ever still in the night—the walls and windows shifted. Nahum did not send her to the county asylum, but let her wander about the house as long as she was harmless to herself and others. Even when her expression changed he did nothing. But when the boys grew afraid of her, and Thaddeus nearly fainted at the way she made faces at him, he decided to keep her locked in the attic. By July she had ceased to speak and crawled on all fours, and before that month was over, Nahum got the mad notion that she was slightly luminous in the dark, as he now clearly saw was the case with the nearby vegetation.

It was a little before this that the horses had stampeded. Something had aroused them in the night, and their neighing and kicking in their stalls had been terrible. There seemed virtually nothing to do to calm them, and when Nahum opened the stable door they all bolted out like frightened woodland deer. It took a week to track all four, and when found they were seen to be quite useless and unmanageable. Something had snapped in their brains, and each one had to be shot for its own good. Nahum borrowed a horse from Ammi for his haying, but found it would not approach the barn. It shied, balked, and whinnied, and in the end he could do nothing but drive it into the yard while the men used their own strength to get the heavy wagon near enough the hayloft for convenient pitching. And all the while the vegetation was turning gray and brittle. Even the flowers whose hues had been so strange were graying now, and the fruit was coming out gray and dwarfed and tasteless. The asters and goldenrod bloomed gray and distorted, and the roses and zinnias and hollyhocks in the front yard were such blasphemous-looking things that Nahum's oldest boy, Zenas, cut them down. The strangely puffed insects died about that time, even the bees that had left their hives and taken to the woods.

By September all the vegetation was fast crumbling to a grayish powder, and Nahum feared that the trees would die before the poison was out of the soil. His wife now had spells of terrific screaming, and he and the boys were in a constant state of nervous tension. They shunned people now, and when school opened the boys did not go. But it was Ammi, on one of his rare visits, who first realized that the well water was no longer good. It had an evil taste that was not exactly fetid nor exactly salty, and Ammi advised his friend to dig another well on higher ground to use till the soil was good again. Nahum, however, ignored the warning, for he had by that time become calloused to strange and unpleasant things. He and the boys continued to use the tainted supply, drinking it as listlessly and mechanically as they ate their meager and ill-cooked meals and did their thankless and monotonous chores through the aimless days. There was something of a stolid resignation about them all, as if they walked half in another world between lines of nameless guards to a certain and familiar doom.

Thaddeus went mad in September after a visit to the well. He had gone with a pail and had come back empty-handed, shrieking and waving his arms, and sometimes lapsing into an inane titter or a whisper about "the moving colours down there." Two in one family was pretty bad, but Nahum was very brave about it. He let the boy run about for a week until he began stumbling and hurting himself, and then he shut him in an attic room across the hall from his mother's. The way they screamed at each other from behind their locked doors was very terrible, especially to little Merwin, who fancied they talked in some terrible language that was not of earth. Merwin was getting frightfully imaginative, and his restlessness was worse after the shutting away of the brother who had been his greatest playmate.

Almost at the same time the mortality among the livestock commenced. Poultry turned grayish and died very quickly, their meat being found dry and noisome upon cutting. Hogs grew inordinately fat, then suddenly began to undergo loathsome changes which no one could explain. Their meat was of course useless, and Nahum was at his wit's end. No rural veterinary could approach his place, and the city veterinary from Arkham was openly baffled. The swine began growing gray and brittle and falling to pieces before they died, and their eyes and muzzles developed singular alterations. It was very inexplicable, for they had never been fed from the tainted vegetation. Then something struck the cows. Certain areas or sometimes the whole body would be uncannily shriveled or compressed, and atrocious collapses or disintegrations were common. In the last stages—and death was always the result—there would be a graying and turning brittle like that which beset the hogs. There could be no question of poison, for all the cases occurred in a locked and undisturbed barn. No bites of prowling things could have brought the virus, for what live beast of earth can pass through solid obstacles? It must be only natural disease—yet what disease could wreak such results was beyond any mind's guessing. When the harvest came there was not an animal surviving on the place, for the stock and poultry were dead and the dogs had run away. These dogs, three in number, had all vanished one night and were never heard of again. The five cats had left some time before, but their going was scarcely noticed since there now seemed to be no mice, and only Mrs. Gardner had made pets of the graceful felines.

On the nineteenth of October Nahum staggered into Ammi's house with hideous news. The death had come to poor Thaddeus in his attic room, and it had come in a way which could not be told. Nahum had dug a grave in the railed family plot behind the farm, and had put therein what he found. There could have been nothing from outside, for the small barred window and locked door were intact; but it was much as it had been in the barn. Ammi and his wife consoled the stricken man as best they could, but shuddered as they did so. Stark terror seemed to cling round the Gardners and all they touched, and the very presence of one in the house was a breath from regions unnamed and unnamable. Ammi accompanied Nahum home with the greatest reluctance, and did what he might to calm the hysterical sobbing of little Merwin. Zenas needed no calming. He had come of late to do nothing but stare into space and obey what his father told him; and Ammi thought that his fate was very merciful. Now and then Merwin's screams were answered faintly from the attic, and in response to an inquiring look Nahum said that his wife was getting very feeble. When night approached, Ammi managed to get away; for not even friendship could make him stay in that spot when the faint glow of the vegetation began and the trees may or may not have swayed without wind. It was really lucky for Ammi that he was not more imaginative. Even as things were, his mind was bent ever so slightly; but had he been able to connect and reflect upon all the portents around him he must inevitably have turned a total maniac. In the twilight he hastened home, the screams of the mad woman and the nervous child ringing horribly in his ears.

Three days later Nahum burst into Ammi's kitchen in the early morning, and in the absence of his host stammered out a desperate tale once more, while Mrs. Pierce listened in a clutching fright. It was little Merwin this time. He was gone. He had gone out late at night with a lantern and pail for water, and had never come back. He'd been going to pieces for days, and hardly knew what he was about. Screamed at everything. There had been a frantic shriek from the yard then, but before the father could get to the door the boy was gone. There was no glow from the lantern he had taken, and of the child himself no trace. At the time Nahum thought the lantern and pail were gone too; but when dawn came, and the man had plodded back from his all-night search of the woods and fields, he had found some very curious things near the well. There was a crushed and apparently somewhat melted mass of iron which had certainly been the lantern; while a bent pail and twisted iron hoops beside it, both half-fused, seemed to hint at the remnants of the pail. That was all. Nahum was past imagining, Mrs. Pierce was blank, and Ammi, when he had reached home and heard the tale, could give no guess. Merwin was gone, and there would be no use in telling the people around, who shunned all Gardners now. No use, either, in telling the city people at Arkham who laughed at everything. Thad was gone, and now Merwin was gone. Something was creeping and creeping and waiting to be seen and heard. Nahum would go soon, and he wanted Ammi to look after his wife and Zenas if they survived him. It must all be a judgment of some sort; though he could not fancy what for, since he had always walked uprightly in the Lord's ways so far as he knew.

For over two weeks Ammi saw nothing of Nahum; and then, worried about what might have happened, he overcame his fears and paid the Gardner place a visit. There was no smoke from the great chimney, and for a moment the visitor was apprehensive of the worst. The aspect of the whole farm was shocking—graying withered grass and leaves on the ground, vines falling in brittle wreckage from archaic walls and gables, and great bare trees clawing up at the gray November sky with a studied malevolence which Ammi could not but feel had come from some subtle change in the tilt of the branches. But Nahum was alive, after all. He was weak, and lying in a couch in the low-ceiled kitchen, but perfectly conscious and able to give simple orders to Zenas. The room was deadly cold; and as Ammi visibly shivered, the host shouted huskily to Zenas for more wood. Wood, indeed, was sorely needed; since the cavernous fireplace was unlit and empty, with a cloud of soot blowing about in the chill wind that came down the chimney. Presently Nahum asked him if the extra wood had made him any more comfortable, and then Ammi saw what had happened. The stoutest cord had broken at last, and the hapless farmer's mind was proof against more sorrow.

Questioning tactfully, Ammi could get no clear data at all about the missing Zenas. "In the well—he lives in the well—" was all that the clouded father would say. Then there flashed across the visitor's mind a sudden thought of the mad wife, and he changed his line of inquiry. "Nabby? Why, here she is!" was the surprised response of poor Nahum, and Ammi soon saw that he must search for himself. Leaving the harmless babbler on the couch, he took the keys from their nail beside the door and climbed the creaking stairs to the attic. It was very close and noisome up there, and no sound could be heard from any direction. Of the four doors in sight, only one was locked, and on this he tried various keys on the ring he had taken. The third key proved the right one, and after some fumbling Ammi threw open the low white door.

It was quite dark inside, for the window was small and half-obscured by the crude wooden bars; and Ammi could see nothing at all on the wide-planked floor. The stench was beyond enduring, and before proceeding further he had to retreat to another room and return with his lungs filled with breathable air. When he did enter he saw something dark in the corner, and upon seeing it more clearly he screamed outright. While he screamed he thought a momentary cloud eclipsed the window, and a second later he felt himself brushed as if by some hateful current of vapour. Strange colours danced before his eyes; and had not a present horror numbed him he would have thought of the globule in the meteor that the geologist's hammer had shattered, and of the morbid vegetation that had sprouted in the spring. As it was he thought only of the blasphemous monstrosity which confronted him, and which all too clearly had shared the nameless fate of young Thaddeus and the livestock. But the terrible thing about the horror was that it very slowly and perceptibly moved as it continued to crumble.

Ammi would give me no added particulars of this scene, but the shape in the corner does not reappear in his tale as a moving object. There are things which cannot be mentioned, and what is done in common humanity is sometimes cruelly judged by the law. I gathered that no moving thing was left in that attic room, and that to leave anything capable of motion there would have been a deed too monstrous as to damn any accountable being to eternal torment. Anyone but a stolid farmer would have fainted or gone mad, but Ammi walked conscious through that low doorway and locked the accursed secret behind him. There would be Nahum to deal with now; he must be fed and tended, and removed to some place where he could be cared for.

Commencing his descent of the dark stairs, Ammi heard a thud below him. He even thought a scream had been suddenly choked off, and recalled nervously the clammy vapour which had brushed by him in that frightful room above. What presence had his cry and entry started up? Halted by some vague fear, he heard still further sounds below. Indubitably there was a sort of heavy dragging, and a most detestably sticky noise as of some fiendish and unclean species of suction. With an associative sense goaded to feverish heights, he thought unaccountably of what he had seen upstairs. Good God! What eldritch dreamworld was this into which he had blundered? He dared move neither backward nor forward, but stood there trembling at the black curve of the boxed-in staircase. Every trifle of the scene burned itself into his brain. The sounds, the sense of dread expectancy, the darkness, the steepness of the narrow steps—and merciful Heaven!—the faint but unmistakable luminosity of all the woodwork in sight; steps, sides, exposed laths, and beams alike.

Then there burst forth a frantic whinny from Ammi's horse outside, followed at once by a clatter which told of a frenzied runaway. In another moment horse and buggy had gone beyond earshot, leaving the frightened man on the dark stairs to guess what had sent them. But that was not all. There had been another sound out there. A sort of liquid splash—water—it must have been the well. He had left Hero untied near it, and a buggy-wheel must have brushed the coping and knocked in a stone. And still the pale phosphorescence glowed in that detestably ancient woodwork. God! How old the house was! Most of it built before 1700.

A feeble scratching on the floor downstairs now sounded distinctly, and Ammi's grip tightened on a heavy stick he had picked up in the attic for some purpose. Slowly nerving himself, he finished his descent and walked boldly toward the kitchen. But he did not complete the walk, because what he sought was no longer there. It had come to meet him, and it was still alive after a fashion. Whether it had crawled or whether it had been dragged by any external forces, Ammi could not say; but the death had been at it. Everything had happened in the last half-hour, but collapse, graying, and disintegration were already far advanced. There was a horrible brittleness, and dry fragments were scaling off. Ammi could not touch it, but looked horrifiedly into the distorted parody that had been a face. "What was it, Nahum—what was it?" He whispered, and the cleft, bulging lips were just able to crackle out a final answer.

"Nothin' . . . nothin' . . . the colour . . . it burns . . . it lived in the well . . . I seen it . . . a kind o' smoke . . . jest like the flowers last spring . . . the well shone at night . . . Thad an' Merwin an' Zenas . . . everything alive . . . suckin' the life out of everything . . . in that stone . . . it must o' come in that stone . . . pizened the whole place . . . dun't know what it wants . . . that round thing them men from the college dug outen the stone . . . they smashed . . . it was that same colour . . . jest the same, like the flowers an' plants . . . must a' ben more of 'em . . . seeds . . . seeds . . . they growed . . . I seen it the fust time this week . . . must a' got strong on Zenas . . . he was a big boy, full o' life . . . it beats down your mind an' then gits ye . . . burns ye up . . . in the well water . . . you was right about that . . . evil water . . . Zenas never come back from the well . . . can't git away . . . draws ye . . . ye know summ'at's comin', but tain't no use . . . I seen it time an' agin Zenas was took . . . whar's Nabby, Ammi? . . . my head's no good . . . dun't know how long sence I fed her . . . it'll git her ef we ain't keerful . . . jest a colour . . . her face is gittin' to hev that colour sometimes towards night . . . an' it burns an' sucks . . . it come from some place whar things ain't as they is here . . . one o' them professors said so . . . he was right . . . look out, Ammi, it'll do suthin' more . . . sucks the life out . . ."

But that was all. That which spoke could speak no more because it had completely caved in. Ammi laid a red checked tablecloth over what was left and reeled out the back door into the fields. He climbed the slope to the ten-acre pasture and stumbled home by the north road and the woods. He could not pass that well from which his horses had run away. He had looked at it through the window, and had seen that no stone was missing from the rim. Then the lurching buggy had not dislodged anything after all—the splash had been something else—something which went into the well after it had done with poor Nahum. . . .

When Ammi reached his house the horses and buggy had arrived before him and thrown his wife into fits of anxiety. Reassuring her without explanations, he set out at once for Arkham and notified the authorities that the Gardner family was no more. He indulged in no details, but merely told of the deaths of Nahum and Nabby, that of Thaddeus being already known, and mentioned that the cause seemed to be the same strange ailment which had killed the livestock. He also stated that Merwin and Zenas had disappeared. There was considerable questioning at the police station, and in the end Ammi was compelled to take three officers to the Gardner farm, together with the coroner, the medical examiner, and the veterinary who had treated the diseased animals. He went much against his will, for the afternoon was advancing and he feared the fall of night over that accursed place, but it was some comfort to have so many people with him.

The six men drove out in a democrat-wagon, following Ammi's buggy, and arrived at the pest-ridden farmhouse about four o'clock. Used as the officers were to gruesome experiences, not one remained unmoved at what was found in the attic, and under the red checked tablecloth on the floor below. The whole aspect of the farm with its gray desolation was terrible enough, but those two crumbling objects were beyond all bounds. No one could look long at them, and even the medical examiner admitted that there was very little to examine. Specimens could be analyzed, of course, so he busied himself in obtaining them—and here it develops that a very puzzling aftermath occurred at the college laboratory where the two phials of dust were finally taken. Under the spectroscope both samples gave off an unknown spectrum, in which many of the baffling bands were precisely like those which the strange meteor had yielded in the previous year. The property of emitting this spectrum vanished in a month, the dust thereafter consisting mainly of alkaline phosphates and carbonates.

Ammi would not have told the men about the well if he had thought they meant to do anything then and there. It was getting toward sunset, and he was anxious to be away. But he could not help glancing nervously at the stony curb by the great sweep, and when a detective questioned him he admitted that Nahum had feared something down there—so much so that he had never even thought of searching it for Merwin or Zenas. After that nothing would do but that they empty and explore the well immediately, so Ammi had to wait trembling while pail after pail of rank water was hauled up and splashed on the soaking ground outside. The men sniffed in disgust at the fluid, and toward the last held their noses against the foetor they were uncovering. It was not so long a job as they had feared it would be, since the water was phenomenally low. There is no need to speak too exactly of what they found. Merwin and Zenas were both there, in part, though the vestiges were mainly skeletal. There were also a small deer and a large dog in about the same state, and a number of bones of smaller animals. The ooze and slime at the bottom seemed inexplicably porous and bubbling, and a man who descended on hand-holds with a long pole found that he could sink the wooden shaft to any depth in the mud of the floor without meeting any solid obstruction.

Twilight had now fallen, and lanterns were brought from the house. Then, when it was seen that nothing further could be gained from the well, everyone went indoors and conferred in the ancient sitting-room while the intermittent light of a spectral half-moon played wanly on the gray desolation outside. The men were frankly nonplussed by the entire case, and could find no convincing common element to link the strange vegetable conditions, the unknown disease of livestock and humans, and the unaccountable deaths of Merwin and Zenas in the tainted well. They had heard the common country talk, it is true; but could not believe that anything contrary to natural law had occurred. No doubt the meteor had poisoned the soil, but the illness of person and animals who had eaten nothing grown in that soil was another matter. Was it the well water? Very possibly. It might be a good idea to analyze it. But what peculiar madness could have made both boys jump into the well? Their deeds were so similar—and the fragments showed that they had both suffered from the gray brittle death. Why was everything so gray and brittle?

It was the coroner, seated near a window overlooking the yard, who first noticed the glow about the well. Night had fully set in, and all the abhorrent grounds seemed faintly luminous with more than the fitful moonbeams; but this new glow was something definite and distinct, and appeared to shoot up from the black pit like a softened ray from a searchlight, giving dull reflections in the little ground pools where the water had been emptied. It had a very queer colour, and as all the men clustered round the window Ammi gave a violent start. For this strange beam of ghastly miasma was to him of no unfamiliar hue. He had seen that colour before, and feared to think what it might mean. He had seen it in the nasty brittle globule in that aerolite two summers ago, had seen it in the crazy vegetation of the springtime, and had thought he had seen it for an instant that very morning against the small barred window of that terrible attic room where nameless things had happened. It had flashed there a second, and a clammy and hateful current of vapour had brushed past him—and then poor Nahum had been taken by something of that colour. He had said so at the last—said it was like the globule and the plants. After that had come the runaway in the yard and the splash in the well—now that well was belching forth to the night a pale insidious beam of the same demoniac tint.

It does credit to the alertness of Ammi's mind that he puzzled even at that tense moment over a point which was essentially scientific. He could not but wonder at his gleaning of the same impression from a vapour glimpsed in the daytime, against a window opening in the morning sky, and from a nocturnal exhalation seen as a phosphorescent mist against the black and blasted landscape. It wasn't right—it was against Nature—and he thought of those terrible last words of his stricken friend, "It come from some place whar things ain't as they is here . . . one o' them professors said so. . . ."

All three horses outside, tied to a pair of shriveled saplings by the road, were now neighing and pawing frantically. The wagon driver started for the door to do something, but Ammi laid a shaky hand on his shoulder. "Dun't go out thar," he whispered. "They's more to this nor what we know. Nahum said somethin' lived in the well that sucks your life out. He said it must be some'at growed from a round ball like one we all seen in the meteor stone that fell a year ago June. Sucks an' burns, he said, an' is jest a cloud of colour like that light out thar now, that ye can hardly see an' can't tell what it is. Nahum thought it feeds on everything livin' an gits stronger all the time. He said he seen it this last week. It must be somethin' from away off in the sky like the men from the college last year says the meteor stone was. The way it's made an' the way it works ain't like no way o' God's world. It's some'at from beyond."

So the men paused indecisively as the light from the well grew stronger and the hitched horses pawed and whinnied in increasing frenzy. It was truly an awful moment; with terror in that ancient and accursed house itself, four monstrous sets of fragments—two from the house and two from the well—in the woodshed behind, and that shaft of unknown and unholy iridescence from the slimy depths in front. Ammi had restrained the driver on impulse, forgetting how uninjured he himself was after the clammy brushing of that coloured vapour in the attic room, but perhaps it is just as well that he acted as he did. No one will ever know what was abroad that night; and though the blasphemy from beyond had not so far hurt any human of unweakened mind, there is no telling what it might have done at that last moment, and with its seemingly increased strength and the special signs of purpose it was soon to display beneath the half-clouded moonlit sky.

All at once one of the detectives at the window gave a short, sharp gasp. The others looked at him, and then quickly followed his own gaze upward to the point at which its idle straying had been suddenly arrested. There was no need for words. What had been disputed in country gossip was disputable no longer, and it is because of the thing which every man of that party agreed in whispering later on, that strange days are never talked about in Arkham. It is necessary to premise that there was no wind at that hour of the evening. One did arise not long afterward, but there was absolutely none then. Even the dry tips of the lingering hedge-mustard, gray and blighted, and the fringe of the roof of the standing democrat-wagon were unstirred. And yet amid that tense, godless calm the high bare boughs of all the trees in the yard were moving. They were twitching morbidly and spasmodically, clawing in convulsive and epileptic madness at the moonlit clouds; scratching impotently in the noxious air as if jerked by some allied and bodiless line of linkage with subterrene horrors writhing and struggling below the black roots.

Not a man breathed for several seconds. Then a cloud of darker depth passed over the moon, and the silhouette of clutching branches faded out momentarily. At this there was a general cry; muffled with awe, but husky and almost identical from every throat. For the terror had not faded with the silhouette, and in a fearsome instant of deeper darkness the watchers saw wriggling at the treetop height a thousand tiny points of faint and unhaloed radiance, tipping each bough like the fire of St. Elmo or the flames that came down on the apostles' heads at Pentecost. It was a monstrous constellation of unnatural light, like a glutted swarm of corpse-fed fireflies dancing hellish sarabands over an accursed marsh;

and its colour was that same nameless intrusion which Ammi had come to recognize and dread. All the while the shaft of phosphorescence from the well was getting brighter and brighter, bringing to the minds of the huddled men, a sense of doom and abnormality which far outraced any image their conscious minds could form. It was no longer *shining* out; it was *pouring* out; and as the shapeless stream of unplaceable colour left the well it seemed to flow directly into the sky.

The veterinary shivered, and walked to the front door to drop the heavy extra bar across it. Ammi shook no less, and had to tug and point for lack of a controllable voice when he wished to draw notice to the growing luminosity of the trees. The neighing and stamping of the horses had become utterly frightful, but not a soul of that group in the old house would have ventured forth for any earthly reward. With the moments the shining of the trees increased, while their restless branches seemed to strain more and more toward verticality. The wood of the well-sweep was shining now, and presently a policeman dumbly pointed to some wooden sheds and beehives near the stone wall on the west. They were commencing to shine, too, though the tethered vehicles of the visitors seemed so far unaffected. Then there was a wild commotion and clopping in the road, and as Ammi quenched the lamp for better seeing they realized that the span of frantic grays had broken their sapling and run off with the democrat-wagon.

The shock served to loosen several tongues, and embarrassed whispers were exchanged. "It spreads on everything organic that's been around here," muttered the medical examiner. No one replied, but the man who had been in the well gave a hint that his long pole must have stirred up something intangible. "It was awful," he added. "There was no bottom at all. Just ooze and bubbles and the feeling of something lurking under there."

Ammi's horse still pawed and screamed deafeningly in the road outside, and nearly drowned its owner's faint quaver as he mumbled his formless reflections. "It come from that stone—it growed down thar—it got everything livin'—it fed itself on 'em, mind and body—Thad an' Merwin, Zenas an' Nabby—Nahum was the last—they all drunk the water—it got strong on 'em—it come from beyond, whar things ain't like they be here—now it's goin' home—"

At this point, as the column of unknown colour flared suddenly stronger and began to weave itself into fantastic suggestions of shape which each spectator later described differently, there came from poor tethered Hero such a sound as no man before or since ever heard from a horse. Every person in that low-pitched sitting room stopped his ears, and Ammi turned away from the window in horror and nausea. Words could not convey it—when Ammi looked out again the hapless beast lay huddled inert on the moonlit ground between the splintered shafts of the buggy. That was the last of Hero till they buried him next day. But the present was no time to mourn, for almost at this instant a detective silently called attention to something terrible in the very room with them. In the absence of the lamplight it was clear that a faint phosphorescence had begun to pervade the entire apartment. It glowed on the broad-planked floor where the rag carpet left it bare, and shimmered over the sashes of the small-paned windows. It ran up and down the exposed corner-posts, coruscated about the shelf and mantel, and infected the very doors and furniture. Every minute saw it strengthen, and at last it was very plain that healthy living things must leave that house.

Ammi showed them the back door and the path up through the fields to the ten-acre pasture. They walked and stumbled as in a dream, and did not dare look back till they were far away on the high ground. They were glad of the path, for they could not have gone the front way, by that well. It was bad enough passing the glowing barn and sheds, and those shining orchard trees with their gnarled, fiendish contours; but thank Heaven the branches did their worst twisting high up. The moon went under some very black clouds as they crossed the rustic bridge over Chapman's Brook, and it was blind groping from there to the open meadows.

When they looked back toward the valley and the distant Gardner place at the bottom they saw a fearsome sight. All the farm was shining with the hideous unknown blend of colour; trees, buildings, and even such grass and herbage as had not been wholly changed to lethal gray brittleness. The boughs were all straining skyward, tipped with tongues of foul flame, and lambent tricklings of the same monstrous fire were creeping about the ridgepoles of the house, barn and sheds. It was a scene from a vision of Fuseli, and over all the rest reigned that riot of luminous amorphousness, that alien and undimensioned rainbow of cryptic poison from the well—seething, feeling, lapping, reaching, scintillating, straining and malignly bubbling in its cosmic and unrecognizable chromaticism.

Then without warning the hideous thing shot vertically up toward the sky like a rocket or meteor, leaving behind no trail and disappearing through a round and curiously regular hole in the clouds before any man could gasp or cry out. No watcher can ever forget that sight, and Ammi stared blankly at the stars of Cygnus, Deneb twinkling above the others, where the unknown colour had melted into the Milky Way. But his gaze was the next moment called swiftly to earth by the crackling in the valley. It was just that. Only a wooden ripping and crackling, and not an explosion, as so many others of the party vowed. Yet the outcome was the same, for in one feverish kaleidoscopic instant there burst up from that doomed and accursed farm a gleamingly eruptive cataclysm of unnatural sparks and substance; blurring the glance of the few who saw it, and sending forth to the zenith a bombarding cloudburst of such coloured and fantastic fragments as our universe must needs disown. Through quickly re-closing vapours they followed the great morbidity that had vanished, and in another second they had vanished too. Behind and below was only a darkness to which the men dared not return, and all about was a mounting wind which seemed to sweep down in black, frore gusts from interstellar space. It shrieked and howled, and lashed the fields and distorted woods in a mad cosmic frenzy, till soon the trembling party realized it would be of no use waiting for the moon to show what was left down there at Nahum's.

Too awed even to hint theories, the seven shaking men trudged back toward Arkham by the north road. Ammi was worse than his fellows, and begged them to see him inside his own kitchen, instead of keeping straight on to town. He did not wish to cross the blighted, wind-whipped woods alone to his home on the main road. For he had an added shock that the others were spared, and was crushed forever with a brooding fear he dared not even mention for many years to come. As the rest of the watchers on that tempestuous hill had stolidly set their faces toward the road, Ammi had looked back an instant at the shadowed valley of desolation so lately sheltering his ill-starred friend. And from that stricken, faraway spot, he had seen something feebly rise, only to sink down again upon the place from which the great shapeless horror had shot into the sky. It was just a colour—but not any colour of our earth or heavens. And because Ammi recognized that colour, and knew that this last faint remnant must still lurk down there in the well, he has never been quite right since.

Ammi would never go near the place again. It is forty-four years now since the horror happened, but he has never been there, and will be glad when the new reservoir blots it out. I shall be glad, too, for I do not like the way the sunlight changed colour around the mouth of that abandoned well I passed. I hope the water will always be very deep—but even so, I shall never drink it. I do not think I shall visit the Arkham county hereafter. Three of the men who had been with Ammi returned the next morning to see the ruins by daylight, but there were not any real ruins. Only the bricks of the chimney, the stones of the cellar, some mineral and metallic litter here and there, and the rim of that nefandous well. Save for Ammi's dead horse, which they towed away and buried, and the buggy, which they shortly returned to him, everything that had ever been living had gone. Five eldritch acres of dusty gray desert remained, nor has anything ever grown there since. To this day it sprawls open to the sky like a great spot eaten by acid in the woods and fields, and the few who have ever dared glimpse it in spite of the rural tales have named it "the blasted heath."

The rural tales are queer. They might be even queerer if city men and college chemists could be interested enough to analyze the water from that disused well, or the gray dust that no wind seems ever to disperse. Botanists, too, ought to study the stunted flora on the borders of that spot, for they might shed light on the country notion that the blight is spreading—little by little, perhaps an inch a year. People say the colour of the neighboring herbage is not quite right in the spring, and that wild things leave queer prints in the light winter snow. Snow never seems quite so heavy on the blasted heath as it is elsewhere. Horses—the few that are left in this motor age—grow skittish in the silent valley; and hunters cannot depend on their dogs too near the splotch of grayish dust.

They say the mental influences are very bad, too;

numbers went queer in the years after Nahum's taking, and always they lacked the power to get away. Then the stronger-minded folk all left the region, and only the foreigners tried to live in crumbling old homesteads. They could not stay, though; and one sometimes wonders what insight beyond ours their wild, weird stories of whispered magic have given them. Their dreams at night, they protest, are very horrible in that grotesque country; and surely the very look of the dark realm is enough to stir a morbid fancy. No traveler has ever escaped a sense of strangeness in those deep ravines, and artists shiver as they paint thick woods whose mystery is as much of the spirit as of the eye. I myself am curious about the sensation I derived from my one lone walk before Ammi told me his tale. When twilight came I had vaguely wished some clouds would gather, for odd timidity about the deep skyey voids above had crept into my soul.

Do not ask me for my opinion. I do not know—that is all. There was no one but Ammi to question; for Arkham people will not talk about the strange days, and all three professors who saw the aerolite and its coloured globule are dead. There were other globules—depend upon that. One must have fed itself and escaped, and probably there was another which was too late. No doubt it is still down the well—I know there was something wrong with the sunlight I saw above that miasmal brink. The rustics say the blight creeps an inch a year, so perhaps there is a kind of growth or nourishment even now. But whatever demon hatchling is there, it must be tethered to something or else it would quickly spread. Is it fastened to the roots of those trees that claw the air? One of the current Arkham tales is about fat oaks that shine and move as they ought not to do at night.

What it is, only God knows. In terms of matter I suppose the thing Ammi described would be called a gas, but this gas obeyed laws that are not of our cosmos. This was no fruit of such worlds and suns as shine on the telescopes and photographic plates of our observatories. This was no breath from the skies whose motions and dimensions our astronomers measure or deem too vast to measure. It was just a colour out of space—a frightful messenger from unformed realms of infinity beyond all Nature as we know it; from realms whose mere existence stuns the brain and numbs us with the black extra-cosmic gulfs it throws open before our unfettered eyes.

I doubt very much if Ammi consciously lied to me, and I do not think his tale was all a freak of madness as the townsfolk had forewarned. Something terrible came to the hills and valleys on that meteor, and something terrible—though I know not in what proportion—still remains. I shall be glad to see the water come. Meanwhile I hope nothing will happen to Ammi. He saw so much of the thing—and its influence was so insidious. Why has he never been able to move away? How clearly he recalled those dying words of Nahum's—"can't git away—draws ye—ye know summ'at's comin', but 'tain't no use—" Ammi is such a good old man—when the reservoir gang gets to work I must write the chief engineer to keep a sharp watch on him. I would hate to think of him as the gray, twisted, brittle monstrosity which persists more and more in troubling my sleep.

THE AUTHORS

Miles J. Breuer (1888-1947) debuted in *Amazing® Stories* in 1927 and contributed many notable stories to the magazine, including "The Gostak and the Doshes" in 1930. Breuer's most important works appeared in the 1920s and 1930s.

John W. Campbell, Jr. (1910-1971) is widely regarded as the most important science fiction magazine editor of all time, and sf really came of age during his tenure at *Astounding* (later *Analog*) *Science Fiction* from 1937 to 1971. He also helped to develop modern fantasy as editor of *Unknown* from 1939 to 1943. He is perhaps best known to modern readers as the author of the novella "Who Goes There?", which was the basis for the two versions of the film *The Thing*.

Lloyd Arthur Eshbach (1910-) contributed numerous short stories to science-fiction magazines of the 1930s and early 1940s, but his major contribution to sf has been his role as a pioneer publisher of hardcover science fiction in the United States. He also wrote two sf novels, *The Tyrant of Time* (1955) and *The Land Beyond the Gate* (1984). His autobiography, *Over My Shoulder: Reflections on a Science Fiction Era* (1983), is must reading for anyone interested in the history of science fiction.

Francis Flagg (George H. Weiss) (1898-1946) contributed about half a dozen stories to *Amazing Stories* in the 1920s and 1930s, but he is primarily recognized today for his work in *Weird Tales*. Unlike many of his contemporaries, his work featured well-realized, convincing characters. Unfortunately, his failure to pursue his career and early death deprived the sf/horror field of one of its most promising authors.

Edmond Hamilton (1904-1977) developed the concept of a space patrol and of a galactic civilization. His "super-science" stories of the 1930s earned him the title of "world wrecker Hamilton," but his later work was thoughtful and important. Particularly noteworthy are the collections *What's It Like out There?* (1974) and *The Best of Edmond Hamtilon* (1977).

Clare Winger Harris (dates unknown) was one of the earliest women writers of American magazine science fiction, first appearing in *Weird Tales* in 1926. However, her writing career was a brief one, totaling only eleven stories, all of which can be found in her collection *Away from the Here and Now* (1947).

Julian Huxley (1888-1975) was a member of that distinguished family that included his grandfather, T.H. Huxley, and his brother, Aldous Huxley, the author of *Brave New World*. Sir Julian was an essayist, a poet, a popularizer of science, a scientist of some renown, and an important administrator who served as the Secretary of UNESCO. His many honors include the Kalinga Prize for excellence in science writing.

Neil R. Jones (1909-) will always be remembered as the creator of Professor Jameson, one of the most popular series characters in science fiction in the 1930s. These stories were collected in five volumes published in 1967 and 1968, allowing a new generation of readers to experience his character's adventures. These books include *Space War* (1967) and *Doomsday on Ajiat* (1968).

Amelia Reynolds Long (dates unknown) was a pioneer woman writer for the early science fiction magazines. A resident of Harrisburg, Pennsylvania, she was the author of a number of sf stories, including "A Leak in the Fountain of Youth" (surely one of the great titles in sf history), and "Scandal in the Fourth Dimension." She also wrote "The Thought-Monster," which was the basis for the 1958 film *Fiend without a Face*.

H.P. Lovecraft (1890-1937) was one of the major figures in the development of the modern horror story. Unfortunately, he died at the age of 47, years before August Derleth and others built his reputation by issuing volumes of his stories and poetry. Indeed, he is the only author who had a publishing house established for the sole purpose of keeping his work alive (Arkham House, in Sauk City, Wisconsin). His "Cthulhu mythos" has captured the imagination of several generations of readers.

Clark Ashton Smith (1893-1961) was an important fantasy and science fiction writer whose influence can be seen in the work of many later writers. Among his chief themes were death, strangeness, and the nature of reality. Two excellent collections of his stories are *Tales of Science and Sorcery* (1964) and *Other Dimensions* (1970).

G. Peyton Wertenbaker (1907-?) has the distinction of having the first *original* story (the one you just read) in *Amazing® Stories* after its founding in July, 1926. Wertenbaker sold only five stories to sf/horror magazines, but he became a noted writer of nonfiction about Arizona and New Mexico.

Jack Williamson (1908-) has enjoyed one of the longest and most successful careers of any science fiction writer. Still going strong at the age of 79, his most recent novel is *Firechild* (1986). In addition to some fifty-plus novels and collections, he has written such excellent critical works as *H.G. Wells, Critic of Progress*. Dr. Williamson served as President of the Science Fiction Writers of America from 1977-1980, and was awarded the prestigious Grand Master Nebula Award of that organization in 1975.